# The Green's Hill Novellas

# AMY LANE

# DSP PUBLICATIONS

Published by
**DSP Publications**

5032 Capital Circle SW, Suite 2, PMB# 279, Tallahassee, FL 32305-7886 USA
www.dreamspinnerpress.com



The Green's Hill Novellas
© 2016 Amy Lane.

Cover Art
© 2016 Anne Cain.
annecain.art@gmail.com



ISBN: 978-1-63216-170-3
Digital ISBN: 978-1-63476-019-5
Library of Congress Control Number: 2015921078
Published June 2016
v. 1.0

Litha's Constant Whim: First Edition published by Dreamspinner Press, June 2010. Cover Art © 2010 Anne Cain, annecain.art@gmail.com. I Love You, Asshole!: First Edition published by Dreamspinner Press, May 2011. Cover Art © 2011 Anne Cain, annecain.art@gmail.com, Cover Design © 2011 Mara McKennen. Guarding the Vampire's Ghost: First Edition published by Dreamspinner Press, October 2010. Cover Art © 2010 Anne Cain, annecain.art@gmail.com.

Printed in the United States of America
∞

This paper meets the requirements of
ANSI/NISO Z39.48-1992 (Permanence of Paper).

Just so you know, you should really listen to Death Cab for Cutie's "Marching Bands of Manhattan" when you read this. Trust me. Put it on loop. It'll hit you right in the feels.


Amy

# Table of Contents

Litha's
Constant
Whim
Amy Lane

# WHIM—OFFERINGS

GREEN'S HILL was a magical faerie commune that rested in an unspecified location in the Northern California foothills. Green was the leader, a beautiful sidhe (or elf) with hip-length, butter-colored hair, a penchant for mortals, and what should have been a minor gift that he'd parlayed into a major one. He had the gift of sex and the ability to gain magical power from the sharing of flesh and the whisper of skin on skin. Using this power, Green managed to gather every supernatural being—shape-shifters, vampires, lower fey, sidhe, all of them—under his aegis and protection. Everybody loved Green and his vampire consort, Adrian, including Whim.

Whim was the second-youngest sidhe on Green's hill, and possibly the least powerful one.

Smaller fey—pixies, nixies, sprites, gnomes, goblins, trolls, brownies—reproduced like rabbits. They were everywhere, hiding in the corners of houses like dust, but sidhe, the big elves, did not, as a whole, procreate a lot. They had sex frequently (for them it was as natural as eating or breathing), but they didn't actually produce offspring. Whim's parents were both sidhe, and in the tumultuous, terrifying (for them) trip overseas on one of the vast sailing ships of the 1800s, they had lost control of their will and their power. Will and power were a sidhe's birth control. Whim was the result.

The youngest sidhe on Green's hill was Bracken. Bracken was (as most elves are) exactly like his name. Fierce and sturdy, prickly, somber, and strong. The terrible, beautiful, painful story of Adrian, Green, Bracken, and Cory—the very mortal sorceress who loved (and was loved by) them all—was the stuff of songs. Whim, however, was not the type of elf that songs or stories were written about. He was beautiful, as were all of his people—with triangular, perfect features; wide, limpid eyes; a full, wide mouth; a clean, proportional nose; and pointed ears—but other than that, he was perfectly average. His hair, which hung—like most of the sidhe's—down to his waist, tended to change color according to his mood, like one big silky mood ring, and he had the attention span of one of the lower fey, but that was why he was named "Whim." He was as insubstantial as the breeze and as reliable as a bumblebee in a hurricane.

At least that was what everybody believed about him, with the exception of Green and Adrian. Adrian, who, as a vampire, had once been mortal, not only told Whim that there was something of substance, of passion, inside his mild, mercurial self—Adrian also introduced Whim to the world of mortals.

Mortals were Whim's secret passion.

Many of the sidhe—including Whim's parents—avoided the mortals, including the mortals-that-had-been, like the vampires and the werecreatures. Sidhe traditions held that their shorter life spans made them incapable of understanding what true life and love and beauty and sacrifice were all about.

*We're sidhe, Whim. I know we've relocated to this wild place, but that is because our leadership in England was corrupt. We need to maintain all of the mystique and magic of being sidhe. Try to remember that as you see the other elves running wild with the rabble.*

Whim didn't care. Adrian had been a mortal once, and so he thought there must be something beautiful and amazing about mortals. It was that simple. Whim hadn't loved Adrian as a lover, although they'd shared flesh on occasion. It had been Adrian's friendship that Whim had loved. Adrian, quick with a joke, quick to blush if he'd just fed, quick to listen, to understand, to forgive. He had forgiven Whim for being an elitist snob, and Whim had ceased to be one. He had forgiven Whim for being afraid to go outside the hill, and Whim had ceased to be afraid. He had forgiven Whim for once forgetting that they were in the middle of sex and starting to sing a bawdy song that Adrian had taught him, and Whim tried very hard to pay attention during sex after that, because he learned that mortals-that-had-been, especially, got a little irritated when their partners forgot that sex was being had.

It had been Adrian's influence that had sent Whim outside the hill for Litha, the time of the vampires' greatest weakness and of the elves' greatest strength:

"Oh, for Christ's sake, mate, get the hell out of here." Adrian had been born in the poorest stretch of London, or so his accent still proclaimed even till the day of his second death. He always claimed not to remember. "Your parents will be doing what your people do during this time. I've taught you how to drive, and we have plenty of cars that have been treated so you can drive them. Your glamour is solid, and unlike Bracken, you can keep your temper for more than two and a half seconds at a stretch."

Adrian and Bracken weren't monogamous at this time, but there had been a period in which they'd been exclusive with the exception of Green. As he talked about his lover, his brother of the heart, his best friend, Adrian's fine-boned face arched wickedly, and he smiled. He loved Bracken—he'd die for him—but that didn't mean that he and Whim couldn't appreciate the vagaries of such a young sidhe. The mercurial Bracken often lost control of his glamour in front of humans. He was practically too young to be let out of the hill. Whim, at sixty, should have no trouble. The Goddess's children all looked young and beautiful, but they had an eternity—if they chose one—to learn about the world. Whim was just old enough to cut loose on an unsuspecting human populace and just young enough to appreciate an adventure.

But still, Whim looked at Adrian, who, at almost six feet tall, was tall for a human and short for a sidhe, and felt a pucker at his brow. Adrian had moonlight-pale hair and sky-spangled blue eyes, and he was almost more beautiful as a vampire than most sidhe—a thing Whim's parents would have said was impossible. Adrian was different than mortals. The world could not possibly offer everything Adrian said it did.

Adrian saw Whim's adoration and shook his head. "There is somebody out in the big world who will give you back that look full measure, Whim. Don't you want to see who that is?"

"Yes," Whim sighed, "but if I do find them, I will probably forget who it is I'm looking for as soon as I see their face."

Adrian laughed then. Whim's attention had never been very faithful, it was true. Most of the other sidhe concentrated on some sort of art or science and mastered it. But as soon as Whim picked up a book of poetry, he was singing a ballad he'd made up himself. He'd tried to master the harp and ended up suspending paper birds from harp strings. Once he'd instigated sex with a female vampire on the cusp of dawn, forgetting that they died with the birth of the sun. The woman hadn't minded, especially because Whim had forgotten what he was supposed to be doing at sunrise and rolled out of her bed and went to find something else to occupy himself—it was considered a case of no harm, no foul. Even among a species considered eccentric in its proclivities and belief system, Whim was an anomaly. To say he was cursed with a butterfly mind was to say cow shit was cursed with methane gas. The two simply went hand in hand, and that was the nature of things.

"Don't worry, Whim," Adrian said then, kindly. "We will know it's for real when you can remember a name."

So Whim had done it, had gone outside the hill to experience full Litha magic, just for Adrian. That first night he had met a mortal woman—an unwary mortal woman, to be outside her husband's home and wishing on the shortest night of the year. Whim had spoken softly to her, had heard her heart's desires, and had touched her bare skin freckled by starlight. He had taken her sweet body in the country quiet. When the morning came, he'd dressed her and put her to sleep next to her husband, with nothing but a pleasant yearning to convince her it had been anything more than a dream.

The experience—the flesh, the power of the solstice night, the mortal woman's sweetness and painful want—had been exquisite. Whim resolved to do it again, and so he had. Every Litha, he had gone into the mortal world and found a mortal who wanted him and only him, even if it was only for the shortest night of the year.

One night, nearly thirty Lithas later, he was wandering along the railroad track in a deserted back field in Auburn. It was there that he met Charlie, and Litha changed for Whim forever.

He started out his wander in a fit of melancholy. The little clearing was on top of a rise, on the other side of a graffiti wall that separated the railroad tracks from the small, low-rent suburb on the other side. Suburb, graffiti wall, even the glaring spaceship of lights below the rise, all of them were new. The area had changed—humans had become more prevalent, and this great, cold-iron track cut less and less through areas of field and forest and more and more through the backs of suburbs and horse pastures—and Whim missed the emptiness. He'd seen the great rabbit warrens of large homes on small plots of land that the humans had been building, and he hated them. Soon, he thought unhappily, Green's hill and the surrounding protected forests would be the only place his kind could walk the earth.

Then he saw a youth in tight jeans and a tank top under a flapping great trench coat, balancing on the cold-iron beam in the starlight, and he forgot his private vendetta against progress and remembered why he was out in the Litha dark.

Litha was the cusp of light and dark, the crux of life and death, the longest day and shortest night of the year. The earth was in full burgeoning strength, and the Goddess's shining ones literally—and with no help from their own magic—tended to glow like beacons of sex and touch. Litha was the night Oberon could seduce Titania with a commoner who had been partially turned into an ass.

As the youth on the railroad tracks looked up and caught sight of Whim walking toward him wearing nothing but jeans and a cloak of color-shifting hair, the boy's mouth curved into a plump little O and his eyes, so dark a chocolate brown as to be opaque in the moonlight, opened as wide as the sky.

Whim looked at him and felt his lips curve into a smile. The boy was like Litha itself: on the cusp of things. He was not tall, certainly not as tall as Whim, who was in the middle of six and seven feet, but not even as tall as Adrian. His chest and jaw would be broad when he filled out, but now, in his late teens, he was all shoulders and elbows, collarbones and angled jaw and bold, assertive nose. His jeans were torn and bleached on purpose, and his tank top was tight to show off the rebellious rings in his nipples and his navel, but that look….

In spite of the sneering of the teenager and the skepticism of the nascent man, the look on his face had been all joyful child, and Whim was charmed.

He drew nearer.

"Be careful you don't get stuck," Whim said gently as the boy played with his feet in the railroad ties. The boy rolled his eyes, and Whim rolled his back. "I am only saying that the train is due very soon, and I cannot touch the rails or the spikes to help you."

That brought the boy up short. "Why can't you touch the rails?" he asked, and Whim looked down at his bare feet and wiggled his toes. The boy's eyes followed.

"The cold iron burns my skin," Whim told him honestly. It was true. Here, on Litha, Whim was caught in all three of a sidhe's vulnerabilities: They drew power from the earth and hence detested coverings for their feet. They were allergic to the cold iron of the humans (the reason all of Green's cars were treated with a salt and herb wash before the sidhe were allowed to drive them). And they could not lie. They could if they really wanted to, but they ended up afflicted with nausea, cramps, and a blinding headache until they burst out with the truth, and Whim had never been tempted to test that particular weakness.

"And don't believe what you hear about foot size and penis size," Whim added for good measure.

"I'm sorry?" There was a curious blink, and Whim felt he should explain.

"Humans believe that foot size is proportional to penis size. You were looking at my feet. They are very large. In fact," Whim said as he held up a forearm, "they are the exact length from the crease of my arm to the edge of my wrist, and so are yours. I know, because I have a friend who makes socks."

"Burns?" asked the boy curiously, and it was Whim's turn to blink. "You said the cold iron burns," the kid enunciated patiently. "That's why I was staring at your feet."

Whim nodded and shrugged and made a very rash decision, which would have surprised no one who knew him. It was Litha. If he breathed in deeply, he could set a shield between himself and this man-child that would deflect bullets and keep even the subtle, warm breeze at bay. With such a shield, he could stand on the railroad tracks and let the train batter him like a wave batters a beach ball and walk away without a scratch or even a blister from the iron itself.

On such a night, with such power brushing his skin, what could this boy do to him, even with the truth?

"My people are allergic to the iron," Whim told him, and his glamour, which hadn't been very firm in the first place because he'd been caught unaware, dropped completely, on a whim. The youth looked up into his triangular features, his wide-set eyes, and saw what he was ready to see.

He must have been ready to see the truth, because his arm rose and his fingertip moved immediately to Whim's curved ears, and he stroked gently, like a child stroking a rabbit's nose. Whim shuddered sensually and purred. The ears of most sidhe were sexually sensitive, and his were no exception.

"You're real," the boy whispered, his voice barely audible in the night quiet. In the rushing darkness, the shushing of the freeway could be heard. It was nearly three miles away.

"You're taking liberties I haven't given you," Whim told him, but he cocked his head and moved his body sinuously anyway. It was his *ear*. It just felt so damned good. "Of course I'm real."

The boy dropped his hand reluctantly, and Whim sighed and straightened his body. "It is dangerous out here for unwary boys. I'm an elf, and even I know that not all strangers mean well."

The boy shrugged, pulled his foot from the space between the two railroad ties, and hopped off the track altogether. "Folks don't care much where I am," he said.

"Don't *you* care where you are?" Whim was there under the moonlight because this was his holiday, a treat to himself. He wanted to feel the warmth of the lingering sun and the faint, cooling breeze. He wanted to smell the new-mown hay, brown grasses, and burgeoning green orchard smells that permeated the Sierra foothills in June. He wanted the absolute aloneness to seep into his bones, because it was so very different than the masses of family that beat in his blood from life on the hill. He cared very much where he was.

"I care that I'm not at home," the boy said on a bleak sigh.

"Well, then," Whim said, feeling a little disappointed that he would not be sharing flesh with someone this night—the boy was too young, after all, "for tonight and tonight only, I will care where you are, and this roof of darkness can be ours."

The boy looked at him with narrowed eyes. "Do you want me for sex?" he asked suspiciously, and Whim gasped a little. He had forgotten that with the changing of the years, human children had become more like sidhe children about these matters.

"I don't even know your name," Whim replied, affronted. "And you are too young, even if I did." The two of them began to walk together through the darkness, using the tracks as a guide but staying well away from them.

"My name is Charlie," the boy supplied with a gratifying readiness, "and I'm eighteen."

"My name is Whim, and I'm…. Well, shit… how old am I?"

"You don't know?" the boy asked, and Whim wrinkled his nose at him.

"Our days pass so ordinarily," Whim replied, wondering. "We sit and we do whatever we want…. There are the solstice celebrations, of course, but no real way of marking our days…. What year is it?"

Charlie told him, and Whim nodded, pretty sure. "Yes, I was born near the beginning of the last century. I am nearing one hundred, but not quite."

Charlie shook his head and stuck his hands in his pockets. "Man, that's messed up. If you live a hundred years, you'd think you'd have something to show for it. Pain, laughter, you know. Something."

Whim looked at the young human with wondering eyes, seeing every feature perfectly with his better-than-human vision. Charlie had fading acne scars and the awkwardness of the young, but… but in that moment, Whim saw something special about him, something indefinable. It was a quality that never left.

"That's exactly what Adrian said," Whim told him, amazed. He'd thought Adrian was the only human—he'd been human once—capable of wisdom. Well, that should show Whim that arrogance was truly an unattractive personality trait. He would find himself struggling against making assumptions of his own superiority for the rest of his life.

"Is Adrian the reason you don't want sex?" Charlie asked suspiciously, and Whim laughed outright.

"Adrian is sex on legs," Whim told him frankly. "One night with you—one hundred nights with you—and Adrian would still play if I asked him. But no. You… you are barely the age of consent. I am not here to give you a yearning for things you can never have. I come out at Litha to give someone a gift, an offering. If they have regrets or loneliness or sadness in their lives, I can give them something magical—a memory that not even time can erase. A moment when their bodies become light and sound, and they're one with the Goddess's shining child. You—you have so much potential in you. You have no regrets yet. Look at you. Your hands are quivering with the urge to paint this night, surreal though it may be. Your eyes are looking at a dark sky and seeing heathered purples and blended greens, a charcoal-tinted rainbow with blood-edged stars. You hear music in the faraway freeway—I can watch it pulse in your throat. Your mind teems with a thousand stories of what is possible this night. I can hear your characters speaking, as though on stage. Myriad talents compete for space inside you, Charlie. You have no regrets—only possibilities." He was very proud when he finished speaking. It was one of the longest speeches he'd ever made on a single topic.

Charlie looked at him very carefully. "You talk really weird," he said at last. "Is that an elf thing?"

Whim looked at him steadily. In the darkness he could see the blush, the sideways slant to Charlie's eyes, the way the pulse throbbed in his throat with a passion waiting to break free. "My words touched you," he said softly. "You're pulling into yourself because you are afraid of what I've said."

And now Charlie looked over his shoulder, squinting into the darkness as though he could make something out. "Man, everybody wants to hear somebody beautiful tell them they're special. Did you think you could tell me something like that and not make me want to cry like a weenie?"

Whim's mouth quirked upward, and he stared at Charlie with more of that renewed appreciation. "My people do not think less of you if you shed tears," he said earnestly, and Charlie turned a shining smile in his direction.

"I'll have to remember that if I ever feel like crying again," he said with mock seriousness. Whim felt a sudden shaft, a sudden flaw in the shape of his heart. He wouldn't be here for Charlie to shed more tears. Not if he held true to the pattern of his butterfly mind.

"We only have Litha," he said with soft regret. "But if it's any comfort for you, I will be sorry to see the dawn."

Charlie didn't have anything to say to that, and he didn't question why Whim would only be there for one night. Whim was grateful. Suddenly, his policy of only mingling with the humans one night a year sounded... artificial, artificial and cowardly, a shield between him and the censure of someone who might not understand the nature of Whim. Especially by the end of the night, when Whim had learned so much about Charlie, and everything about him was real and brave.

Charlie had just finished his senior year in high school. He had earned scholarships to a performing arts school—a full ride, in fact—but his father wanted him to join the military. Charlie didn't want to go. He planned to tell his father the next morning that he couldn't join the military. For one thing, the military did not appear to *approve* of specific ways of sharing flesh, and Charlie was gay.

"I never understood that word," Whim said, frowning.

"You're not gay?" Charlie asked, clearly disappointed.

"I'm sidhe," Whim told him. "Most of us are pansexual. We don't discriminate among genders or species." Whim especially had no trouble with that. He tended to bed whomever he wanted, depending on... well, his whim.

Charlie raised his eyebrows and mouthed the word "species" with some appreciation, but then Whim asked him what he intended to do with his art scholarships and his family life, and he moved on to the answer.

"I guess now I'm going to have to really live up to all that bullshit I was just spouting and tell them," he answered obliquely.

Whim blinked. "You didn't mean it when you said it?" He was puzzled and let it show. Charlie flashed a crooked grin.

"What—you mean everything you say?" he asked snidely.

Whim nodded, his eyes open very wide. "I have to. I forget that humans and vampires and were-folk can lie, but we cannot. I did not realize you were lying." Whim pulled his head back, a little disappointed.

"I'm not lying now," Charlie said, his voice firm. Surprising Whim, he caught Whim's chin with his fingers and made the taller man look down, into his eyes. "I mean every word I said, I swear. And I'll never bullshit you again."

Whim nodded, touched yet again. Maybe it was the boy's youth that touched him, he thought optimistically. Youth would pass. But he did not think that was the reason this boy seemed to yank at his heart.

"You are a very good person, Charlie," he said gravely. "This night is much more exciting than I had anticipated."

"Even though you're not getting laid?" Charlie asked, incredulous. "Because having not been laid yet, I can only tell you, I was really hoping you were up for it!"

Whim took a deep, deep breath and exhaled through his nose. The problem, he thought crossly, was that human young were so beautiful at this age. There was an aching softness to even the strongest jaw, and a terrible vulnerability to simple things, like clavicles and biceps and limpid eyes that spoke of an awful, stomach-churning need to be cared for.

"I do not think so," Whim said, wrapping an arm around Charlie's shoulders. They trembled underneath the old ratty trench coat, and Charlie tucked right into him as though his slight frame was made to fit. "I think I'm up to good company and comfort tonight, if you don't mind."

They had reached a stand of woods by now, also carved by the cold iron of the railroad track, and Whim, with Charlie at his side, ventured into it. It was not too terribly deep or thick, but in the darkness it would have been daunting to a human, especially since the moon was not full and the light was poor. Charlie followed Whim's footsteps without hesitation, and Whim turned toward him, trying not to censure.

"Please tell me you do not trust other humans the way you trust me!"

Charlie's lips quirked up. "You just turned down sex. Twice. And you won't even stand on a railroad track. Odds are good you're not going to gank me with a shiv as soon as the light gets dark."

Whim stopped and mouthed "gank me with a shiv" and then shook his head. "Whatever. You must promise me to take care of yourself, Charlie. Elves don't reveal their true selves to just anybody. You're special. Please be careful."

Charlie's long-suffering sigh was the only response. They found a nice place to sit and spread Charlie's trench coat on the ground to sit upon it—he'd been sweating under it anyway, pure affectation on a night with a low temperature of eighty degrees—and then Whim spent the rest of the night talking with the boy and trying to convince him why his life, of all mortals', was important.

It was a beautiful conversation. The night smelled lovely, and other than the two trains that passed that way during their time, there was no sound but the shush of the mortal road a few miles away and the occasional animal tracing delicately padded paths through the underbrush. Whim switched topics often, as he usually did, but Charlie seemed able to follow him, and their voices hummed into the breeze-touched summer night. Once, Charlie stopped talking abruptly and looked up, his eyes large. Whim turned his head and saw a family of rabbits venturing out in the predawn chill. Charlie shivered, and Whim stood regretfully.

"Is it over already?" Charlie was plaintive as Whim shook out the coat and put it over Charlie's shoulders. Whim didn't need to guide him through the trees or across the field this time, because the darkness had become tinged with silver.

Whim reached down and grabbed his hand, and he was gratified by the way their fingers threaded together. "This Litha has passed," he told the boy logically.

"Does it have to end now?" Charlie asked. His voice was tired and had taken on an edge, like that of the child he no longer was.

"It doesn't, no," Whim told him thoughtfully. They had reached the railroad tracks by now, and Charlie took a step up to the rail so that Whim, down the rise a little from him, could look him in the eye.

"Then see me tomorrow," he demanded, and Whim shook his head.

"Tomorrow, you'll be no older than you are today," he muttered— but it was hard, so hard, because the boy's face was so amazingly appealing. His skin was pale, and in the predawn light, Whim could make out the barest print of dark brown freckles.

Charlie made a grunt of impatience, grasped Whim's face in both chilled hands, and pulled his face so close Whim could see gold flecks glimmering in his chocolate brown eyes. They stood, panting gruffly at each other, and then Whim heard it—the approaching train. Charlie must have felt it through the soles of his battered sneakers, because he gave an evil little smile and hauled Whim the last few inches and kissed him roughly.

Whim groaned and wrapped his arms around that skinny, all-ribs-and-elbows body and opened his mouth and returned the kiss, then pulled back roughly. "You can't do that," he panted, Charlie's taste still on his tongue. "You can't steal kisses from the sidhe."

"Why not?" Charlie wanted to know. Then he hummed in his throat, and the sound was so wanton, so innocent and greedy, that Whim wrapped his arms around Charlie's body again, and *he* fed Charlie's hunger this time. It was an openmouthed, gleefully carnal sort of kiss, and Whim used his preternatural strength to hoist Charlie up in his arms and haul him down the hill even as the train rounded the corner. Thousands of tons of indifferent cold-iron death chilled their secret little island of serenity with its ear-shattering scream.

Whim didn't care. Charlie tasted so good, and his hands on Whim's stomach were eager and questing, and his touch was…. Whim shuddered and pulled him even closer, growing hard and full against Charlie's upper thigh.

Charlie's own decent-sized erection was burgeoning through his jeans against Whim's stomach, and that alone was what made Whim pull away from the kiss and pant into Charlie's neck.

"Dammit," he muttered. "It's almost dawn." People at Green's hill would start missing him if he wasn't back by dawn, and he'd been keeping his expeditions at Litha a secret from everyone but Adrian.

"Are you going to disappear at dawn?" Charlie wanted to know. Then he laved a tongue around Whim's ear, and it was all Whim could do not to just sit down, right there on the open ground, and let this boy have his body like a Litha sacrifice.

"You can't steal kisses from us," Whim muttered again. "You can't…." He was trying to warn Charlie, because this entire moment was ill-advised.

Charlie hmmmed into his ear, and Whim let out a sound much like a whine, if a sidhe had ever been undignified enough to whine.

"I'm serious!" Whim pulled his head away—still holding the boy, of course—and made sure they were eye to eye. "You understand? Stealing kisses is like… stealing joy, like humans get from drugs. Stealing kisses will turn you into a junkie…. Unless you get your next… mmm—" Because Charlie was looking so wicked and so wide-eyed and so happy that Whim just had to steal his own kiss even as he lectured. "—taste," he breathed and then tried to start again. "Unless you get your next taste willingly, the want alone can kill you." It was true. That part of faerie lore held its roots in fact.

"But I got my next taste willingly," Charlie teased, playfully nuzzling the corner of Whim's mouth. "Doesn't that mean I'm good?"

"More than good…." Whim groaned and turned his mouth into what he promised himself was going to be one more voracious, youthful, *gleeful* kiss. Oh *Goddess*, did this kid taste like hunger and joy and everything Whim yearned for when he made his Litha pilgrimage. He opened his slanted mouth and took in Charlie's wicked, rapacious want, and grabbed Charlie's bottom as the boy wrapped his legs around Whim's waist and ground up against him.

Charlie was groaning and whimpering in his passion, and Whim reached between their bodies to the snap on Charlie's jeans, gratified when the only thing between Charlie's flesh and Whim's bare stomach was a thin layer of rapidly slickening cotton.

Then he hauled Charlie closer and sank blissfully back into that glorious kiss while this very mortal, very human man-child rutted up against his skin as though he was life and sanity and beauty and pleasure, all in one simple, befuddled elf.

Charlie's movements became frantic, almost frightening, and Whim's supernatural strength alone kept both of them from buckling to the ground as Charlie stroked himself violently against Whim's body. After a moment, a dazzling, terrifying moment, Charlie came, groaning into Whim's mouth, and Whim was shocked to find his own vision blackening, his own body shuddering, a glorious climax rocking his entire body even as Charlie's spend coated his abdomen through his child's white underwear.

Trembling, Whim sank to the ground, catching himself on one hand and keeping Charlie in his lap while Charlie panted and shuddered in his arms and dawn flirted with the horizon.

"God… holy Jesus shit damn fuck…"

"Holy Goddess, merciful God, damnable other…."

The oaths may have been blasphemous, but the sentiment was reverent, and they simply sat, holding each other for many long, shaking breaths.

Whim's palm was planted firmly on the soil beneath him, and he felt the added power of Litha drain out of his body, back into the earth that spawned it. He was still strong, though, and the sex had made him stronger. With a scoot of his bottom, he leaned forward, raising his arm up to enfold Charlie completely into his arms, to protect him and cherish him. That is what sidhe were taught to do with lovers who moved them in unexpected ways.

"Are you sure you have to leave?" Charlie asked mournfully, his voice muffled in the cocoon of Whim's arms, and Whim was going to say, *No. No. I'll take you with me. You can be my mortal, or I'll give you the gift of the were-folk and you can be a mortal-that-was. Just be mine… be mine….*

That's not what happened, though. What happened was a ferocious, agonizing pain that exploded along Whim's forearm, and he yelped and stood up, dumping Charlie on his ass.

"*Owwwwwwwww*…." Whim had never truly felt pain before, and he had no stoicism on which to rely. He turned his face to the pale silver-gold sky and howled, holding his forearm out in front of him as it blistered madly, even as Charlie stood and cradled it against his chest.

"My God, Whim! What happened?"

Whim gasped and looked at the wound with a hurt so deep it felt like wonder. "It's a cold-iron burn," he mourned. "Goddess, Charlie, what do you have in your pocket?"

Charlie's pale features blanched so white they were gray. "Oh God, Whim, I'm so sorry…. I even forgot it was in there. I was going to…." Charlie's lower lip began to tremble, and suddenly Whim's burn was soothed—temporarily, anyway—with blissful salt tears. "I never meant to hurt you," he muttered. "I'm so sorry. Jesus, do you really have to go?"

Whim nodded miserably. "I need to go home. Green can cure this. Someone can cure this. But I don't have what we need. Look…." Before their eyes another blister formed, another half inch of skin turned red around it, and a blister in the center popped and ran blood. Whim raised his free hand to Charlie's cheek and rubbed the cheekbone with his thumb. "I need to go."

"Can I meet you again?" Charlie pleaded. "Not tomorrow." Because Whim was going to say no. "Next Litha. I'll be here. I'll meet you here."

"Will there be houses?" And Whim hated the trembling in his voice. He hated to see the hills run rife with houses.

"No." Charlie raised his hand and cupped Whim's cheek, wiping a tear away with a bony thumb. "I swear, there's no development here. I know. There'd be signs. It's not even for sale. No houses. I promise, Whim. I'll be right there—by the trees. I'll be waiting for you next year, okay?"

Whim nodded, feeling like a child. But he wanted to see Charlie, and he had to go. The pain… it was overwhelming. A detached part of him said that within half an hour, he wouldn't be able to drive.

*"I'll be there before then,"* said a voice in his head, and Whim recognized Green and almost wept. He was a child. He was Green's child, and Green had heard his pain.

Carefully, Whim bent down and brushed Charlie's lips with his own, trying hard not to wince when the movement jostled his arm. "I'll be back at Litha, Charlie. Remember, you made promises tonight. I take those seriously."

Charlie nodded and wiped his cheek with the back of his hand. "Jesus, Whim. The least I can do is be here when I promised, right?"

Whim smiled weakly and gave him one more kiss before straightening and turning toward his car. Sidhe could move extraordinarily fast when they wished, faster than mortal sight.

To Charlie it would have looked as though he disappeared.


To Whim, it looked exactly like he drove (badly) to the McDonald's parking lot right off Interstate 80 and the Foresthill exit. Green met him there, butter-colored hair in a tight braid, with Bracken—dark to Green's light, pine tar-colored hair whipped by the wind—on the back of the cycle.

Whim's vision was going in and out by the time they pulled up, but that didn't keep him from pulling his arm back as Bracken approached.

"Green!" Bracken complained, and Green wrinkled his nose in irritation.

"Tell him what you're doing, brother. Words aren't just for hurling insults, yes?"

Bracken growled. "Sorry, Green." This time, when he bent down, he was much gentler. "Whim, I'm going to use my power to make it bleed. That way, when Green heals it, there will be no poison left in the wound. You feel me?"

Whim nodded and trusted, because Green was his leader and wouldn't do him harm. And because Bracken was bigger than he was, and his power was terrifying.

But the wound didn't hurt at all when it bled, and Green's countertouch on his wrist made the skin grow back in gentle layers. Whim gave a sigh of relief and leaned his head on the car seat, and Green scooted in next to him to offer an arm and a shoulder.

"All better, brother. So, are you going to tell me what you were doing out of the hill?"

"Adrian said I could," Whim told him. "I met a mortal."

"And you stayed long enough for him to hurt you?" Bracken snapped, alarmed, and Whim pushed his head out of the car to retaliate.

"It wasn't like that! He stole a kiss!"

And now Green was alarmed. "He stole a *what?*"

Whim had never heard that sort of panic in Green's voice. "I stole it back," he defended. He tried not to pout. "And that's when things got out of control."

"Is that when he pulled the gun?" Green asked, his voice tender.

"What gun?" Whim asked guilelessly, and Green pinched the bridge of his nose as though his head hurt.

"Whim, how did you burn your arm?"

"On Charlie's pocket," Whim said obediently.

"Is Charlie the man who stole a kiss?" Green asked again, trying to make things simple.

"No. Charlie is the boy I didn't want to kiss," Whim said. Then he humphed. "But he stole the kiss, and he tasted soooo good."

Green took another deep, even breath. "Whim, please tell me you at least had your glamour on when you were out seducing mortal children."

"No," Whim said, missing Green's frustration entirely. "But that's not why he kissed me." Whim knew Green and Bracken were exchanging glances over his head, but he couldn't help it. They were his thoughts. He knew where they were going.

"I'll bite," Bracken said after a moment. "Why did he kiss you?"

Whim looked at his grumpy younger brother—at least as the sidhe reckoned relationships—and smiled giddily. "He kissed me because he liked me. We talked all night. He must have liked me for me."

Bracken shook his head, as though blinded by something, and he and Green met eyes again. "Well, good, brother," Green praised. "Are you going to see him again?"

Whim nodded enthusiastically. "Yes—yes. We will see each other next Litha."

Bracken made an odd choke-gurgle, and Whim looked at him as he started coughing so hard, Green had to reach out of the car and thump him on the back.

"Goddess, Whim, do you think you'll remember his name by then?" Bracken asked, and Whim was surprised.

"Of course I will," he said. It was Charlie, after all.

"I'll believe that when I see it etched in wood," Green muttered, and then he gave Whim a gentle, one-armed hug. "Come, brother. Brack will drive you back, and I'll take the bike. Let's get you back to the hill before June tries to fry you like an onion, yes?"

The sun was already a skin-sizzling glare, and Whim nodded distractedly. "Yes. Yes, let's get back to the hill." A picture was forming behind his eyes, and he was trying to make sure the sugar-drunk butterfly that was his mind would land in this place and stay. It would be the perfect thing, he thought, barely hearing Bracken and Green talking around him, to make sure he never forgot Charlie's name.

# Charlie—Covenants

Until Charlie saw the blisters on Whim's arm, he'd never thought that the gun in his pocket would hurt anybody but himself.

But Charlie looked up and Whim was gone. Charlie was there, with come sticking on his crotch and the tatters of his ill-advised plan of killing himself and making the world sorry lying around his feet.

Somebody thought he was beautiful. Somebody thought he was worthwhile. A beautiful somebody—a somebody beyond the dream of *anybody's* imagination.

And Charlie had just paid that somebody back with a fistful of pain.

Right there, standing in that wonderful, miserable dawn, Charlie made a particular resolution: never again would he take the good and give only the pain. He'd rather be the one eating the pain before that happened. He couldn't bear that he'd hurt a kind, funny, generous person because he'd been stupid enough to think a gun in an empty field was a way out of a painful decision.

He went home, took a shower, and told his parents he was gay.

They didn't take it well. But they didn't throw him out, either. He still got to live at home. His college money was still there. His mother was going to be a weepy mess and his father might not talk to him for a year or two, but all in all, it was a hell of a lot better than lying dead in a vacant field. The lying dead part had been his plan before he'd looked up and seen this mesmerizing, beautiful, amazing… *creature* walking toward him in the light of the sliver moon.

And then that *creature* had turned out to be Whim. He was aptly named—he was sort of like a crazy uncle or a child with ADD. Getting the guy to stick to one topic had been impossible, so Charlie had been content to follow his thoughts like a playful breeze. It had been fun. Entertaining, insightful, and unexpectedly sweet.

It had been worth the weirdness and anxiety of living in a house where he was suddenly gay (at least to his parents). Of going off to school where he didn't even have a small, tightly knit peer group to retreat to. Of allowing himself the luxury of smiling at other boys and flirting with them, too, when he'd been afraid for his life in high school. Of touching another boy's hand and feeling his body respond.

That conversation alone had been worth turning some of those boys down, just so he could let Whim be his first.

He studied art and music and acting and settled on acting. After hours, he studied sex. He studied grooming, hygiene, and technique, and experimented on his willing, panting body as often as he could get in his dorm room alone. He decided he liked sex very much—and would like it even more when someone else participated.

He really wanted his first someone to be Whim.

He had no illusions after that, really. Whim had made it clear that he'd only be found in that clearing on Litha, and as much as Charlie would like to indulge in the fantasy that Whim would come to that clearing one day and take him away from his life and to some magical place where creatures like Whim were commonplace and where they *cared* for each other the way Whim had seemed to care for Charlie on sight, he was realistic.

He might only ever have one other night with Whim; he wanted to make it count, dammit. If an elf was going to come out of nowhere and steal his heart, every blessed moment of the theft was going to be fucking magical. With only the slightest emphasis on fucking. Honest.

So Charlie learned how to flirt and taught himself how to come and allowed his heart to ache for the shortest night of the year. The night came, hot and muggy, and found him waiting in the clearing by the woods with what he deemed to be the essentials of the encounter—a picnic blanket, a sleeping bag, a basket of fruit, bottles of water, a pocketful of wet wipes, a box full of condoms, and a jumbo-sized bottle of lubricant.

The one thing he'd learned best from college was the value of coming prepared.

Still, that didn't mean his smile wasn't uncertain when he saw Whim ambling along the railroad tracks in the light the oppressive clouds let in from the half moon. But Whim looked up and saw him, and suddenly he smiled—and he literally glowed. Literally. He cast a shadow with his brilliance, and Charlie decided that casual anticipation was a joke anyway and hurtled across the clearing into his arms.

"You came!" he said breathlessly, Whim's big hands cupping his bottom and his legs firmly wrapped around Whim's waist. Whim gazed at him with something so close to adoration that it made Charlie's heart stutter in his chest.

"I promised," Whim told him gravely. "You packed fruit. I can smell it. What do you think they ate here before they grew fruit? Did you know things like peaches and oranges did not originate in California? How was school?"

Charlie laughed helplessly. He had forgotten that Whim's conversation was exactly that—whimsical. He wiggled a little so Whim put him down, and then he grabbed Whim's hand and led him to the picnic itself, ready to be the maître d' to their first real date.

"You did not answer my question," Whim said imperiously after he was seated with a paper plate of cut melon in his lap. He picked up the melon pieces between his thumb and fingers and scooped them elegantly into his mouth, and Charlie thought with admiration that Whim could make any act look sexual.

"Which one?" Charlie asked, his own mouth full. He really loved fresh fruit, and on a hot summer's night, you couldn't lose.

"How was school?" Whim closed his eyes as though to savor the taste of the fruit, but his head was still slightly cocked. It was clear that he was waiting.

"Fun," Charlie said, thinking about it. He spoke then of getting on stage, of writing his own pieces, of the joy of knowing people he hadn't grown up with—even, when Whim showed no signs of jealousy, of the few hurried kisses, the touches on the hand, the shy bouts of flirting that had taken place in between times.

"Did you take a lover?" Whim asked after listening with uncharacteristic single-minded attention. He almost sounded hopeful.

Charlie blushed and cast him a slantwise look in the moonlight. His cloak of hair—and Charlie wanted to see it in the sun, because he was pretty sure it had just shifted from chartreuse to magenta, but the moonlight made nearly every color a variation of silver—hung sideways as he balanced his lean torso on his elbow, and his face was rapt with attention for Charlie and Charlie alone.

"No," Charlie said truthfully. If Whim couldn't lie, he couldn't either—at least not for the sake of pride. "I kept, uhm, thinking about solstice night, you know?" Nervously, Charlie began to pack up the picnic, putting the paper plates in a bag and the Tupperware container of fruit into the box he'd brought to hold it, but he needn't have worried about telling the truth.

Whim's slow smile had charm and heat behind it. "How very symbolic," he said softly, "but I'm pretty sure they sacrificed virgins at Beltane, so we're just going to have to make love instead."

Charlie couldn't help it. His grin literally hurt, it stretched so far, and a warm chuckle rumbled out of his chest. "I'm so glad," he said when his stomach stopped shaking with laughter, "because I went to a lot of trouble to seduce you." He sat back on his heels and began to sweep off the picnic blanket.

Whim grinned back and then sat up in a fluid movement that belied how totally relaxed he had been seconds before, scooting out of Charlie's way so he could fold the thing up, leaving them on the opened sleeping bag. "You seduced me last year. I was just waiting until you were ready for consummation." And suddenly he made one of those abrupt conversational shifts that had marked their time the year before, and Charlie had a little bit of whiplash following him.

"Here. I want to give you something. I started making toys this year. Tiny ones. They're… they're…." And now Charlie could swear Whim was blushing. He could feel the heat that big, powerful body put out under the oppressive summer sky. "Green and Adrian say they're beautiful," he confessed and reached into the pocket of his jeans.

What he pulled out was not what Charlie expected. It looked like a case for glasses, the kind that opens and shuts powerfully on a spring, but it was more square than rectangle, and it was made of finely etched wood. For a moment Whim paused, closing his eyes, and a glow from his hands surrounded the thing, making it easy for Charlie to see the details of the wood.

"That's my name," Charlie said, surprised. The letters were embellished with oak leaves and wildflowers and things, and he looked at Whim, moved. Then Whim smiled happily and opened the case, and Charlie's breath caught.

It was a train, moving perpetually through the night, with a stand of oak trees below it and a clearing and a graffiti wall on the other side of it. There was even, carved in the tiniest detail, a family of rabbits venturing timidly from the bole of an oak tree. It was their time, their place, and Charlie had to swallow hard past a lump in his throat.

"Here," Whim said excitedly. "Blow—gently."

Their heads were together over the glowing toy, and Charlie puffed out his cheeks and made a tiny burst of wind. The train rocked and the bunnies wiggled and the trees swayed back and forth, and Charlie was caught up in the wonder of the moment.

"Wow," he said in a shaking voice. "Whim… this is… this is *amazing*. You *make* these?"

"Yes," Whim said, sounding shy and pleased. "This is my first one. Green has started selling the others. He owns many businesses, and one of them is a curiosity shop in the little mall on Main Street. I'm adding to the family income," he added with obvious pride.

"Whim, who's Green?" The name had come up before, and Charlie couldn't tell if it was a parent, a lover, a boss, or what.

"He's our leader," Whim said distractedly, blowing on the little scene again to watch the train rock. "Adrian is his consort. They keep us safe."

"Safe?" Charlie asked, startled, and Whim looked up at him, his face very sober as he closed the toy carefully and the glow around his hands diminished.

"Our world is secret, Charlie. And not all sidhe or vampires or werecreatures are friendly. The hill is sanctuary, but not everybody wants to stay there all the time. That's what a leader does—keeps his people prosperous and safe. I make toys for Green to sell, and Green comes to heal me when thoughtless lovers leave guns in their pockets. It's a trade."

Charlie blushed. "I'm so sorry about that," he muttered, looking away.

Whim took his hand and pressed the toy into it firmly. "I am not sorry for anything about that night. I am certainly not sorry you decided not to use the gun."

Charlie fiddled with the box for a moment, stroking the reverence of his own name. "I'm sorry that you were kind to me and I hurt you," he said at last. "I was being a dumbass. I don't even know if I would have used the damned thing. I just…." Charlie looked up and found Whim's eyes, rapt on his face. "I hurt so bad last year. I hurt so bad, and you looked at me and thought I was beautiful, and some of that hurt went away. Enough of it to be brave. Meeting you was a gift. Having you show up here again, it's more than I could ever wish for. I'm… I have nothing to give you back."

Whim blinked and smiled. He was kneeling next to Charlie, and almost shyly he leaned forward and kissed the bare, pale skin peeking out from the strap of his tank top. Charlie shivered and turned to him, looking at his eyes in the moonlight.

"Whim, what color are your eyes?"

"Somewhere between blue and green and gray," Whim answered. His smile curved down at the ends and became melancholy. "Like my hair—and my name. Inconstant. Childish. Even for a sidhe."

"You showed up tonight," Charlie told him earnestly. "You're about the most dependable person in my life."

Whim blinked rapidly as though surprised and stunned, and his eyes grew shinier under the cloud-lit sky. "I will show up next year, if you like," he said, and Charlie grinned.

"We haven't even had sex yet. What if it's awful?"

Whim closed his eyes and breathed in lightly, sticking his well-proportioned nose into the hollow of Charlie's neck and scenting his skin. "It will be wonderful," Whim whispered. "It already is."

Charlie shivered and sighed and tilted his head back. Whim kissed up his shoulder and along his neck and then up to the curve of his ear.

"Wait," Charlie said, before his vision went dark and his mind went completely blank. Very carefully, as though it were a glass butterfly, he took the precious little box, wrapped it in a fold of the picnic blanket, and then put the blanket in the cardboard box that held the Tupperware. He looked up self-consciously to find Whim watching him in bemusement.

"It's important," Charlie said with conviction, and Whim nodded, understanding.

"Good," he said. "So is this." And then he skipped the preliminaries and captured Charlie's mouth in a kiss.

Whim tasted like every good thing in the world. Like melon and peaches, chocolate and buttered toast, ham and sweet peppers, every taste individual and explosive on his tongue. And the kiss deepened, and Whim invaded his mouth, and Charlie stopped thinking about food and started tasting things like *desire* and *want* and… oh… oh God… *hunger.*

Whim leaned back and pulled Charlie with him, rolling so they were side by side on the sleeping bag, just kissing and using their fingertips and the flats of their hands to explore. Charlie's tank top was rucked up, and Whim's palms glided over his back, cupping his shoulders and hauling him closer. Whim cocked a leg up, and Charlie tangled his legs in with Whim's so he could grind his groin up against Whim's stomach because, jeez, elves were tall, and Charlie wanted the contact.

For his part, Charlie pressed his hands against Whim's bare chest, rubbing his thumbs against Whim's nipples and enjoying Whim's catch of breath immensely. Whim bucked against him and then pulled back from the kiss with a pouty little frown.

"Stop that," he muttered.

"You liked it!" Charlie protested, laughing with arousal and joy.

"I could orgasm from that alone," Whim told him crossly, "and I'm trying to make this good for you, so…."

Charlie grinned at him unrepentantly and took each nipple deliberately between a thumb and forefinger and pinched gently, just the way he liked his own nipples pinched.

Whim growled and kissed him savagely, his hard frustration taking kissing to a whole new level for Charlie. Charlie *liked* it! He returned the kiss with ferocity, still grinding, and then he stopped and shuddered a little when Whim spurted some precome.

"See?" Whim sounded peevish, and Charlie smiled against his lips—but not for long. Whim pulled away from him and kissed down his chest, stopping at his nipples and suckling and licking until Charlie cried out and gibbered, knotting his fingers in Whim's bloodred hair convulsively and begging for, God, anything, anything, but not this wonderful, frightening escalation to an orgasm the likes of which might crumble the earth beneath their bodies.

Whim knew what to do. He pinched Charlie's nipples one more damned time, and Charlie begged some more for form, and then Whim kissed his way down the soft skin of Charlie's stomach, and Charlie thought his heart would stop when he sucked in air. Whim's hands deftly unfastened his jeans and stripped them down his hips and off—he'd taken his shoes off when they'd sat down—and Charlie's naked virgin body was gleaming in the light of a half moon.

Whim pushed himself up on his arms and looked at him—just looked at him—a little half smile on his face. "Do you doubt it?" he whispered, and Charlie gazed up at him, his erection throbbing and his hips wiggling in arousal.

"Doubt what?" he whimpered, and Whim popped a finger into Charlie's mouth. Charlie sucked on it, hard, and Whim lay next to him, his head propped on his hand, right near Charlie's middle, and used that slick, air-chilled finger to trace a line from the tight, furred swelling of his testicles and up his turgid, erect cock.

"Doubt that you're beautiful," Whim breathed, and Charlie wanted to hold him, just wrap his arms around that clean, long body and hold him, but Whim grasped his cock firmly and squeezed, and Charlie's vision went dark as his whole body threatened to explode.

Whim chuckled with an evil little accent, bent and extended a pointed tongue to taste the head. Charlie whimpered and buried his hands in Whim's hair, and Whim licked again and then again and then, when Charlie was squirming beneath him, popped his lean mouth over the bell of Charlie's cock and slid his lips down to the base, swallowing as it bottomed out in the back of his throat. Charlie groaned, because it was going to happen… happen too soon… but oh God….

Whim did it again and one more time and….

"Auuuuuughhhhhhhhh… God… *Whim*!" And Charlie was coming and coming and coming and coming and Whim's head kept bobbing until Charlie's fingers relaxed and he fell back, panting and sweating and flaccid, recovering from a climax that seemed to have cleared the clouds from the moon.

Whim pushed himself up next to Charlie and lay on his side, patiently waiting for Charlie to find something to say. Charlie turned his head sideways, reached out a shaking hand, and pushed Whim's tangled hair away from his face.

"Damn," he said after a moment, and Whim's smile was brighter than stars.

"My people don't believe in damnation," Whim said practically, "but it's a very good word and I'm happy for it."

Charlie's shoulders shook, and he cupped Whim's cheek. "That was amazing," he said more coherently. "You… uhm…." His eyes darted down to Whim's crotch. His cock was thick and trapped against the leg of his jeans. "You want I should, uhm… you know?"

Whim nodded enthusiastically. "Reciprocation," he agreed, rolling to his back and shucking his jeans. He didn't have on any underwear, Charlie noted with raised eyebrows. "Reciprocation is an *excellent* word."

Charlie did the same thing Whim had: he explored. He discovered that Whim's nipples were even more sensitive than his own, and he spent a while tasting them, playing with them, and nibbling delicately on them, until Whim put both hands on the back of Charlie's head and *pushed*, and Charlie obeyed.

He lay on his stomach, propping himself up with one arm, and decided that Whim's cock was truly a thing of beauty. It was large, long and thick, although not, he had to admit, quite proportional to his feet, which was probably a good thing. Under the gray sky, it gleamed like marble, even when he grasped it at the base and slid his hand smoothly up, a tiny, shining bead of precome leaking out. Charlie tasted it, sticking his tongue out like a cat's, and then licked up the broad, flared, uncircumcised head, pulling the foreskin back so he could ply his tongue on the ridge. Whim shook, quaked, trembled like a rabbit's soft bunny nose with every new discovery, and the sound he made when Charlie stretched his lips over his teeth and popped that thing in his mouth....

Ooooohh....

That sound alone made Charlie hard all over again.

But this time was for Whim, for all Whim had given Charlie—although it appeared that Whim had a lot more stamina than Charlie did, because Charlie's mouth was getting tired and his fist was cramping, and Whim was still highly aroused but showed no sign of going over the edge to climax.

Then Whim started giving him explicit directions, and Charlie's prick got even harder.

Whim widened his legs and folded his knees up, and Charlie, using a copious amount of spit, began to stroke the area behind Whim's balls. A little bit of precome spurted, and Charlie swallowed, gratified, and Whim kept begging, piteously, and Charlie gave him what he wanted.

Sliding his finger on that sensitive area—Whim called it his taint, and Charlie liked the word—he then let that curious, probing finger slide down, down, into the cleft of Whim's bottom, and then into the shadowed recesses of his ass.

He found the entrance, and Whim whined even as Charlie gulped at that magnificent prick in the back of his throat. Charlie let more spit dribble down, down over Whim's testicles, into his cleft, and took that moisture and rubbed it on the tight pucker that strained for his touch.

Then he breached it gently, and Whim shouted and fisted one hand in Charlie's hair while Charlie stroked with that one finger and, in a sweet, breathless moment, Whim was coming, pouring come down Charlie's throat. He couldn't swallow it all, but he kept trying, until finally Whim lay still, panting and shaking under Charlie's cheek, and Charlie was using the heel of his hand to wipe away the slickness that coated his chin and lower jaw.

Whim hauled him up by the armpits until he was sprawled and sticky on Whim's narrow chest, and then Whim reached up and licked the spend off his chin with little laps, like a delicate kitten.

Charlie whooshed out a breath and fought to find Whim's mouth. His lover allowed himself to be captured, and they kissed, long and long and gloriously, until both their bodies were aroused again. But neither of them was in a hurry to move.

"*Whim*," Charlie groaned into his shoulder. "One night is not going to be enough…. Can't you stay more? Longer? A summer?"

Whim framed his face with both hands. "The thing I am afraid of," he said after a long, cricket-chirping pause, "is stealing away your life from you, Charlie. I could take you to my hill, change you into a werecreature or a vampire, and you would be mine forever. Or for a much-lengthened lifespan. You know, if you wanted to be a werekitty or a werewolf or a puma or something."

"They have werekitties?" Charlie asked in bemusement, and for once Whim was the one keeping the conversation on track.

"But you have so much to do in your world," Whim continued, his face tense and taut with this thought. "You have… *Goddess*, Charlie, there is so much you can accomplish. So much I would rob you of, should I take you with me now. You need to have another lover. You need to feel what the world is like without me. You…." Whim looked away for a moment—to their surroundings, to the railroad track that still cut a swath through this vacant field, to the graffiti wall that separated them from everything real in Charlie's human world. He looked back, and his face was pinched and unhappy, and his eyes were shiny, and not with joy.

"Charlie, I want you to go out into the world and live, and come back to me and tell me of your life. Can you do that? For a few years, can you do that? I would not miss the man you are becoming for all the Litha nights under the sky."

Charlie bit back bitter, bloody disappointment, and he nodded. He'd told himself, hadn't he? He'd known. Whim was his for a night. *This* night. He would be Charlie's on Litha, and wasn't that more than a mortal could ask?

Still, he didn't object when Whim raised a hand to his cheek and wiped his eye with a gentle thumb. Whim took the tear to his lips and tasted, and he made a sound like a man would make if a scalpel made of starlight incised the flesh nearest his heart.

"I know that taste," he whispered. "It's the taste of my own tears, Charlie. But I beg you to meet me here anyway, so we can have laughter too."

Charlie sniffed. "What sort of moron would turn down another night like this?" he asked, trying to keep his chin under control. He failed miserably, and Whim took his mouth and kissed him hard, and their bodies, naked now, resumed their delicate dance of flesh as they kissed and kissed, their wet cheeks rubbing together and the taste of their combined tears sweet and bitter on their tongues.

They made love again—and again—although the condoms in Charlie's picnic box never came into play. (Whim told him as the night wound down that Charlie wouldn't need them anyway, not with Whim. Apparently elves didn't get those kinds of diseases, and they certainly didn't spread them, and Charlie was relieved to hear that.) When Charlie sounded disappointed, sometime near the break of dawn, because they wouldn't get to actually do *that,* Whim had laughed gently.

"We'll get around to *that,*" he promised. "Is it horribly vital that I'm the first person to invade your flesh?"

Charlie looked at him soberly. "Yes," he said with emphasis, and Whim nodded, accepting that this was important.

"If it's that vital, it can wait until next year," Whim said quietly, running his fingers through Charlie's floppy bangs. "Tonight my flesh is sated, but I cannot get enough of touching you and watching you and talking to you. I would rather spend our last hour that way, if we may."

Charlie nodded—his body was about wrung out anyway—and they talked quietly until the first light of dawn cracked over the edge of the hill. Whim stood with regret, and both he and Charlie slid their jeans on (after making free use of the wet wipes), and Charlie tucked himself into Whim's arms to be enfolded into his careful embrace.

"Goddess, boy," Whim muttered, "I shall miss you. There is no lying about how much I will miss you."

"Someday, Whim?" Charlie asked plaintively. "Someday?"

"Someday," Whim told him. "I promise. We don't take that lightly. Someday, when your living is done here in this world, I'll take you to my hill and you can be a big tomcat—my big tomcat—and chase sunbeams and play music and do whatever you wish, and we will have every night in a soft bed to touch each other's skin."

Charlie nodded against his chest, forcing himself to be content with that, and then he raised his face for one last kiss.

"Close your eyes," Whim whispered, and he did. He felt Whim's lips against his own, and then on his forehead, and then a faint breeze.

When he opened his eyes, Whim was gone.

# WHIM—SACRIFICES

THE NEXT Litha, Whim was there when Charlie arrived, and he watched his human walk purposefully through their little field with an eye that was both critical and pleased.

He was growing up. His body was no longer ribs and clavicles, elbows and ears. His face had grown into his nose a little, and his chin was growing strong and square. He still wore ripped jeans and was in a tank top and the ratty trench coat, but Whim was starting to wonder if those were Charlie's real clothes or if he was dressing that way so Whim would know who he was.

Whim would always know who he was.

The illusion of complete adulthood vanished anyway, because as soon as Charlie saw Whim he stopped his purposeful walk and started tear-assing across the field, vaulting into Whim's arms with enough force to propel Whim backward a few feet as Charlie wrapped his legs around Whim's waist and met Whim's mouth with a ferocious kiss.

Charlie's taste hadn't changed either, nor his passion, nor the way he closed his eyes when Whim kissed his ears or his neck. He tasted his way down Whim's body with enough enthusiasm for Whim to know he'd had other lovers since they'd last met, but when he took Whim's erection in his mouth—after they'd both scrabbled furiously to get out of their clothes—he made a deep, primal sound in his chest. When he pulled back, a shudder ripped through his body.

"Thank God. I was starting to wonder if it was my imagination, but it's not. No one tastes as sweet as you. No one feels like you do under my hands...." His voice choked a little, but he silenced the sadness with the taste of Whim's erection and his fingers began the walk that Whim had coached him through the year before, and Whim saw black stars in his vision and bucked and all but screamed into the clear night. There was a three-quarter moon on this solstice—it made their clearing look knife-edged in light.

Whim had his turn then, rediscovering Charlie again and adding some things he was pretty sure they hadn't done the year before. Charlie whimpered in surprise when he found himself manhandled and turned on his stomach, and then he grunted when Whim wrapped an arm around his waist and hauled his bottom up in the air. Whim pulled a little bit of plump cheek into his mouth, laving with his tongue and suckling on it hard, and Charlie made a series of sounds into the sleeping bag that were a hysterical cross between laughter and arousal.

Whim let go of Charlie's flesh with a wet smack of his lips. "You've bathed," he said with satisfaction, reaching around to grasp Charlie's cock with a sure hand.

"I… oh gosh… I *prepared*…." Charlie was gasping and not very coherent, but Whim got the gist—his body was clean inside and out—and Whim took that as a big hint. Charlie wanted everything, and Whim wanted to give it to him. Still, he teased, separating Charlie's bottom and touching his tongue to the pucker between the cheeks. Charlie made a squeaking sound that Whim took as invitation, and he was more generous with his kiss. In fact, he spent a bit of time there, licking, stretching, using his fingers to make sure the ring of muscle was relaxed and ready, and Charlie's shameless begging, his innocent passion, had Whim aroused and (with a little help from the bottle in Charlie's trench coat pocket) poised at Charlie's entrance in far shorter a time than Whim would have imagined.

He reached down first and hauled Charlie upright, so for a moment his chest brushed Charlie's shoulders and he could whisper in Charlie's ear. "Mine," he promised. "Mine, for Litha, forever. Mine."

And then he thrust inside, and Charlie moaned, "Yours. God, Whim… I'm yours… always have been… *now now now now now*…."

And Whim obliged.

It was different than other sex, where Whim felt his own flesh alone, no matter how considerate he tried to be of the nerve endings of his partners. For one thing, Whim felt no urge to sing. For another, he was focused—as he always had been—completely and utterly on Charlie. Charlie's every grunt and groan, every frenzied cry, every gibbering word begging for completion, all of it was Whim's agenda, his feedback, his evaluation. When Charlie groaned loudly and went down on his elbows, yanking furiously on his own cock in order to climax, Whim was there reaching around, because he didn't want Charlie to have to do anything this time but scream with pleasure and come.

Which he did, and then—only then—was Whim prepared to finish, and the sweetness of spending inside Charlie's body…. Whim would stop often in the following years, out of nowhere, and shudder and smile wistfully because he had possessed such joy.

Afterward, there was touching, soft conversation, and huddling under the extra blanket Whim had brought. It was one of those summer nights where the ocean roaring of the wind seemed to blow the last of the orange sunset away in tatters, and once the night was securely, dazzlingly purple, it was chilly. The two of them pulled the blanket over their heads and held a flashlight under it and whispered like children, and once again Whim caught up on Charlie's year.

It was a good Litha. They were *all* good Lithas. Whim always considered himself the most honored and blessed of sidhe to see such a good man grow from such a troubled boy.

That year Charlie was excited because he was in plays. The next he was excited because he was *writing* them. The year after he was *producing* them and involved in community outreach programs that used drama as therapy. He was writing public service messages and watching young people put on programs that would benefit their community. He coached the youth of his community to speak out on every subject from the environment to tolerance, through simple plays about responsibility and tenderness. Whim was so proud of his playful lover for being responsible for such amazing, creative work!

When Whim asked him where he'd gotten the idea to use his gifts to help people, Charlie said, "From you, Whim. Where else?"

Charlie grew a little taller, but mostly his chest grew broad and filled out, and his waist and hips stayed trim and narrow. He developed a patch of chest hair that dwindled to his navel and then established what Charlie called a "happy trail" to his privates. He went from being clean shaven—in the mornings, too, because no stubble would grow—to having a goatee, to having sideburns, to being clean shaven again but with stubble in the mornings, because that is what human men did as they grew older. His hair stopped being floppy and in his eyes and started being cut short and sticking up, and with variations, that's the way it stayed.

One year, his eyebrow ring disappeared. The next year, he didn't even have the scar from where it had been.

He never stopped greeting Whim by running into his arms and wrapping his legs around Whim's waist, for which Whim was profoundly grateful.

He did take other lovers, some serious and some short-term. He would tell Whim about them every year, saving up the best or brightest stories to make Whim smile or wonder or be proud.

One year he grew sober when Whim asked about a lover, saying that this wouldn't make a good story.

"I'm here for sadness too," Whim told him, and Charlie looked away.

"Except you won't be, Whim," Charlie said, his face bleak. "I'll go home, and Steven will be gone because he didn't understand about Litha, not at all, not even a little, and I'll be alone again for another year."

Whim caught his breath. His fault. His Charlie was alone, and it was his fault.

"Do you want to stop?" he whispered. "Do… do you want to leave me on Litha too?"

Charlie shook his head adamantly, but he couldn't smile either. "I'd give up a thousand lovers, Whim, just to spend Litha with you. You know that, right?"

Whim nodded, swallowing. It had never occurred to him—although it should have—that their moments of Litha magic could hurt Charlie as well as heal him. The thought of hurting his boy… his man… his lover… it tore something terrible in Whim's chest.

"Do you like your life, Charlie?" Whim asked, hoping he'd say, *No, Whim. Take me away. Rescue me.*

"Yes!" Charlie said unexpectedly. "I love it. I have a sweet little house, and cats who love me. I have a job I'm proud of. I have a lover— even if it's once a year—who makes my life magic. I'm grateful, Whim. Everything you gave me—I haven't wasted any of your gifts, you need to know that."

Whim's face fell. "Oh," he said in a small voice. "You are happy. Then of course you must stay."

And now it was Whim who waited, anxiously, for the moment when Charlie might let him know that it was okay for Whim to take him home.

Charlie was not the only one who changed, though.

Whim had found his calling in the graceful little toys, and although his choice of subject matter would vary from moment to moment, it appeared he'd finally found a thing that could capture his butterfly mind and make him focus on something that would help his people. He made a special toy every year for Charlie, usually based on some story Charlie had told him from the year before. The year after Charlie produced his first play, the toy had a stage, tiny actors dressed in costume, Charlie in the audience, looking very grown up. The year Charlie bought his house, Whim had created the house itself—down to the cat sitting in the window, twitching its tail. He was patient. He could remember. He knew that Charlie would be waiting.

He took fewer lovers now, and the ones he took, he cared for, cherished, and remembered. Not once since he'd met Charlie in that clearing on Litha had he ever forgotten he was with somebody or burst into song. Whim had always considered himself insubstantial and only partially there in any moment. Thinking about what Charlie could be doing, at any moment in any given day, made each day worth remembering. He kept his feet—and his mind—securely on the ground as time went by and discovered that he, too, could offer something real to the world.

*"You're actually pretty flippin' scary there, mate," Adrian told him, his arm securely wrapped around the shoulders of the mortal sorceress he'd brought home one night. She appeared to be an ordinary mortal, but she had become invaluable to the hill. "You become any more of a grown-up and you'll be just like Green."*

*Cory smiled at him shyly, her plain face radiating an inner beauty that Whim was unsure mortals could see. She was, Whim thought painfully, barely older than Charlie had been when he and Whim had first met. Whim was touched with the frightening urge to take Adrian aside and yell at him.* The girl is too young. Don't lock her into love with you now. Don't play with her emotions the way you and Green can do. Give her room to grow, dammit! *But given the powerful, frightening magic this girl could do with little more than a thought and some strong emotion, Whim refrained. She belonged on the hill, probably since birth, while for Charlie, it was a choice. It had to be.*

*Whim smiled sadly back and bowed. "I could never be like Green," he said through a swollen throat. "For one thing, my hair is usually purple."*

*This had made Cory laugh as though charmed, and Whim resolved to make her a toy someday, because she could truly become his queen, and he loved her just as he loved Adrian and Green as his princes. But he didn't love any of them like he loved Charlie.*

The Litha Adrian brought Cory home was Whim and Charlie's eleventh—Charlie had told him that the year before. It was an unsettling time at the hill. Adrian had not just brought home a new lover from outside; Green had taken to her as well. There was an enemy threatening them all. The vampires and werecreatures seemed to be in constant danger. Mitch, one of the werekitties that Whim loved the most, had been killed, leaving his mate Renny despondent and empty. Every vampire, elf, and werecreature was huddling on the hill like ancestral humans around a fire.

Whim, who only went out during Litha, began to worry that he wouldn't be able to make his moment with Charlie.

But he *had* to make his moment with Charlie, he thought plaintively. He *had* to. It was the only moment they would get. Charlie had his life, his happy life, and he only needed Whim on Litha.

When the longest day of the year dawned and Whim realized that the situation with their enemy was going to be resolved *that night*, he did something unprecedented.

He left the hill without Adrian's permission, and he did it during daylight.

The magic little clearing he and Charlie had made theirs looked smaller and plainer during the day. The sun was *hideous*. One of the reasons Whim only came out at night during the summer was that elves did not do well in the heat, and as he struggled across the clearing to the trees where they usually met, a sleeping bag and picnic basket in his arms, he thought crossly that no wonder the long grasses were brown. The sun had apparently killed everything in the area with incredible malice. Even the dirt was hot and painful under his bare feet, and Whim realized with a shock that if he stayed here in this unfriendly place for the entire day, he would become ill. Green *always* kept the temperature in the hill cool so that his elves might prosper, and Whim was hit with the sad realization that it hadn't just been artifice and random rules keeping him out of Charlie's life.

If this field alone, this place he loved, was this hostile on a summer's day, how bad would the rest of the mortal world be? Charlie really did need to come to Whim, and Whim fought off a moment of despair that he would ever be ready to do that.

Whim was patient now. He had learned. He could wait.

But not today. Today, he set down his bundles by the tree and passed a geas—a spell—that said that only Charlie could see them. (For Charlie, they would probably glow.) He left a note, as well as Charlie's toy for the year. This year it was a tiny drum set. Charlie had joined a band after work hours, and the drums were his favorite. When you blew on it, the cymbals crashed and the tympani rattled.

The note was brief and, Whim hoped, not too worrisome.

*Charlie—Serious hill business tonight, but I will still be here. Even if you have to wait past dawn, I will not break our promise.*

He hoped it was not unfair. For the first time he cursed that he and Charlie had ignored basic modern conveniences such as phone numbers or e-mail addresses (not that Whim could use a computer, but there were such things on the hill) because it would make the separation less hard for Charlie if he could talk to Whim every day.

Whim longed to talk to Charlie every day. But he could not live in this world, he thought miserably as he trekked back to his car. At least not in the summer, and probably not during any other time. This battle that the hill had planned on the other side of the foothills terrified Whim; it would be loud and violent, and if it had been for any other reason than to protect Adrian and Green, he might very well have retreated to the cowardice of his kin and abstained.

But it *was* for Adrian and it *was* for Green, and the least he could do would be to show up and think of creative, capricious ways for their enemies to die. They *were* fighting a rogue vampire kiss, he thought with some optimism. Maybe he could simply make them fly into trees.

In either case, Whim needed to live on the hill. The human world only worked for him during Litha, or perhaps other nights with magic in them. And Charlie needed to want to be something more than mortal. He didn't even need to quit his beautiful job, but he needed to commit to the hill, and that was a decision Whim couldn't pressure him into or beg him to make. It had to be Charlie's own.

Whim looked longingly at the picnic basket and the sleeping bag sitting forlornly in what appeared to be an abandoned back lot. In the light of day, it needed some serious magic to take on the glamour of the Litha night.

# Charlie—Discipleship

Charlie was seriously worried by the time Whim showed up. The note itself had sounded sad, almost like a desperate promise. Charlie wondered what was going on in Whim's life to take up so much of a night that even Charlie could see meant the world to Whim. He could still remember the terrible (but not bitter) disappointment on Whim's face when he'd said, "You're happy, so you have to stay."

All those years of wishing that he could follow Whim, and now his life was too good to leave? Whim didn't have to feel bitterness. Charlie felt it for him. Damn… damn, damn, damn, and damn. After living with that moment in his heart for a year, Charlie was pretty much ready to drop everything not to have to live with it again. He was working as a high school counselor these days, doing his music and his drama as extracurricular activities, and he was prepared to simply not show up for work one day, leave his house and, hell, leave his cat, and simply walk away, a victim of the night, to make sure he never had to feel Whim's abandonment again.

And now, Charlie thought he'd do all that plus walk on fire just to be sure Whim was all right.

He was and he wasn't.

He arrived in the cold of the night. Charlie, who had long since abandoned the ratty trench coat, was wrapped in the blanket, sitting with his back propped up against their tree and nodding off, when Whim appeared at the far side of the clearing, walking unevenly and dazedly to where Charlie was sitting. For a moment, Charlie's breath froze in his throat. It looked like Whim was covered in blood.

He was across the clearing in moments, and Whim put up his hands to hold him off. "It's not mine," he said abstractedly. "You don't need to get it on you."

"Fuck that." Charlie evaded the warning hands and took Whim's arm, leading him to their place with gentle movements. Looking up, he could see the tracks Whim's tears had made through the even spatter of blood on Whim's face. "C'mon, Whim. Come here. Come tell me what happened."

But Whim didn't, not right away. He sat on the sleeping bag and let Charlie cover his shoulders with the blanket, and when that didn't seem to work, he let Charlie get under the blanket with him and just sit, warming their bodies in the soft breeze. Eventually Whim laid his head on Charlie's shoulder and murmured, "You humans here, you don't have princes. You have presidents. You had one you thought of like a prince, didn't you?"

Charlie was confused for a moment. "Like JFK?" he asked, completely thrown out of his element.

"Yes," Whim said. "Do you think when that prince died, it was worse for the people who ate breakfast with him? Who saw him be happy with his family? Who maybe shared his bed? Although that's frowned upon, I know. Do you think those people grieved for a friend *and* a prince? Do you think they wondered which one hurt more?"

Something about this question was making Whim openly weep, and Charlie could only answer honestly. "I think they probably did, yeah," he said softly. "I think the leader and the man were probably very, very different, but they'd miss them both. I think they maybe grieved more for their prince than for other men. Why?"

"Because my prince died tonight," Whim told him on a sob. "My prince died tonight, so horribly and so quickly that I'm wearing…." He shuddered. "We're *all* wearing his blood. And his mates… they did such horrible things in the wake of his death. Green… Green *sang* the hearts of his enemies into his hands, and the girl-sorceress… Goddess…." Whim turned a helpless face to Charlie. "She's barely older than you were, Charlie. She's a child. And she did such a terrible thing out of grief. And I'm glad. Isn't that awful? I'm glad she did it, because he was my friend and my prince and I wanted to kill and kill and kill and I didn't have to. She did it for me. She just pulled magic out of the air and did such horrible things and I was *glad.* Oh, Charlie… there's a big shredded emptiness where my heart is supposed to be, and the only way I know it's beating is because you're next to me to hear it."

Charlie was helpless in the face of Whim's grief. He could barely track the events as they tumbled out of Whim's mouth in a disorganized jumble, but he'd heard of Adrian. He'd heard of Green. In the same way Whim asked about Charlie's life, Charlie heard bits and snippets of life on Green's hill and of the gentle men who inspired such loyalty from his Whim. And now Adrian was dead, and Green was in pain, and this girl-sorceress Cory (who was new, granted) was lost like a child, and Whim was not much better.

There was nothing to do but hold him, comfort him, tell him that Charlie would be there for as long as Whim needed him.

Whim turned a tear-ravaged face to him with the slightly open mouth of a six-year-old. "But I'll always need you, Charlie," he said with such stricken earnestness that Charlie had no recourse but to believe him with his whole heart.

"I'll always need you too," Charlie told him, and whatever that was worth, it seemed to quiet Whim down. The sobs eventually ceased, and Charlie eased Whim's head into his lap and sat there, still leaning against the tree, and watched the sun rise. Charlie was half expecting him to just vaporize in the gold light of dawn, but the reassuring weight stayed there on his thighs, and the lovely curtain of hair stayed under his hand like coarse satin. When the sky was truly light, Charlie looked down and saw that the hair was scarlet and black today—the color of old blood.

"Whim?" he said softly. "Whim, we need to leave. I don't want you to just go away, not like this. Can you come home with me, just for a day or two? I'll take care of you, Whim. I swear, nobody will know you're there. You'll be just as secret at my house as you've always been."

Whim sighed. "Everybody at my house knows you," he said, surprising Charlie badly. "But yes. I don't want to leave you. Not yet. Not like this." There was a pause, and Charlie felt guilty because a corner of his heart was overjoyed to hear this. Then Whim said, on a note of complete practicality, "But we'll have to take my car."

"Car?" Another surprise. "You drove a car?"

Whim nodded and sat up, pushing his tangled hair out of his face. The color had changed a little—it was now a murky, mottled brown. Grief, yes, but not so fresh. "It's specially treated," he explained, and then he shrugged. "If we drive cars that haven't been blessed with a salt wash and herbs, the cold iron in the engine eventually makes us sick."

Charlie blinked and stood up, offering his hand to Whim, who took it and rose gracefully. Charlie was almost surprised to see Whim turning and gathering the sleeping bag and the blanket, putting them in his own picnic box. He turned to Charlie suddenly, and now his hair flashed a bright orange.

"Did you see the box?" he asked, a trace of the joy that Charlie was used to in his voice.

Charlie nodded. "It was beautiful," he said earnestly. "They're always beautiful. I have a shelf for them, you know. A place of honor in my house. I'm glad you'll get to see it."

Whim nodded and continued packing, hoisting the box and the sleeping bag up easily. He turned toward the car, but not before casting a baleful look at the sun.

"It's hot already," he sighed. "The heat isn't good for us either."

"That doesn't surprise me in the least," Charlie said with a slight smile. Everything about Whim pointed to the fact that he was very strong and very fragile. That he should have great magic and great physical vulnerabilities was pretty much par for the course. They walked across the field and then took a gap in the graffiti wall to the suburban neighborhood that sat behind their magic place. In the daylight, the suburb looked older and a little worn down, and Whim's car, a fairly new SUV but not too fancy, didn't look particularly out of place on the curbside. Charlie should know—his own car, a white Honda, was parked about a block away in front of a friend's house.

He might have seen Whim's car, or one of them, every Litha night for the last eleven years. The thought was somehow disturbing.

"Whim, if you drive here, how is it you just disappear?"

Whim paused in the act of throwing the stuff in the back hatch and fished out Charlie's toy before he closed the hatch. "We can run really, really fast," he said simply. "It only looks like I disappear."

Charlie held an imperious hand out. "Here, give me the keys," he said, and Whim pulled them out of his pocket. "Why do that? Why not just walk with me back out to our cars?"

Whim got into the car first and did the seat belt just like Charlie, although Charlie was pretty sure Whim had told him they were almost invulnerable to things like car crashes.

"I was hurt that first night—and you needed magic," he said when Charlie had started the car. "Something beautiful. I didn't have much I could give you. And after that… well, you expected it, and I didn't want to disappoint you."

Charlie shook his head, and then he shook his head again when Whim reached out and pressed play on the iPod sitting in the jack. Christmas music started to play, and Whim began to bob his head happily.

"You are magic," Charlie told him, smiling sadly. "And you have never disappointed me."

Whim looked at him, his smile old and wise. "I will," he said with certainty. "You're a grown-up now. You have higher expectations."

Whim seemed both happy and sad to see Charlie's little white-painted house sitting on the half acre of unfenced land. He definitely approved of all he saw, including the nicely mown, well-watered lawn, which he sank his bare feet into blissfully.

"It's beautiful, Charlie," he said sincerely. "Do you think your cat will like me? We have werecats at the hill, and I like them very much. Mitch and Renny like to curl up at my feet when I work." Suddenly he made a hurt whimper, and Charlie looked at him sharply. "Mitch isn't alive anymore," he remembered. "And Renny's damaged. Oh damn."

Charlie looked at him in alarm. Whim had stopped still on Charlie's lawn, a tall, pale man with alien features and hair the color of old blood. His neck drooped with dejection, and his whole body was smeared with the rust-colored remains of his fallen prince.

"We need to get you inside," Charlie said gruffly. "Let's give you a shower, get some food into you. You'll feel better then."

"Do you have oatmeal?" he asked hopefully, and Charlie was relieved to remember that he did.

After the shower and the oatmeal—Whim liked his with honey and butter and walnuts, but Charlie didn't have any walnuts—Whim fell asleep in Charlie's bed, wrapping his long body around Charlie and holding him to his chest like a teddy bear.

Charlie was tired too, but he spent long moments in that secure embrace just staring at that lovely, inhumanly beautiful profile. Even in sleep, he looked sad. Whim had loved the house, Charlie thought with a tight swallow. He'd loved the hardwood floor, he'd loved the comfortable furniture in eclectic colors, and he'd really loved the specially carved shelf Charlie had made for his toys. He even loved the cat. But his face, his heart, had been so transparent, even as he'd said, "This window is wonderful, Charlie. You must be happy to eat your oatmeal here every day." He'd loved it, but it had hurt him, because Whim was obviously not suited for this world, and Charlie's nice house and happy life were not things he'd ask Charlie to leave.

Over the next three days, though, Charlie found a reason to leave them. Whim woke up after only a few hours of sleep, ready to make love. He hadn't cared about Charlie's morning breath or the sweat that invariably coated his body in the summer. He just wanted to touch skin to skin, to put his mouth on Charlie's body, from his ears (sensitive!) to his chest to his, well, everywhere. Charlie had let him, had reciprocated, had ended up doing a sleepy, happy, awkward (Whim's body was *very* long) sixty-nine before he was even close to awake. And that was only a prelude.

Whim grieved. He lapsed into stunned silences in the middle of conversation, and he could be found at any moment, standing or sitting starkly still, staring into space and weeping. He also helped with the dinner dishes, petted the cat to distraction, put on work gloves and helped Charlie with the bathroom repair he'd been planning, and painted a playful and stunning—Charlie was forever impressed by Whim's artistic gift—mural of cats lounging in magnificence on Charlie's bathroom wall. And yes, Charlie was a little surprised at that one. But Whim asked for the latex paints and nonmetal equipment, and Charlie obliged. Two hours later, the bathroom wall was a living testimonial to Texas the ginger cat and any friends or relatives Texas might have.

He also made love with a frequency that would have left a rabbit sore, but Charlie wasn't complaining. Every touch, every smile, every time Charlie came in his mouth (Whim was unfailingly generous—it was almost as though he'd been taught "sex manners") convinced Charlie that Lithas weren't an anomaly; they weren't a magic pocket of time with a mystery lover. Litha was magical because of Whim. Whim was magical in broad daylight, in the dark of a moonless night, or when he was ambling over Charlie's lawn in his bare feet on a bright, dry morning, singing a plaintive version of "The Little Drummer Boy."

The morning of Whim's fourth day, Whim woke up suddenly from a dead sleep and said, "They're missing me. Oh, Charlie, Green is worried sick. I need to go."

Charlie was caught flat-footed, horrified. "Go? Go? Whim—you… now?"

Whim's smile added a whole new level to the mourning he'd been doing since he'd arrived. "I want to take you with me."

"In a heartbeat."

"But I can't."

Charlie's beating heart plummeted to his toes. No. Not a rejection. Not after this.

"I wanted to…. Goddess, Charlie, I was going to ask you this year. Small"—a little quirk of his lips—"wonderful house be damned, I… I need you. I miss you. My years used to fly by, without anything to anchor them. Now they crawl by, from Litha to Litha. I was going to ask you.

Beg you. I was going to make you every offer under the sun, fall to my knees if I had to—"

"You don't!" Charlie burst out, hurt, moved, confused. "You just have to ask."

"Ask what? Ask you to leave a good life for a country at war?"

Charlie opened his mouth, surprised by the analogy, surprised by the idea. "A country? It's a place…."

"It's a *people,* Charlie. And we just lost our prince. And now we'll be besieged by enemies. Adrian left his vampires to his beloved—the girl, Charlie. A nineteen-year-old mortal girl-child is in charge of a kiss of vampires. Do you have *any* idea how badly this could go?" Whim took a shuddering breath and wiped the back of his hand across his cheek. "We lost six shape-shifters in this attack, Charlie. They're the first ones to die. They're our weakest members. Stronger than humans, yes, and longer-lived. But in my world they're cannon fodder."

Whim shook his head, his hair a mournful, aching twilight color, and took both of Charlie's hands in his, even as they sat up in Charlie's bed, naked—both physically and in any other way two people could be.

"Can you wait another year, beloved?" he asked, his voice raw. "Can you wait until I at least know what I am asking you to become a part of?"

Charlie searched his face and saw only sorrow. "Beloved?" he asked, playing for time. Whim's face fought against collapsing again, fought to stay composed.

"It's our word at the hill, our endearment. Can I say it? Will you be my beloved, even if I can't take you home with me?"

Maybe it was the word. Maybe it was the taut way it passed through Whim's throat. But Charlie was convinced. This denial—it hurt Whim possibly more than it hurt Charlie. Charlie had a life without Whim. Whim didn't like his life without Charlie.

"Yes," Charlie whispered, and it was his turn to pinch the bridge of his nose and squeeze his eyes shut. "I'll be your beloved. And, beloved, I will be soooo sorry to see you go."

Whim kissed Charlie's forehead then, and Charlie closed his eyes and tried to imprint this feeling, this warmth of having Whim there near him, the smell of him, the sound his breathing made in the silence. One more year, he thought resolutely. He could wait one more year.

"Whim?" he asked, trying not to whine. "Could you do me a favor?"

"Anything."

"Could you let me see you into the car? Don't just disappear on me. Not this time."

Whim's eyes, which really did move from blue to green to turquoise in the light, flashed bright turquoise, and his hair grew tints of gold.

"That I can do," he said simply. Then he proceeded to kiss Charlie, pull him down into the bed, and make love to him through simple touch and taste one last time.

Putting Whim into the car hurt, but it felt like a more temporary hurt than just having him disappear. Whim kissed him on the forehead and promised to drive safely and begged him one more time to wait, just one more year, and Charlie promised. And then he was gone.

THE YEAR seemed to slog by, and Charlie threw himself into his job. Counseling was grueling work. By the time he got the paperwork down, he found he'd been ignoring the students. And when he turned his attention to the students, he was suddenly ass-deep in paperwork. And none of it, *none* of it felt like a winning situation.

He got a small parcel at Christmas—a perfect miniature of his bedroom, complete with a blue bedspread and a purring Texas the cat on his bed. When you blew on it, the wind chimes outside the bedroom window made the sweetest sound and Texas twitched his tail. Charlie put it on his shelf with the others and stood looking at the little parcels of Whim's devotion to him for a long, long time. If Whim could make it a year, then he certainly could.

In February, he went to a gay bar the day after Valentine's Day.

It was an unusual move for him, but his whole life had become Placer High School and the needy students and beleaguered administration, and even his band had become a point of stress because nobody had time to rehearse, and dammit, he just wanted company. He hadn't had a lover since Whim, and that was unusual, and all of his friends had their own girlfriends or boyfriends or family. Mostly he just wanted someone to talk to on lover's day. He would have tried the regular bars to look for a girl to talk to (he got along with women just fine—in fact, he missed his mother frequently now that he was out of the house), but this was Auburn and he didn't want to get the shit kicked out of him. So Auburn's one hole-in-the-wall gay bar was where he ended up, and he was just about to give it up as a bad idea when someone sat next to him.

Charlie was surprised to find he knew the guy, and even more surprised that he was old enough to drink.

"Jesus, Daniel," Charlie said, "has it really been three years since you graduated?"

"Five, Mr. Fratelli," the kid answered, smiling a little over his beer. "But seeing you here is still like watching your dog sit up and talk."

It should have been a good conversation. Daniel had always been a quick kid, funny with the one-liners, happy and easygoing. He'd been in one of Charlie's first theater groups, and he and Charlie had gotten along very well in that way some teachers and students can. Charlie had never, ever thought of him as more than a kid, a student, somebody to mentor, somebody to help.

Daniel needed a lot more help now.

He'd recently been diagnosed as bipolar. He had no health insurance, no job, and his parents were on the verge of kicking him out of the house because of his sexuality and his refusal to be discreet with his bed partners—even Daniel had to admit he'd been less than circumspect.

When Charlie had asked him, alarmed, if he should be drinking, Daniel had given a fuck-it-all shrug. "Hell, with the meds, it'll just make it easier for the razor blades to slide in."

Charlie experienced a horrible frisson of truth. He meant it. Just like Charlie had meant it the night he'd gone wandering the railroad tracks with a gun.

Oh God. Whim. Charlie closed his eyes and wished so hard for Whim that he was surprised the elf didn't just show up there in the bar, ready to take him away from the pain of the world and the hard choices it held. When he opened them, it was still Daniel sitting on his bar stool, smelling of alcohol and despair.

"Don't say things like that," Charlie said softly, placing a careful hand on Daniel's as it sat near his on top of the dirty bar. "Some of us care about you."

Daniel turned to him with the greedy love a drowning man shows a rope, and Charlie thought dismally about June, when Whim would be coming for him.

*Whim, forgive me. I owed the world for you, and now it's time to pony up.*

# WHIM—SUPPLIANT

HE'D FELT it, in February, the dreary month when it seemed the siege of his people would never end. He'd felt Charlie's remorse, a single bloody shaft right to his chest, but he showed up for Litha anyway.

The sullen young man Charlie brought with him and left at the gap in the graffiti wall looked as though he would rather Whim hadn't, but Whim was too heartsore to care.

"I'm sorry, Whim," Charlie said, walking the rest of the way across the clearing. He wasn't running and jumping into Whim's arms, and that hurt too. Whim looked up to where the boy sat. Dark blond hair, maybe, and probably hazel eyes. Whim didn't care. He was the boy who would take Whim's boy away from him, and Whim didn't care what he looked like.

"You're not coming," he said back. "Ever."

"It's not forever!" Charlie burst out, and then he looked hurriedly behind him and grabbed Whim's hand, pulling him into the trees, dropping his voice. "Me and Daniel, it's not forever, Whim. It's not you and me. It never was. It was never supposed to be."

"Then why?" The terrible shaft of betrayal seemed to ache where it landed.

Charlie sighed. "Because you saved me, Whim."

"You don't owe me."

"I don't…." Charlie blew out a breath and scrubbed his hands through his hair. Whim could see one or two threads of silver in it now, not too much, but still, his mortality was glimmering in those silver threads. "I do, but that's not why I love you. It's not why I've shown up here, year after year. But I owe somebody. God. The world. Somebody. I came here twelve years ago to kill myself, and the universe sent me you instead. Don't you see? Don't you see how wildly out of balance that is? This is me, giving back. This is me, sacrificing a year of my life, of happiness with you, to make up for all of the time I've had that I wouldn't have had if you hadn't shown up."

Whim felt his face relax, and some of the pinched misery that had taken up his anticipation of this night faded away. The pain in his chest eased to a dull throb. His people understood good works. They understood giving back. They understood a debt to the Goddess. Whim took several deep, trembling breaths and tried very hard to understand Charlie.

"He thinks this is forever," Whim stated, wanting to know if Charlie knew that.

Charlie shook his head. "Daniel is really troubled, Whim. His disease makes him selfish, and sometimes unkind. He doesn't know forever. I just need to get him to a place where he'll take his meds, take care of himself, learn to exist on his own. Once I know he's not going to… to rob the world of all he's got to offer, then I can let him see how wrong for each other we are."

Charlie's voice deepened with irritation then, and Whim was heartened (as petty as it was) to see that Charlie didn't really love this boy. Not like he loved Whim. But still….

"A relationship based on pity, Charlie?" Whim asked, not liking that idea either. "Is that what you think you and I have been? Is that what you think he wants?"

Charlie took Whim's hands then, regardless of eyes that could be watching, and held them up to his stubbled cheek. "I do not doubt, nor have I ever doubted, that you love me for me, beloved," he said solemnly, and Whim's heart actually started beating again without feeling like it was pumping through a sucking chest wound.

"Yes?" Whim asked pathetically, and Charlie eased closer and wiggled, looping Whim's arm around his shoulders.

"Not once," Charlie reassured, leaning against him. Whim's whole body gave a sigh of relief. He had known he wouldn't get sex this night, but he hadn't counted on getting a full dose of Charlie, either. Apparently Daniel the chaperone was going to have to live with the idea that Whim got to stand as close as a lover, even if they couldn't make love.

"What about him?" Whim asked, wanting Charlie to see how this could all go wrong. "Nobody wants to be someone's pity lay as a long-term relationship."

Charlie looked up at him, his chocolate-colored eyes dancing with their first glance of humor for the night. "Pity lay? Did you just say pity lay?" he asked, inviting Whim to oh-please-laugh with him a little.

Whim could never deny Charlie a damned thing. "I watch movies," he replied loftily, and then he sobered. "But this is important, Charlie. You both could end up hurt. Anything that hurts you is always a bad thing."

Charlie leaned his head against Whim's chest, and for a moment there was only the sound of their breathing, loud among the trees, and the sound of the train far off in the distance, not ready to roar through their Litha yet.

"When he becomes unsatisfied with pity, then he'll be well enough to move on," Charlie said with a combination of heaviness and hopefulness, and Whim had to concede. It was the best scenario this plan had to offer. He would have to hope.

"I brought your toy," Whim said out of nowhere, because his basic nature had not changed in all these years.

"I thought the one at Christmas was my toy," Charlie said, content just to lean on him.

"Yes, but I thought this would be good-bye," Whim explained, reaching into his pocket. "I made you a special one, for good-bye."

"You knew?"

Whim shrugged. "I… I felt something…. I felt you beg me for forgiveness, in the winter." Whim looked away. "I couldn't think of what else it would be."

Charlie moaned a little and took the small wooden box from Whim's hand. "I don't want to look at it if it's a gift of farewell," he muttered, but he took it anyway. He opened it, and Whim summoned the light from his hands so Charlie could see. There was Whim, tall, loose-jointed, standing in their clearing, his arm poised to throw a stick across the green. Standing near him was a cat, a large one that came up to Whim's thighs, getting ready to pounce as soon as Whim threw.

Charlie blew on it softly, and Whim's arm extended and the cat's legs moved, and for a moment, Charlie could see what Whim dreamed for them. Charlie could have been that shape-shifting cat, and he and Whim could have spent their days together.

"We'll live this, Whim," Charlie whispered, looking at it. "I swear. Tell me that it's okay. Tell me you can make it another year. Tell me we can be this, this right here, someday. Please. It hurts so bad right now, being here with you and being so close. Tell me this can be us."

"This can be us," Whim said, believing it.

"Tell me you'll be okay," Charlie said hopefully, and Whim closed his eyes and murmured his first lie.

"I'll be fine," he said, and the first attack of stomach cramps was truly horrible. He kept his body still and breathed evenly, and Charlie didn't even flinch against him.

"Are you sure?"

"If I know we can be together at the end, I'll survive," he said, and this was the truth, so the nausea and muscle aches eased back a little. But not entirely. Charlie must have heard something in his voice then, because he didn't press.

"Then so can I," is what he did say, and Whim used the opportunity to change the subject.

"Do we have the night?" he asked. "I mean, I know making love is out, but can we sit and talk? He's right there. I'm not going to simply man-nap you into the night. Can we… can we talk?"

Charlie nodded and cast Daniel a weary glance. "I told him it would be boring. I told him that's all we'd do. If he wants to fall asleep over there while we talk all night, I think that's his choice, right?"

Whim had brought the picnic blanket and some food, and Litha was almost like it had been. Before they really started, Charlie ran Daniel a peanut butter and jelly sandwich and some melon that Whim assured him he wouldn't be able to eat. Charlie told Whim about continuing with the job as a counselor but learning the workload so he could still work on his music and write, and Whim told Charlie about the year at the hill.

It had been an eventful year. Their little sorceress had proven herself again and again. Between her and Green and Nicky and Bracken, her other lovers, they had made the hill a place with hope again.

"Bracken *bonded* with her. Can you believe that, Charlie?" Charlie didn't understand, so Whim had to explain about bonding. When a sidhe bonded with a lover, it was an awesome kind of magic—it literally bonded the two together for the lifespan of the most mortal of the couple. Bracken had bound himself to a mortal. He had sacrificed the potential of thousands of years, just to know that she wouldn't leave the world without him. Bonding was also based on fidelity. Cory had previous bonds, so she would be allowed to keep those lovers. Bracken had only Cory. If he were ever unfaithful, it would be Bracken who died while she mourned him.

Charlie was overwhelmed. "That's an amazing sacrifice," he said, looking at Whim with awed eyes.

Whim blushed. "I'd make it for you, if you became a were-animal," he promised, and Charlie squeezed his hand hard. Whim changed the subject then and explained how the combined power of Green and Cory and their lovers made their hill and their people strong.

"Not invulnerable," he warned Charlie. "There are still threats sometimes." But powerful. People were afraid to attack them now. All of Green's followers bore Green's mark, and to commit treason was to be punished horribly.

"Would you like to see my mark, Charlie?" Whim asked, and as Charlie looked, fascinated, Whim pulled down his T-shirt (another first) and showed him the tattoo between his neck and his shoulder. Most of the time a sidhe *couldn't* tattoo. A tattoo was a wound, and they healed such things. This one had been blown through his body with magic, though, and his own permission, with the power of touch, blood, and song, the basis of all elven magic, and it meant that Whim belonged—truly belonged, in spite of his oddness and his time spent alone in his own head and his little workshop and his butterfly mind—to the hill that he loved.

His mark showed a gamboling cat with a bloody rose in its teeth, playing with limes and acorns. "All the things are symbolic," Whim assured him, not wanting to talk too much about it. "But the cat is definitely you."

Charlie had smiled. "You really want me to be a cat, don't you?" he asked rhetorically, and Whim knew his smile was a little foolish, but he didn't care.

"I really like cats," he said solemnly, and that earned him Charlie's first real laugh of the night, and for a moment Whim forgot that his stomach was going to explode. "Newcomers get a tattoo as they become a vampire or a werecreature… or a friend," he added.

Charlie asked questions about the hill politics, and about Whim's prince and his queen, and Adrian's best friend and former lover, Bracken, the youngest sidhe at the hill. Whim's tongue tripped as he tried to explain the marriage ceremony that would happen in two nights' time, and he thought he was doing a horrible job of explaining all of it—but Charlie proved, as he had always proved, a quick study for these things.

"It's like Arthur and Guinevere and Lancelot," Charlie said in evaluation, "but like they really worked it out instead of making a hash of it."

Whim was delighted, and something in his heart righted itself in spite of the nasty, cramping nausea, and he began to hope again, truly hope, that he and Charlie would someday get to live that promised future. "Yes. Yes, exactly," he said, a little bit of happiness bleeding into his voice.

Charlie took his hand and kissed it. "That's awesome, Whim. It's like, you know, if something that epic and big can happen and work, then maybe just you and me, we can work too."

Whim nodded earnestly. "It works that way, Charlie," he said, excited at the thought. "Renny, the werekitty who was so heartbroken after her beloved died, she found a new lover. It's strange because he's a policeman, but sometimes even the strangest things can work if there is big love magic surrounding it."

"Big love magic," Charlie said wryly, lifting his eyebrows. "Well, we'll have to hope for that."

Hope. Sometimes it was the driving force behind the oxygen pushing itself into a body's lungs, wasn't it?

They talked until dawn, and then Charlie stood and looked beyond the railroad tracks to the graffiti wall where Daniel sat, dozing in the gold light. Whim stood and took his hand, and together they walked to the clearing, the decision to part right before the railroad tracks unspoken and mutual.

Charlie turned to Whim when they got there. "Promise me you'll be here next year," he begged, and Whim nodded.

"How could I not be?" Whim told him sincerely. Charlie stood on his tiptoes and pressed his mouth hard to Whim's, and Whim closed his eyes and savored the taste.

"Promise me you'll be okay until then," he whispered, and Whim nodded.

"I'll be fine." Then he gritted his teeth against the cramping, the sweats, and the pain.

Charlie's eyes searched his face, not liking what he saw, but he still turned and left. He got to Daniel and shook him awake, and Daniel stood and blinked, scowling when he saw that Whim was still there. Charlie sighed and, after making sure the other man would follow him, disappeared through the gap in the graffiti wall.

As soon as he was gone, Whim fell to his knees and vomited bile onto the scorched ground at his feet. When his body was done with the first round of heaving—and after two such heinous mistruths, odds were good he'd be sick all day—he looked up and saw Daniel hadn't quite followed Charlie. He was still there, looking with surprise and, to his credit, some concern as Whim humiliated himself in the middle of a vacant lot.

"What?" Daniel asked, almost against his will, and Whim didn't have any evasions or half-truths in him.

"I lied," he said achingly, feeling his stomach buck inside him again for round two. "I said I'd be okay…." And with that, he heaved again and again, and when he looked up, miserable and trembling, Daniel was gone.


WHEN WHIM later thought about that year, he thought of it as "the year of malaise." He felt sickly, sad, and not himself from the moment he got up off the ground and staggered back to Green's hill.

It was a hard year to feel like shit at Green's hill. Cory, Green, Bracken, and their accidental lover, Nicky, were all happy, and the hill felt more secure—a safe place to bring a lover. Even the new and deeply troubled alpha werewolf managed to settle in with his family and achieve something like peace, and given how damaged he'd been, that was saying something. The hill itself was built like a vast apartment building right in the center of one of the smaller mountaintops in Foresthill, with a wraparound window on three-quarters of the hill, showing the side of the elves and nothing but hillside on the side of the vampires—so as not to let light in. Ever. It was hard to be alone in the hill proper. More and more, Whim found himself retreating to his tiny workshop in one of the buildings outside the hill, singing melancholy songs to himself while he poured all of his hope into his tiny toys.

He didn't take a lover once that year, and this behavior alone was an anomaly among elves. His hair was a perpetually shifting shade of storm-cloud gray and mournful blue.

It wasn't until June arrived, when his heart usually lifted and soared with anticipation at seeing Charlie, that this sickly sadness became ominous.

It wasn't until the week before Litha that Whim realized it wasn't just his heart that was sick about Charlie, but that something about Charlie was truly, physically sick.

Whim panicked. He had the realization while working on a toy just for Charlie, one showing a boy in a trench coat, dancing to music in his own head. He was thinking so deeply about his boy, his *man,* that suddenly he pictured him.

Charlie's body hurt. His arms and hand were hooked up with tubes and wires. The hand with the biggest, clearest tube and the biggest, most painful needle was pale and thin, and the veins stood out like blue railroad tracks, carrying death to their destination.

*"Charlie!"*

It was the same way Whim had known Charlie was going to break his heart, but this time Whim needed Charlie to hear *him.*

*"Heya, Whim. Is it Litha yet?"*

The quality of Charlie's reply let Whim know that he was drugged heavily and in pain.

*"You'll hold on till Litha for me, won't you, Charlie?"* Oh Goddess. Oh please. Three days. If Charlie could hold on three days. *"I can't heal you in that place, Charlie. I'm not strong enough. Please, Charlie. Hold on until Litha. I'll be there. I swear I'll be there."*

He crashed into Green's bedroom, his hand tearing through the lock on the door and everything. *Nobody* opened that door. *Nobody* violated the privacy of Green's sanctuary. For one thing, it took a lot of magic power to violate the lock itself, and usually Whim would have said he wasn't up to the job.

As it turned out, Green wasn't in there, but his little sorceress was. She was sitting cross-legged on the giant hand-carved bed in cutoff shorts and a white T-shirt so big as to be the sail on a large vessel, her neck drooped over a book. She'd been crying, and she looked up at Whim in surprise, the curly red ponytail at the back of her head bobbing like a child's.

And then she'd smiled gamely through her tears, and for the first time since his frightening vision, Whim knew hope.

"What's wrong, Whim? You look like shit."

The words were coarse, but the expression on her freckled face was all concern, and Whim found himself on his knees, his arms propped up on top of the bed like a petitioner before his goddess, telling her the whole story. Litha, Charlie, his desire to bring Charlie to the hill—all of it tumbled out of him, and when he finished with, "Goddess, Cory… he's so sick! I can't heal him alone… how can I heal him alone? I don't even know if he'll survive becoming a werecat!" He dropped his head on the coverlet and sobbed softly, only vaguely aware that her hand was on his head, stroking through the tangle of his murky green-brown hair.

"Shhhh…," she soothed. "Shh…. He's still alive, Whim. We just have to make a plan. I'm supposed to be good at plans."

"I'm not," he said in a clogged voice. "I'm only good at stupid things—"

"Stop that!" Her voice was sharp enough to make him look up. "You're good at joy, Whim. You're good at joy, and kindness, and it sounds like that's all this guy has ever wanted in his whole life."

"I can't heal him in a hospital, Cory," Whim confessed miserably. "I'm not that powerful. The needle in Charlie's arm alone hurt me." And then he showed her the skin of his arm, which was reddened and swollen as though healing from a cold-iron burn.

Her eyes widened, and she laid a hand on his cheek. "Jesus, Whim, you're already partially bonded to the guy. Touch, blood, and song— you've already got a link. We can do this. We can heal him. I've got an idea. Here. Here's the plan."

Whim trusted her. She'd saved her lovers on more than one occasion, and she'd saved the hill on every level that counted. Cory could do this. Cory could make the most of Whim's gifts, even though he was the least powerful sidhe on the hill.

So Whim put his trust in his queen, and then she laid out a way to save his Charlie.

While she was outlining what needed to be done, Green walked in, his hand tender on the back of her neck as she spoke.

"Luv," he interrupted at one point, "you know we can't…."

Cory nodded and met Whim's gaze with her own tear-reddened eyes. "We can't leave the hill on Litha, Whim," she said apologetically. Whim knew. Adrian had died on Litha. The entire hill mourned. That kind of grief carried a powerful magic all its own—and not the lovely, healthful magic that Green was usually so good at, and that Whim needed now.

"That's okay," she said, looking hopeful. "Green, I think I know the perfect healing elf for the job."

"What about the werecreature?" Green asked. Charlie would need to be bitten—there was no doubt about that. Besides needing to fit in at the hill, the fact was, the bite of a werecreature would clean the sickness out of Charlie's blood as he changed form. Neither of them offered a vampire's bite, and Whim was grateful. He would rather Charlie be mortal and full of life than immortal and yet pallid and pulseless.

"Renny?" Whim asked hopefully. Renny loved Whim. Whim thought he would need all the faith he could get.

Cory's face softened as she looked at him, and Green nodded behind her. "I'll ask," Cory promised. "I'll ask. And you can do this, Whim. All elves can heal a little. You'll make this work, okay?"

And then they finished planning how Whim was going to save his Charlie.

# Daniel—Gifts

By the time the police officer, the elf, and the tiny girl crashed into Charlie's hospital room, Daniel had seriously grown the fuck up.

The past year had been hell. Charlie had been diagnosed with leukemia in January. Six months of feeling ill, out of sorts, and (even Daniel had to admit) brokenhearted had turned out to have a physical cause, and Daniel had panicked.

"I can't do this!" he'd yelled. "I can barely care for myself!"

Charlie had nodded, accepting, and said, "Fine, Daniel. I've got insurance. I've got family. You do what you need to do."

Daniel hadn't made it out the front door. Charlie had saved his life—figuratively, literally, spiritually—in every way possible. He found that he wouldn't be much worth saving if he didn't hang in for the rough stuff.

And it had been *very* rough. Charlie had needed chemotherapy, radiation, long car trips to specialty clinics, and an up-close-and-personal relationship with a barf bag. It still hadn't been enough. In May, he'd been diagnosed as terminal. By the middle of June, he'd been in the hospital, waiting to die.

Hanging on until Litha.

It had made Daniel's vision go red at first, how much faith his Charlie had in that tall, alien-looking freak he'd met in the abandoned lot. But something about the way Charlie talked about Whim, something about their simple faith in each other, finally touched Daniel's heart. Charlie had always loved Whim more. That he had given Daniel a year and a half of his life had been a true gift, a true sacrifice, and Daniel had been damned ungrateful.

He'd even started to think of ways to help Charlie escape the hospital, just so he could spend his last moments saying good-bye to his Whim.

As it turned out, he didn't have to.

The door to the ICU room blew open, and a man in a local sheriff's uniform said, "Dammit, Lambent, I'm supposed to be here to make it official."

A tall man with fiery red hair and a ruddy complexion snapped, "Come off it, Max, I've numbed the minds of anyone we've run into. It took us three bloody days to find this bloke, and I'll be damned if I let Whim down now."

Daniel, who had stood up in outrage next to Charlie's bed, suddenly felt hope. "You know Whim? You can get him to Whim? It's the only reason he's hung on this long." Daniel looked at Charlie, who had barely come out of his pain enough to recognize his visitors. "He only wants to see Whim again."

Lambent nodded, and something in his appearance melted away. He suddenly had the same triangular features Daniel had seen on Whim, only broader and redder, and the same pointy ears. Not a man, Daniel thought distantly. An elf.

"Well, we're here to make that happen. Renny, luv, if you will…?"

And with that the girl, a tiny, tiny girl with flyaway hair and a loose cotton dress, turned into a giant brown tabby cat before Daniel's very eyes, the dress pooling at her ankles. Daniel, who had spent more hours than he could count looking at the tiny, perfect toys under the glass bubble of the shelf, especially the one featuring Whim and the big brown cat, felt a certain amount of hope.

Delicately, the girl-cat padded up to Charlie as he lay in his hospital bed and sniffed at him mournfully. She turned to Lambent and gave an unhappy mrowl, and Lambent nodded.

"Hear you, luvie." Deftly, he turned off all of Charlie's machines and pulled the tubes from his skin. Then Renny took Charlie's hand in her mouth and bit gently, just hard enough to let a little bit of blood seep out. She licked at the wound until it stopped bleeding and then stepped out of the way for Lambent, who picked up Charlie's wasted gray body in his arms and sighed. "It's going to be close," he told them all. "It's going to be close. The bite won't work unless he's stronger. I can give him a little strength until we get there, but in the end, it's all going to come down to Whim."

Maybe because he was desperate enough to hope, Daniel saw a faint glow around the two of them, but that was put out of his head as he trotted out of the hospital behind them. Not a soul tried to stop the motley little group, and Daniel figured maybe that was magic too.

The clearing looked magical by moonlight, as well. After a truly terrifying ride with Max-the-cop behind the wheel of a big SUV, Lambent led the way with Charlie still in his arms. Charlie had come to a little in the car, and his first word had been "Whim."

"No, Charlie," Daniel said, feeling a little like shit just for bearing the news. "We're going to see him."

"Good. Thank you, Daniel."

For the first time since Charlie had gone terminal, Daniel felt something that wasn't tinged with anger. Charlie knew him. Charlie cared. It wasn't Daniel's fault that he wasn't Whim.

Whim was there in the moonlight, standing with his bare feet planted in the earth, his arms extended to take Charlie from Lambent, who relinquished him gently.

"You're charging a good bit, brother," Lambent said softly, and even Daniel could see the glow that surrounded Whim as he cradled Charlie in his arms.

"I'm not very strong," Whim worried. "I couldn't do this without Litha… without our magic place…. Oh, Charlie, you're so thin!"

Whim didn't even mention the hair, which had fallen out with radiation and never grown back.

"I held on for you," Charlie mumbled. "God, Whim… you're the first thing I've smelled since the hospital. You smell so good."

Whim chuckled weakly. "Are you ready for this, Charlie? It's going to mean you and me together until death. And you're a werekitty now. That's going to be a very long time."

"Take me home, Whim," Charlie begged. "You promised. Take me home."

"I'll die before I break that promise," Whim muttered, and then looked at Lambent as though begging for something. Lambent, for all he seemed arrogant and demanding, gave him a gentle kiss on the cheek and pressed a small silver knife into Whim's hand.

"It can't be me," Lambent said gently.

"You're a healer, Lambent, and I'm not that strong…."

"You've got the love, brother. All the love in the world. You'll do fine. It's near midnight, and that's when you'll be strongest. He's not going to be strong enough to change into his other form and get this shite out of his blood unless you heal him first. His wound is still open from the bite—hurry."

With that, Lambent grabbed Daniel's arm and hauled him back. Together, he and Daniel stood with the big brown cat and the cop who kept petting her and watched the tableau of Whim and Charlie in the center of their magic place on Whim's most powerful day of the year.

None of it made sense to Daniel. Whim used the silver knife to make a small cut on his finger and then took Charlie's hand in his own, opening the wound and rubbing the blood together. The wounds began to glow, and then Whim began to sing.

From where Daniel was standing, it sounded like "The Little Drummer Boy."

Even the stoic cop's eyes grew wide. "Interesting choice," he observed, and Lambent shushed him even as he nodded a rather befuddled agreement.

And then none of them had words. The glow increased, grew brighter, intense, a blinding mixture of blue, red, and gold light, culminating in a cornea-blasting silver that engulfed the two lovers in the clearing.

Whim kept singing, though he fell to his knees still cradling Charlie's wasted body against his chest, and the light swirled and blurred around them. Still, it didn't seem to be enough, not to cure Charlie, not to help Whim, until Whim's voice, ragged and cracked and bleeding, tore across the clearing. "*Please, Goddess, please....*" And then the glow exploded around them until the little gathering of watchers had to cover their eyes.

When the glow faded and Daniel could see past the spots playing in his vision, he blinked and saw a miracle.

Charlie was sitting up in Whim's arms, and his hair had grown back. He was still thin and looked as though he *had* been ill, but even in the moonlight, Daniel could see that his face was flushing and his cheeks had color and his breathing was even and healthy.

That was it. His miracle. Charlie was going to live.

He took one excited step across the clearing when a hand on his arm stopped him. He looked in surprise to see the girl there instead of the cat. She was naked and apparently didn't give a shit, and she was glaring up at him with unfriendly amber eyes.

"You don't think he's yours again, do you?" she asked in a feline growl, and some of Daniel's glee faded.

"I… I thought he was here to say good-bye. I…. Now that he's going to live, I mean… he's got a life now, right?"

"Not with you," the girl said, her voice flat.

"Renny," Max-the-cop warned, and Renny gave him the equivalent of a cat flipping its tail. Max rolled his eyes, muttered something that sounded like, "No sex for you," and then let her finish.

"They're *bonded*, Daniel," she hissed. "Whim just pledged his life to Charlie's, as long as they're faithful. That means if he goes back to you, Whim just gave up his life so you can have a security blanket."

Daniel sucked in a breath and looked back to the two of them, murmuring in the middle of the clearing as though nothing had happened, telling each other the important things in their lives. He didn't bother asking how this tiny girl-cat would know what his relationship with Charlie was like. That was the least of his worries. She spoke the truth. He'd been prepared to give Charlie up to death. He'd even reconciled himself to it. He'd spoken promises about caring for himself, living up to his potential, becoming the man he'd promised to be instead of the clinging, careless boy he'd been when Charlie had taken him into his life. Did Charlie's life really make those promises less valid?

He swallowed hard and nodded soberly at Renny. He understood, he thought painfully. He got it. He walked thoughtfully to where the two lovers were, and this time Renny let him.

"You will like the hill," Whim was saying softly. "Especially as a cat. There are lots of things to play with. The sprites love to play with the werecreatures. One of them will adopt you immediately, I'm sure."

Charlie's hand, whole now, not withered for all his thinness, was splayed over Whim's chest. "I want to play with you instead," he said, and his voice was Charlie's voice—playful, demanding, irrepressible.

"Later," Whim muttered. "After I've held you for about a thousand hours."

"Yeah." Suddenly, Charlie became aware of Daniel, and a moment of conflict crossed his face, a reluctance to shoulder a burden he knew he must, and that moment was enough for Daniel. "I… I can't…. Whim, I need to make sure Daniel is okay…." And before Whim could even be hurt by the moment of duty, Daniel made his decision.

"I'm fine," Daniel said through a tight throat. "I'm fine. You go be happy, Charlie. You've earned it."

Charlie looked at Whim. "Can we make sure he's taken care of, Whim? There's legal stuff and—"

"I'm on it," said the cop, coming up behind Daniel. "In fact, I'll even give him a ride home. Ouch! Dammit, Renny, I'm helping!"

Daniel looked down and saw Renny was a cat again, and she'd just shoved her claws into Max's leg. Giving the cat equivalent of a chuckle, she turned her fuzzy butt toward Max and Daniel and led the way to the car.

Daniel knelt for a moment and gave Charlie a kiss on the cheek. "Bye, Charlie," he said gruffly. This was better than seeing him die, he told himself. He could be happy, just knowing that Charlie was happy out in the world.

"Bye, Daniel," Charlie said back, but he could barely look at Daniel long enough to say it. His eyes were all on the clean, beautiful profile of the elf who had just saved his life for love and love alone.

When Daniel got to the graffiti wall, he turned around for one last look. Whim had sunk to the ground completely, crossing his legs and keeping Charlie securely on his lap. Lambent had produced a blanket from somewhere and draped it over them, and was now leaning back against a tree, his cheek on his knees, looking prepared to doze quietly until the lovers were ready to go.

Charlie was leaning his head on Whim's shoulder and looking at him with more devotion than Daniel had ever felt for another human being, much less earned for himself.

Daniel swallowed hard against the lump in his throat and left the future tomcat and the elf named Whim to their faithful Litha night.

A YEAR later, Daniel came back to the clearing.

No one had told him to come; no one had invited him. But he had lived through the year, had dealt with his grief, had taken care of himself and come out complete.

Of course, Whim's people had helped. Two days after Litha, the police officer had shown up, catlike girl at his side, and given him a forged death certificate as well as a will—notarized—that said Daniel got Charlie's house and all of his possessions.

The only exceptions were thirteen of the fourteen cunning little wooden toys sitting on Charlie's glass-cased shelf.

The one that Max and Renny left was the one Whim had made when he thought Charlie had been going to say good-bye—the one showing the cat and the elf in a clearing, playing with an undisguised joy.

Daniel took it as a sign. He took his medication, kept his job, fed Texas-the-depressed-cat, and mowed the lawn. He made peace with his parents, consoled Charlie's folks, got to know Charlie's sisters, and attended family dinners. He came to learn all of the lessons Charlie had been trying to teach him when he'd been there, and he wondered if he ever would have grown up enough to learn them if Charlie hadn't left.

He realized that his love for Charlie had been the love for a caretaker and not that of a beloved, and he grew up enough to be grateful that Charlie had cared.

He showed up at the little back lot, magical only one night a year, so he could show Charlie he was okay. So he could say good-bye.

They were there. Whim wasn't throwing a stick like the scene in the toy, though. He was doing something even better. He waved his hands, and two light spots traveled across the ground, playing with each other and dancing in an impressive display of light. A big chocolate-brown tomcat chased them with all of the playfulness Daniel remembered. He pounced on one and leapt to the other and frolicked across the meadow to the next, and Whim's laughter traveled across the quiet of the Litha midnight like the chiming of bells.

Daniel found he was smiling—tearful, yes, but smiling. God, they were so damned happy.

He was going to turn away then, but Whim must have seen him from the corner of his eye. The elf turned and raised a silent hand in salute. He forgot to turn off the light he was generating with his magic, and for a moment Daniel was blinded as it hit him in the eyes. He almost missed the next part.

Very slowly, and very deliberately, Whim bowed.

Dammit. That was it. Daniel wiped his cheek with the back of his hand and bowed back. "You're welcome," he whispered, and then to Charlie, who had turned and was gazing at him serenely from gold cat eyes, "You're both welcome. Thank you. Thank you both."

He turned and left the clearing just as the train passed by, separating him from the two figures in the moonlight, and he realized in his bones that Charlie's decision to leave had been the right one. Looking back had never been an option for Whim and Charlie anyway.

# Whim—Blessings

As soon as Daniel disappeared, Charlie ran across the field and then took a giant cat leap. He turned into a human in midair and landed, legs straddling Whim's waist, hands wrapped around Whim's shoulders, pulling Whim down for a kiss.

Whim kissed him, kissed him ravenously, kissed him as though they hadn't made love that morning and nearly every morning and every night since Charlie had come with him to Green's hill.

They always kissed that way.

"He's gone?" Charlie asked him between kisses.

Whim had no words for Daniel. "Mmm-hmmm...."

"Good," Charlie said breathlessly. "Good. Good...." And then he kissed Whim some more. His body was strong and wiry, like it had been his entire adult life, and his hair was thick and a little long, growing over his ears for the first time since he was a teenager.

There was a three-inch tattoo on his naked chest, right over his heart, and had been since the night Whim had healed him. It showed a rose, dropping blood over an acorn and a lime. The blood changed colors according to Charlie's mood. Charlie knew what it meant now, and Whim liked to touch it quietly while it glowed the colors of cherries and melons and bananas.

Whim held him now, strong and healthy and as gleeful as he'd ever been, and Whim kept holding him, kept falling into his exotic, familiar taste, as he walked unsteadily to where the trees were. They'd come prepared tonight, and their blankets and their picnic were waiting for them. This year, Green had even given them a special basket and had their favorite foods made. He and Cory said that someone should celebrate Litha, since they could no longer take joy in it.

And Litha it was—their Litha—and when they were together, there was always much to celebrate.

I Love You, Asshole!
Amy Lane

# In the End

ONCE UPON a time, he'd had a last name and a girlfriend, and he'd been completely straight. He wasn't sure what happened then. There had been a dark shape swooping in front of his car, a body thunking off the hood, a terrible crunch of metal, and a feeling of unreality. Part of his steering column snapped in half and penetrated his femoral artery, and his soul began to detach from his body as the blood that held the two of them in the same space pumped out.

Things got weird after that.

Absolute cold, the silence of a frozen sea, the faint promise of warmth and light, and then….

Something fiery burning along his veins, pulling him back through that sea, causing it to splinter and scathe, penetrate and scrape, flay the skin from his flesh and bind it back together with a cold so penetrating, so icy, it felt as though his blood vessels were lined with blistering pustules, bursting with scorching, raw pain.

It felt a little like… a lot like… a *whole lot* like….

The need to come when someone wouldn't let you breathe and had your cock in a vise.

Marcus expelled his last breath on a scream, bit down hard on something that felt an awful lot like cold flesh, and pulled blood into his body in an orgy of carnage until his stomach filled to bursting….

And he came.

He felt like panting then, in the aftermath, and his chest even cooperated for a few tries. But as he blinked hard and looked around him, his chest stopped moving, and he was too distracted to notice.

His clothing was shredded, and his shredded body was *healing*, knitting up flesh like some sort of reverse time-lapse photo even as he watched. He was covered in blood—not just from the injuries that no longer existed, but spilling from his mouth and over his chest, and there was… a man's thigh, in tattered jeans, pulling away from his face even as he took stock.

There was also a man's mouth licking gently at Marcus's naked thigh, where he'd seen the steering column enter and the blood pump out before the whole frozen-lake-of-silent-fire thing.

The hole where the steering column had been was all gone, and what was left was smooth, rapidly cooling skin.

The man who'd been… suckling on his thigh? Really? The man who had pale white hair turned his head and grinned at him, flashing red, whirling eyes. His mouth and chin were covered in blood, and—

"Where are my pants?" Marcus asked, his voice resounding so loudly in his ears that he almost wept.

"Mr. Desarno! Ohmigod!" Marcus was on the side of the road, naked from the waist down and covered in blood, and there was something wet and white mixed with the blood on his chest, and Marcus watched as the man who'd been… suckling… on his thigh rolled over, tucked his equipment in his jeans, and buttoned up, commando style.

He was lying on the side of the road, naked from the waist down and covered in blood and *come*, and someone he knew was there to see him?

Oh God… he knew that voice. Recently. Where…?

"Mr. Desarno, you're going to be a little disoriented, okay?"

He knew that voice. Where… where…? He blinked, and his teacher's brain kicked in.

Adult education, last year. She'd been in her twenties, and fragile. He remembered that she'd been so… on the verge of just not showing up, just not earning her GED, just not being a part of the world at all. Twenty-three years old, and she was just ready to disappear.

"Gina?" His voice was still too loud in his ears. "Gina Victorine?"

"Mr. Desarno! Thank the Goddess! You changed! You were dying, right, and I remembered you, right? And Adrian was taking me flying, and… we couldn't just let you, you know? We couldn't just let you die."

The blond-haired man with the whirling eyes who'd been sucking Marcus's blood sat up and gave them both an insouciant grin. "Well, technically, luv, he *is* dead."

Marcus stared at him, and the man gently placed Marcus's hand on his own throat.

Nothing happened. Nothing moved. Nothing pumped, breathed, or twitched.

He was dead. Dead, naked, and covered in blood.

"Mr. Desarno, you're going to be all right, okay?"

Marcus blinked. He was going to be all right? Or he was going to be dead? One thing was certain.

"All things considered, Gina," he said slowly, "I think it's better if you call me Marcus."

# A Ten-Year Vampire Primer

Gina Victorine had apparently found herself—or at least a family to take care of her. It was unfortunate that she'd been found when she was half-dead of an overdose, but Adrian—the blond man who had pulled Marcus over into the vampire world—had helped her out as well.

Gina and Adrian had been the best mentors a newly fledged vampire could have.

It was terrifying, at first. Marcus was a gentle person, a history teacher, a baseball coach for his nephew's team, a suitor so bashful he'd dated his girlfriend for nearly six months before he'd gotten laid.

The first time he ripped Adrian's jeans off his body to gobble his cock and suck blood from his thigh was about five minutes after Gina and Adrian got him back to their home, Green's hill, and got him out of the shower.

He was a naturally curious person, so he should have been worried about the house (dug into the side of the hill, with a wraparound window facing out from three-quarters of the hill and the "darkling"—the vampires' quarters, which were completely covered in earth—taking the other quarter), but he wasn't. He should have registered that his room—complete with a shower cubicle with a curtain in the corner and a big sturdy bed in the middle—was almost like a padded vault as opposed to a real guest room, but that wasn't what he was curious about either.

What he *was* curious about was… flesh. The throbbing of it. The slickness of the skin over it. The blood… glorious blood… *fabulous* blood… *delicious blood…* pumping underneath and through it.

The next thing he knew, he had a mouthful of Adrian's thigh, and Adrian was coming on his ear.

And Marcus was mortified. He'd stepped out of the shower, had a towel around his hips, and was trying to come to grips with the fact that what should have been a cold shower didn't really bother him that much, and then Adrian had stuck his head into the bathroom and said, "You okay, mate?" in that lovely cockney accent of his, and then….

Well, Marcus needed another shower. He'd come all over his towel.

Adrian explained it to him a little later because one shower turned to two, and then three, and then Adrian had brought in a young man with a lovely *warm* body, and Adrian explained that he was a shape-shifter, and he didn't mind being gnawed on or fucked into oblivion because his blood supply replenished quickly. Marcus's attention wandered, and the young man had looked so lovely, and Adrian handed him a bottle of lube, and suddenly Marcus's cock completely took over. And only *then*, after the young man was panting and dilated and laughing in reaction and a little pale from blood loss, did Marcus think he could hold a thought in his befuddled head.

The tall, blond-headed vampire climbed naked into bed with him. Marcus should have been embarrassed but, considering all of the other things that had happened to him and that he had done that night, was not.

"What you have to understand, mate," the man said soothingly, stroking his hand down Marcus's back as he clutched his pillow to his chest for comfort, "is that you're like a big baby with a sex drive. You want to eat, you want to fuck, and not much else is going on up there." Adrian tapped Marcus's head through his curly black hair. Italian—everything about him was Italian, from his olive skin to his dark eyes and regularly plucked unibrow.

"But...," Marcus muttered. "But... *men*, Adrian. I've never in my life...."

He'd just fed—a *lot*—and he would learn that the full-body blush that coated him would only happen when he was full of other people's blood.

"Shhhh...," Adrian whispered, soothing his shoulders and generally showing Marcus physical kindness. "I get it, mate. The thing is, Gina tells me you're a gentleman. A good guy. A nice man. I'll be honest. Until you're over this blood-madness thing, you're only going to see men in this room, and I'll tell you why."

Marcus pulled out of his misery and the strange lethargy that was hitting him as dawn approached, and he turned his head. He noted—in a purely objective way—that Adrian had the most blessedly blue, sky-spangled eyes Marcus had ever seen.

"Why?" Marcus asked somnolently, wondering what those eyes would look like behind him as Adrian buried himself in Marcus's flesh. His cock stirred, interested, and for a moment his body was paralyzed with indecision—the approaching sleep or one more bout of... of... *lust*.

"Because you *are* a gentleman," Adrian told him, his eyes going from blue to that alert red Marcus had first seen. "You're a nice guy, and the guilt for what you would do to a woman—even if she's willing—I've seen it drive some blokes mad."

"I don't want to hurt anyone," Marcus mumbled, and Adrian nodded.

"Oh yes. And the women here are mostly shape-shifters or vampires—they're tough. But *you*—" Adrian tapped his bare chest. "You're a kind man, Marcus. You've got that thing in your head that wouldn't forgive yourself for fucking a girl bloody. No—your body is on high alert, and all it wants is to feed and to fuck, mostly at the same time. You'll be more comfortable if you're with someone you feel could fight back or hold his own. Don't worry, mate. We've done this drill before. We'll keep you supplied. But get ready for a bumpy ride. It'll be weeks before you're civilized enough to be in the room with a live body and not be tempted to eat its throat and fuck the corpse. I won't lie—for a gentle man, it will be damned uncomfortable. But you'll learn. You'll be a gentle man again. Just trust me, right?"

Marcus felt the lethargy take over, dulling the bloodlust, dulling the regular fuck-me lust, and he had enough wherewithal to ask, "Why am I so...."

"Sunrise." Adrian embraced him gently, and then the sun did, and he wasn't sure what happened for the next eighteen hours.

Adrian was right, of course. Marcus would learn that, in spite of his reluctance to lead like a general, Adrian was very good at leading a person to be the best version of himself. The next day, after Marcus had fed from Adrian himself—and the wounds had healed, and Adrian had fed from someone else out of Marcus's sight—Adrian brought in a young-looking man, naked, as they all seemed to be in this room. Marcus had to admit it cut down on cleaning.

Adrian told Marcus to think about feeding, and suddenly his canines lengthened alarmingly. Adrian showed the same face to Marcus, and then, after asking the young man's permission, he took hold of a tender wrist and delicately punctured a vein. The blood ran freely, and Marcus felt hunger stir in his belly.

Adrian told Marcus to do the same, and because he wasn't voracious and desperate with it, he managed. The tooth poked, the blood spilled richly out, and Marcus clamped his mouth over the vein, suckling eagerly. The young man's head fell back, and he sat naked between the two of them, writhing, groaning even when Adrian lapped at his wrist to close his own wound and Marcus continued to feed.

Marcus's hunger wasn't overriding anymore… or at least his hunger for food. Now that he wasn't out of his head, the hard-on was a surprise.

But it wasn't to his dinner. The boy—Marcus would find out later that he was older than Marcus; he'd been turned into a shape-shifter while still in his teens—took one look at Marcus's arousal, took his healing wrist from Marcus's dazed grasp, and bent his head, opened his mouth, and proceeded with a blow job so exquisite, Marcus was pretty sure he wouldn't need sex for at least….

Another fifteen minutes.


IT GOT better. After a month, they let Marcus out of what amounted to a giant vault in the basement, where they kept new vampires locked up so they didn't go running amok through the rest of the hill. Marcus had to admit—if Adrian had been a less skilled tutor, and if there hadn't been a steady procession of warm bodies coming through his room nearly every hour, they might have needed to lock that thing on him.

Blood and body lust were *not* comfortable obsessions.

But it was a condition Marcus learned to live with.

A month after Gina had flown in front of Marcus's car, causing him to swerve off Foresthill Road and down a gulley into a tree, Marcus was told to feed deeply and then taken to meet Green.

Green wasn't human either—but he wasn't a vampire, and he wasn't a shape-changer, and for the first five minutes of their acquaintance, Marcus simply stared at him, blinking and trying not to be a fool.

Green had hip-length, butter-colored hair, astonishing emerald-colored eyes, and pointed ears.

Yes. Pointed ears. He also had a face that was almost a perfect triangle—wide-set eyes, wide cheekbones, pointed chin. He had attenuated fingers and toes (and bare feet), a torso that was unusually long and narrow (and no shirt), and was at *least* six and a half feet tall.

The look he gave Adrian was heavy-lidded with affection, and Marcus had to reevaluate everything he knew about this world—again.

There had been a steady stream of willing bodies through Marcus's little vault, all of them male. Marcus, half-numb with his new, frightening drives, had simply assumed that this would be his life now—willing body after willing body. He'd even started to forget that he'd liked women when he'd been alive. He'd never been fucked into the mattress before by another man, and he'd certainly never sucked another man's cock or fingered a tightened sphincter or fucked a willing ass or a willing mouth before his induction into the vampire world, but he found, when his mind cleared of the bloodlust, that he enjoyed these things.

He'd started a vague assumption that this was who he was now.

Looking at the unadulterated sweetness passing between Adrian and Green, he suddenly remembered the look in his girlfriend's eyes when he'd finally made his move and kissed her like they would end up in bed together. He remembered the way she sighed when he was inside her and the way her little yelps of passion had made the entire world crystallize and shimmer with heat and desire.

He wasn't aware he was weeping until he wiped his hand across his eyes and saw that it was covered with a mixture of blood and brine, and his vision was red with it.

They were meeting in the front room of the hill, which had a wraparound window overlooking a canyon silvered with starlight. Before Marcus could even wipe his eyes, the room was empty of everyone except Green.

"Marcus, is it?" Green asked gently, and Marcus nodded, beyond words. "Come here, Marcus. There are some things I'm not sure you know."

The first thing that Marcus didn't know was that making love to Green was like making love to sunshine on a summer's day. For a vampire, it was both heartbreaking and precious to have that touch of warm flesh without the promise of iron-rich blood beneath. (The elves bled sugar-sweet ichor—it was the vampire's equivalent of fifty-year-old scotch.)

The second thing Marcus didn't know was….

Everything.

Green's hill—Adrian's home—was a commune, perhaps the only place in the world where every preternatural being in the world was welcome, and most gathered. Green was a sidhe, a high elf, the kind with all the power, but he wasn't the only fey creature in the place.

In fact, the fey creatures outnumbered the vampires *and* the shape-shifters, and if you counted the tiny ones, the little sprites who mostly just looked like glowing lights unless you got close, and all the kinds of not-so-tinies, the pixies and nixies and brownies and gnomes and trolls and ogres and yunwi-tsunsdi (Native American pixies) and every other creature from folklore who lived there, the fey outnumbered the vampires and shape-shifters in astounding numbers.

And Green didn't give a shit. They were *all* his children.

As Green's flesh merged with Marcus's that night, he didn't fuck. He stroked, he touched, and he *talked.*

"Different than with women, mate, right?" he said, palming Marcus's cock with a touch so fantastic Marcus almost came just then. "But you like women, and that's good. So do I."

That surprised Marcus. "Yeah?" he asked, arching into Green's touch, his kind words, his complete understanding of Marcus's *complete* confusion.

Green moved his head down and took a lazy swipe with his tongue. Marcus's cock tingled, and something wondrous short-circuited that whole blood-fuck circuit in his body, and for the first time in ever, he just wanted to *fuck.* But not now. He wanted to talk to Green more.

"Absolutely, mate, and they're one of the world's wonders. Don't worry. You'll have a woman in your bed again, right?"

"Right," Marcus groaned as Green used his mouth some more.

"And in the meantime," Green said between licks, "you can practice being as good a vampire as you were a man."

It was only as Marcus's body washed hot and cold with orgasm that he remembered his girlfriend. She had already mourned him, attended his coffinless service, and was probably moving in with his parents to share their grief, and he'd been fucking and feeding without even thinking about her pain.

Green swallowed and wiped his mouth and then moved languidly to Marcus's side. He pulled a tissue from the side of his big hand-carved bed and began carefully wiping Marcus's blood-brine tears from his cheeks.

"I'm sorry, Marcus—I'm sure it was a lot to lose."

Marcus nodded and took the tissue and tried to hold himself together. He failed miserably and ended up sobbing into Green's arms until Green stood up, holding a hefty armload of vampire as though he were a child, and ran him down to the darkling, both of them as naked as day.

When Marcus awoke the next morning, he was starving, but not so hungry that he savaged the throat of the young shape-shifter who had been waiting in his room for the sunset. The young *female* shifter, he realized somewhat amazedly, as she all but purred and shivered in his arms.

It wasn't until they'd brought the act of feeding to a natural—and mutually satisfying—sexual conclusion that he realized something else.

He was in a different room.

THE ROOM was one of the largest in the hill; Marcus was never comfortable having it to himself. Gina explained, not long after that first morning, that Adrian was trying to make him welcome. Gina had been a good person in real life but so unhappy in the human world that she'd been on the verge of self-extinction. Marcus was different—he'd been recruited by force. Gina had been distraught, and Adrian had felt bad for both the new vampire and her unintended victim.

The room was the hill's way of telling him he had his space to be angry if he didn't feel like fitting in. As Marcus grew more accustomed to Green's hill—and to being a vampire—he found he wasn't angry at all.

He was sad at first. When he was allowed out of the hill at night (and oh! the freedom of flying, the amazing roar of the wind in his ears and the peculiar cold wonder of the earth from two hundred feet in the air!), he took one opportunity to sneak away from the hill and go see how his family was doing.

He sat in the darkness below his parents' window and listened with his new, improved, super vampire hearing, just to hear their conversation.

That wasn't what he heard.

Yes, he heard their words and their sorrow… but he also heard their blood pounding through their veins, and even though he'd fed that night before he left, he *wanted* it.

He was appalled. For a terrible moment he was literally torn, half of him consumed with the alien urge to storm into his family's home and *devour* them—rip their veins from their flesh and guzzle the blood as it pumped, hot and iron-oxygen fresh, from their cooling flesh.

He fought it. It took slow, stiff movements, and then, in the back of his mind, he heard Green's words.

*You can practice being as good a vampire as you were a man.*

He took two running jumps and flew.

He confessed to Adrian later, both that he'd gone farther than he promised and that the compulsion to… to *eat* the people he loved had almost driven him insane. He and Adrian were not lovers—not on a regular basis, anyway. But Adrian had made him—had literally willed him to swallow, willed his brain to spark when there was no oxygen and no electricity, and the only thing driving his sentience was magic. There was a bond; when Marcus had become calmer and not needed to fuck or feed off anything that moved, he could sense it and realized it was what had kept him from losing his sanity in the first place. So on this night, instead of sex—raw sex, tender sex, any sex—Adrian had folded him up in a very brotherly sort of embrace in the few moments before dawn.

"Most of us can't be trusted around our loved ones for over a year after we've changed," he told Marcus seriously, his sky-spangled eyes intent. "Love can be an all-consuming emotion, brother. In our state, it takes some practice to separate the eating from the embracing—you were lucky."

Marcus shuddered in Adrian's arms, suddenly so supremely grateful for the kindness at Green's hill that he didn't have words. He would have given up his nice bedroom—attached bathroom, solid oak furnishings, two king-size beds, oak paneling, nice, soft-green wool blankets and everything—and just lived in that vault in the basement with the crappy shower. He would have given up anything just to know that he had people who would love him through this change and do it unconditionally.

"How long did it take you, Adrian?" Marcus asked, feeling the dawn lethargy overtake him.

"That's different," Adrian said, voice sad. "The only person I'd loved when I was alive was Green."

Marcus would have asked more, but the sun rose, and they slept.

TIME PASSED. In one way, it seemed to pass furtively, slowly, with no sun to mark the changing of the days. But in another, the world seemed strangely fluid, timeless, and ten years of death went by far faster than someone who had lived thirty-three years of life could ever imagine.

For one thing, people were not idle at Green's hill.

There was no clock to punch, there were no deadlines, work evaluations, or paychecks, but the hill *was* a collective. There was simply a gentle expectation that if you had a talent or a gift or an area of expertise, you would lend yourself to making things run smoothly.

Marcus, who had taught the concept of group work to his high school classes for *years*, found himself being a part of the group with very little effort. Once he had earned his new room by simply not being a blood-fucking savage, he found that he was needed to tutor the younger werecreatures—many of whom had dropped out of school and life before

Adrian found them and offered them a way out of going nowhere—to get their GEDs, and he enjoyed that.

He also enjoyed helping Adrian check up on Green's businesses and on Green's people, who either ran them or frequented them; he was good at that too. He would watch in fascination, though, as Adrian would start chatting up humans, male or female, and begin the process that would make the change in that young person's life—permanently.

Marcus's new leader had an eye for kids like Gina—kind, clever, and very, very lost. It became a fascinating game to walk into a group of twentysomethings and try to guess which one would be Adrian's choice to join the hill.

It wasn't always who Marcus thought he'd choose.

Marcus would go for the sweet ones, the gentle ones, the ones who seemed too fragile for this world. Sometimes Adrian would go for those people too, but sometimes he'd go for the tough kids, the ones with the foul mouths, the ones with the anger and the history of trouble. Marcus asked Adrian why once and was met with that fuck-me grin and love-it-or-lay-it shrug.

"The ones who are too gentle will grow bitter in this life, mate. You need some strength to survive as a vampire or a shifter. The ones who hide their gentleness under a tough mouth or some violence with their fists— those are the ones who will survive with their goodness intact, yeah?"

Marcus had to admit that it seemed to work for Adrian. He was never wrong about his choices. Never.

And life wasn't all work either at Green's hill, and that helped make the time speed by. One winter awakening, about five years after his arrival, Marcus was missing his family particularly badly after the (admittedly spectacular) Christmas/Solstice holidays. That was when Gina came to his room holding an armload of gear.

"What's this?" he asked, catching the parka and the boots and the gloves and the skis—skis? Damn… he hadn't been skiing since….

"You used to love to ski," Gina said, hopping over to his bed like a little girl. "I remember, you know, when I was in your class. You'd always let us out early on Fridays so you could go up the hill. I mean, you did, didn't you?"

They had been lovers on and off in the past years, but it hadn't been serious. Marcus had come to appreciate that monogamy did not always figure in the seriousness of a relationship here, and he, like everyone else who'd been recruited to this life, found that Adrian and Green were the gold standard for the emotional depth he wanted out of a real relationship. Gina was not that person, but that didn't mean they weren't friends.

"I did!" Marcus said, surprised. Of course, flying was easier now, and it had the same rush, but still…. A human memory crafted of snow-cut crystal made his skin tingle with the remembered feeling of wind on his face, the smell of pine and cold, and the color of the platinum moon as it bounced off the drifts.

With wonder he said, "I used to love *night* skiing!" and then he smiled into her eyes, gave her a kiss, and said, "Thank you! Are you coming with?"

Gina had been a very plain girl, with thin, sallow cheeks and frightened, darting eyes. She was a very beautiful vampire, with a sort of austere, aloof face and slanting, mysterious, very *brown* eyes, and the look she gave him was all vixen.

"I thought you'd never ask!"

They were loaded up and in the car less than an hour later, and Green had even arranged for them to have tickets to the lodge and a special room, so they could stay as long as they liked.

They made it a tradition to disappear to the ski lodge that week every year. Sometimes they brought other lovers (Marcus always assiduously picking female lovers, in spite of what he'd learned during his blood frenzy), and sometimes they simply brought a shape-shifter for food and company. It didn't matter—what mattered was that Marcus had friends at Green's hill and not just bedmates, and it mattered that his passions survived his change to a vampire, and it mattered that he had found a good life now that he was dead.

On the fifth year of their traditional ski trip, and Marcus's tenth as a vampire, the mountains were heavy with wet snow. Earlier in the winter, the cold had been intense, but now the peaks were covered with a slushy sort of ice, making the drifts treacherous and ensuring that only the experts went up the hill to the more advanced runs near Donner Pass.

Marcus and Gina were in their element—the cold didn't bother them, and although the wet was uncomfortable, it would have been far worse for the poor humans braving the hazards with them. Gore-Tex was not yet common, and the most comfortable humans were wearing fleece-lined leather.

One of the few to brave the Black Diamond run with Marcus was wearing an outfit in all black, lined with fleece, with waterproof gloves and a set of ski goggles that Marcus was pretty sure he'd seen on television during the last Olympics. His hair was artfully slicked back from a faint widow's peak, and his face was narrow, with a square jaw and pointed chin and a truckload of arrogance. As the stranger had walked by the Green's hill party at the snow lodge (they'd brought a couple of shape-shifters and Adrian for this trip out), Adrian had flashed a little fang and cracked quietly that he looked more like a vampire than any vampire Adrian had ever seen.

Marcus had laughed at Adrian's joke, because it was true. But as a schoolteacher who had always worn jeans and a polo shirt on the dress-up days, he also hated the stranger on sight.

They ended up sharing a lift, though, and for a few moments as the lighted track of the hill drifted eerily beneath their feet, there was an equally cold silence between them.

To Marcus's surprise, the stranger spoke first.

"You're a hell of a skier," the guy said, and Marcus blinked at him, surprised.

"Thank you," he muttered, flustered. He didn't like the compliment—he had been average as a human. All of his speed, strength, fearlessness, and skill came from the knowledge that he was already dead. Anything that happened to him on the slopes from this point on would be uncomfortable but not fatal. "You too."

The compliment was sincere. At first he'd assumed that all the flashy gear was just that—for show—but as the other man had zoomed gracefully down the slopes as though he, too, had nothing to lose, Marcus had been impressed. It was a style and panache he'd never had when he was alive, and he was gracious enough to give the other guy credit.

To Marcus's surprise, the guy looked pleased, and from the other end of the ski lift, Marcus could scent the blood rushing under his skin. He was blushing. Wasn't that interesting?

"I skied a lot as a kid," the guy was saying, that blush getting stronger. "I wasn't good enough to make the Olympic team, but damn, did I have fun trying out."

"I'll bet!" Marcus was interested in spite of himself. "What were your events?"

The other man smiled. It could have been a predatory smile, just like a vampire's, but it wasn't. In fact, there was a little bit of hidden sweetness in it, like Adrian's. Marcus wondered if he ever would have spotted that sweetness under the shark's smile if he hadn't scented the blush and been able to see clearly the eager expression on the man's face in the dark, under the full moon.

"I liked the long downhill events, myself. I loved the slalom—man, that was a rush." The man looked at Marcus sideways and pulled off his glove, sticking out a hand that was probably freezing without the covering.

"I'm Phillip Chambers—pleased to meet you."

Marcus was charmed. He smiled back and found that it was genuine, the kind of smile that his grandmother used to tell him had dimples in it. He took off the light knit glove he wore, held out his hand, and shook, liking the firmness of the other man's hand, although it was almost as cold as *his* was, beating heart or no.

"Marcus," he said, so used to not having a last name that he didn't think to use it now.

"Jesus, your hands are cold!" Phillip exclaimed, and Marcus put on his light glove quickly, feeling a little embarrassed. "Marcus what?" Phillip was in his early thirties, and his eyes, a lighter, almost hazel brown, crinkled in the corners with his smile.

"Marcus has to get off the lift!" Marcus improvised, and together he and Phillip laughed as they lifted their toes up and glided through the snow at the top of the mountain. Together they slid to the edge of the Double Black Diamond and pulled their snow goggles over their heads. Marcus pulled his hat snug over his curly black hair, and Phillip gave him a grin—this one *definitely* predatory and decidedly competitive.

"Wanna race?" he asked, and even that was unnecessary.

"Oh *hell* yes!" Marcus nodded, and together they rocked forward and backward and forward and backward, and Phillip counted, "One, two, three...."

And they were off the edge of the hill, hurtling down through the flake-flurried night.

It was like flying, Marcus thought in the back of his mind, but better. They twisted, they turned, they danced through a frozen ocean of crystal-sharded dark. They zoomed like little kids on roller skates, and Marcus heard Phillip's joyful cackle as they hit the end of the run neck and neck, knees bent and poles tucked under their arms as they tried to streamline their bodies.

They both twisted their bodies and rooster-tailed neatly to a stop, regarding each other laughingly for a moment, both of them pulling off their goggles at the same time.

"That was *awesome!*" Marcus breathed, not conscious that he *was* breathing, as he hadn't been for quite some time.

"Amazing!" Phillip echoed, and Marcus grinned at him. Their gazes locked for a moment, and although Marcus didn't detect a thing about Phillip's breathing or blood pressure that would indicate arousal, he was suddenly, subtly reminded that although he made it a point to share a bed with women only, in that first frenzied year, he had truly liked men too.

The thought made him self-conscious and shy again. He remembered that it was freezing, and while he might not be affected by the cold, Phillip was definitely only human.

"So," he said, trying to hide his disappointment, "you'll probably want to go back to the chateau and—"

"Do you want to go again?" Phillip had apparently not even heard his socially weak attempt to back off.

"Absolutely!" Marcus grinned back at his new friend. "You couldn't keep me away."

# Darkness, Blood, and Filtered Light

Marcus didn't realize how foolhardy he was, choosing to go on that second run, until he heard Adrian's voice in his head halfway down.

*"You've got half an hour until sunrise, mate! I hope you know what you're doing!"*

Shit! Half an hour?

*"I can make it."* He hoped he could make it. It had taken them half an hour the first time down.

*"Fly!"*

Jesus. Adrian didn't usually command, but when he did, it was because he was worried about you. Crap.

*"Human here!"* Marcus gave Adrian a visual of Phillip, who was right on his tail, whooping because Marcus had unconsciously picked up speed. Marcus went a smidge faster, and Phillip let out a holler that seemed to shake the ground.

*"Hold up, mate. What's that?"*

Marcus could feel it too. He risked a longer look back and watched as Phillip faltered to look behind him as well. Marcus took advantage of the fact that the human wasn't watching him to lift his skis up off the snow for a minute and take a good, long look at what was behind him.

*"Fuck!"*

He wasn't sure who said it—himself, Adrian, or Phillip—but it didn't matter. The last icy-wet snowfall or Phillip's whoop of excitement or the sudden cracking cold of dawn—it didn't matter. The cap of snow on the mountain had endured quite enough and was crashing down on their heads with the wrath of an angry Norse god!

*"Get out of there, fuck it all! Blow!"*

But Marcus couldn't. Phillip had laughed at him and had offered him friendship and had raced him down a mountain, *twice*. Gina and Adrian hadn't left Marcus to bleed to death on the side of the road, and Marcus couldn't leave his new friend to die horribly in an avalanche either.

Marcus leaped right out of his skis and hovered horizontally for a second while a startled Phillip zoomed right into his arms. He grasped his new friend under the armpits and hoisted him up, up, up, up....

And not quite over the avalanche as it caught up with them.

Marcus could have let go by then—he could have. But he didn't. He held tight, his body flush behind Phillip's as they were tumbled about like pebbles in a blender, ass over toes over shoulders over nose, until his own body felt battered, and he knew for a fact that a couple of his bones were knitting together as they crashed against chunks of ice and boulders and tree limbs in their free-fall hurtle down the mountain.

Marcus knew Phillip's bones wouldn't magically knit together like his. He hunched his shoulders protectively and didn't let go—not even when they were both skewered through the stomach with a tree branch like pieces of chicken on a shish kebab.

Adrian's voice was a constant song of *"Get out of there, oh Christ, mate, get out of there get the fuck out of there get out of there oh Jesus, Marcus, get yourself safe!"*

The panicked, crushing thrill ride stopped abruptly, freezing the two of them in a bubble of air under a solid four feet of snow. Marcus ripped the tree branch out of their bodies, laid his new friend down on the tiny, coffin-like space of the rocky bottom, and took stock.

It wasn't good. Phillip was already convulsing, his body bloody, blood gushing through his mouth and nose. His stomach wound would be fatal if the awkward, misshapen breaks in his limbs didn't kill him first.

Marcus looked at his new friend longingly. God, he was happy at Green's hill, but besides Adrian, he couldn't think of a single other person he could have shared a night like this with—and Adrian would have wanted it to end in bed.

And now, with regret, so did Marcus.

He couldn't help himself. He was bleeding too—he felt his old vampire's blood dripping sluggishly down his repairing nose, and he knew what would happen.

He hoped it would happen.

He locked his mouth over Phillip's and kissed him, thrusting his tongue into that glorious blood-coated mouth and praying he swallowed.

*"C'mon, Phillip, taste it. Swallow. Have enough life in you to swallow."*

*"Marcus?"* Adrian's voice was unmistakable. *"Marcus—you need your will…. Oh Jesus, I can feel you using it…."*

Marcus was not good at vampire tricks. It had taken a while to learn to spell his prey with his eyes to calm them down. He didn't like wiping people's memories. While the other vampires could go outside the hill, brainwash their prey, and spend a pleasant evening with a lover or dinner or both, Marcus stuck to the hill and the willing shape-shifters and the people he knew. In school he'd led by personality, by being passionate about his subject, by making students see that behaving well was in the students' best interest.

Marcus did not *will* anyone to *do* anything.

But he willed Phillip to swallow his blood, and he willed Phillip to live.

*"Jesus, mate!"* Adrian's voice in Marcus's head was a little bit panicked, and then he felt a lovely thing. He felt Adrian's will there with his own, even as he locked mouths with this man, this stranger, this friend, and together they *willed* the other man to want to live.

There was a movement in Phillip's mouth—was it a swallow? Was it his final breath? Then there it was again—a swallow! Another! Marcus's canines had popped out, and he used one to rip across his wrist. He pulled away from the compulsively clutching fingers in his hair and on his back and gave Phillip his bleeding wrist.

*"It's rich blood, Phillip. It's rich; it will feed you. Drink, brother. Guzzle it until you're sick."*

*"Fucking awesome, brother."* Adrian sounded tired. *"Now just give the shifters until dark to find you—and try not to let him rip your head off before then, because that's one wound we can't repair."*

Marcus was suddenly *exhausted*. He'd lost a lot of blood, he realized. He'd been wounded and now Phillip was drinking his reserves, and he would be *ravenous* when he woke up.

Phillip would be worse.

But the sun…. He could already feel it, shining on the other side of the mountain, pulling slowly up to peep over the peak…. Not yet… not yet….

Phillip's suckling motions on his wrist stopped abruptly, and Marcus's soul flew somewhere Marcus had never seen.


MARCUS WOKE up with a mouthful of warm shape-shifter arm, when nothing around him was warm. He opened his eyes, locked his jaw, and fed.

The shape-shifter—a comfortable armload of soft woman named Stephanie—sighed and melted into his arms, and a pained, tightly wound something in Marcus's chest relaxed. *Goddess*, he had never been that hungry, not since his first awakening. He gave a blessing and a thank-you to the Goddess and to Adrian for making sure he wouldn't have to roam the world so hungry he was almost mad with it.

Then he heard a startled yelp and a growl, and he shook off his feeding torpor because something bad was happening.

Stephanie's mate was her husband, Joe, and he was a thirtysomething lumberjack-shaped person with an easy disposition. His alternative form was a big Newfoundland dog—and that was the thing currently backed up against the side of their little snow cave, nursing a torn throat and whimpering.

Phillip had apparently gone full-bore scary vampire when he'd awakened, and now the three of them were trapped in the snow cave with him. Fucking *aces*!

A vampire's feeding face was a more, well, intense version of his or her regular face. Phillip had possessed a narrow-jawed, high-cheekboned sort of aesthetic beauty before he'd changed, and now? Now he looked like Dracula on steroids, with hollow cheeks and an outrageously pointed mouthful of teeth (dammit, it *was* just his canines, right?) and the whirling red eyes that indicated extreme hunger or emotion.

Marcus swallowed his last mouthful of Stephanie and shouted, "You two! Get out now!" and then jumped in front of Phillip to hold him off while the shape-shifters escaped.

Phillip screamed at him, an anguished, confused, enraged scream, and Marcus felt his own feeding face come on.

"Fuck that!" he snarled. "C'mon, man—you're safe, you're fed, now back the fuck down and fucking *down* or we're going to have to take you out right here and now!"

If anyone he'd ever known in either life had ever heard him snarl like that, they would have been shocked—but dammit, he *knew* what would happen if Phillip couldn't get control of himself. It was why Adrian always picked his people so carefully, and why no one was *ever* supposed to make another vampire without his approval or Green's.

Marcus had just gone to a hell of a lot of trouble to *save* this guy; he was damned if he was going to have to ask for Adrian's help to kill him!

"What did you do to me?" Phillip growled, wiping his hand in front of his mouth. It came back caked with old blood and new blood. Marcus swallowed hard, in a particularly human gesture that he'd seen Adrian make but had never felt the urge to make himself.

"I changed you," Marcus said, and it cost him to say it without apology. "You were young, and you were vital, and you were dying, and I didn't want to see that happen. You got a problem with that?"

Phillip looked at himself wildly, at his torn clothes, the smooth flesh under the savaged hole in his stomach, the blood, saturated and frozen to almost every stitch of clothing he was wearing.

"I'm *starving*!" Phillip screeched. Marcus looked down at his pants, and sure enough, Phillip's body was starving for more than blood. Marcus swallowed again and subtly unbuttoned his torn and bloodied jeans.

This was probably going to be painful.

"What are you doing?" Phillip demanded, distracted. Marcus watched the way Phillip's eyes zeroed in on Marcus's fumbling fingers. Some of his wildness eased, and Marcus tried to remember how badly he'd savaged his first lovers.

*"You didn't."* Adrian's voice was soothing in his head. *"You were rough but not brutal. You're going to need to prep yourself, though, because he won't think to. And you're going to want to be on your back, so he can feed when he comes."*

*"Thanks, Adrian."* Marcus knew his inner voice was far more nervous than his real voice, but that was okay. Adrian wouldn't mind.

*"I'm in his head too, right? I'm keeping him calm. C'mon, mate. It all starts with a kiss."*

"You're going to want to fuck me silly," Marcus explained, trying very hard not to feel like prey. This guy was a leader, right? A very, very alpha male, right? Marcus had been unprepared for that urge to just fuck things into the ground. It had been very, very un-Marcus of him. This guy—maybe he could handle it.

"I don't like guys." Phillip's voice lacked conviction, and he watched as Marcus bared the lower half of his body with a distracted fascination. Marcus sighed. He might be tougher than the average human, but it was still cold in their little snow cave now that the shape-shifters were gone. He measured the discomfort of the cold next to the discomfort of the ground and then took off his parka and laid it down so it could cushion his back and bare ass.

"You're going to like sex," Marcus told him, keeping his voice soft and confident. He walked forward slowly, as though hunger was not even now *raging* through Phillip's body and threatening to consume them both. He got close and stopped, pretended to breathe, because he knew the rhythm was soothing. Phillip's eyes were whirling a little less frantically now, and Marcus nodded. While he was nodding, he stuck two fingers into his mouth and suckled, wetting them with saliva, before reaching around to his backside.

He gasped when the first one penetrated without a hello or how-are-you, and Phillip's eyes started to whirl a little more quickly. The second one helped the first one to stretch, and his cock, which had been a shriveled thing afraid of the cold, began to wake up and generate its own heat. Marcus leaned forward and put his tongue out, slowly licking Phillip's bottom lip, tasting the remains of the blood—and Phillip's fear.

"You're going to like sex with me," Marcus said softly. He pulled his fingers out and hoped that had been enough prep—Phillip wasn't going to stay this calm for long. "I'm your friend, and I'm almost indestructible, and I can take anything you need to dish out. C'mon, Phillip—you're one of the few creatures on the planet who get to live twice. Let's live."

Their fangs clashed as Phillip growled in his throat and bore Marcus to the ground, and Marcus just kept opening his mouth and letting Phillip plunder it, delving deeper and deeper. Marcus spread his legs wide and laughed a little when Phillip ripped his leather pants in half without even thinking about it, just to be able to grind his cock into the crease of Marcus's thigh.

Phillip kept grinding, hard and harder—hard enough to bruise viciously if Marcus had been a human—and Marcus rocked his body to help. It happened so quickly, Marcus was surprised. He hazily remembered the first time he'd taken another man. He'd remembered the fingers and the stretching, but the intent to fuck—to thrust into another human body—that had been there. Marcus had *needed* that. As Phillip ground up against him, grunting and whining, rutting frantically, Marcus realized that this man was different.

Marcus kissed him back a little harder, swallowing Phillip's whimper of confusion, swallowing his fear and his hunger and his savagery. Marcus would make it better—he would. Marcus framed that lean face with both hands, remembering the playful human, the shy competitor, the little boy in what looked to be a corporate shark's body. That man *would* survive. Marcus would make sure if it.

"*Jesus* God…." Phillip pulled back a little, and his eyes were whirling faster.

"It's okay, brother. Just let it come."

Phillip howled into the cradle of Marcus's neck and shoulder as his cock spat come between their bodies. Marcus tilted his head, thrust his neck against those thrusting canines, and gasped with the pain. Phillip wasn't gentle—he *couldn't* be gentle—and Marcus wasn't aroused enough to find the pain sweet. It was okay. It was okay. Phillip was okay, so this would be too.

Stephanie and Joe wriggled back in through the opening above their little ice cave in their human forms almost as soon as Phillip came. Marcus wasn't surprised—they had probably been listening in along with Gina, Adrian, and the other people in their party, waiting to see if he was going to need any help. Stephanie offered her wrist to Marcus immediately, and Joe, after a moment of steeling himself, gave a bare arm to an almost somnolent Phillip as he lay sprawled over Marcus's half-naked body.

Phillip ate automatically, like a baby, and Marcus was grateful for what Stephanie gave him, because he was drained and tired from the sex and the blood loss and using his will with Adrian to bring Phillip back to life. The thought of getting Phillip out of this cave and to Green's hill seemed almost impossible.

It wasn't.

Adrian hopped in after Steph and Joe with a wool blanket for Phillip and some new clothes and a jacket for Marcus. After Steph and Joe changed back to their dog forms, they got a boost out of the hole. Adrian took Phillip in his arms and lifted him out the roof of their little cave, and Marcus followed him.

"*We're doing the distance home,*" Adrian said as they flew. "*You up for the trip?*"

"*Damned well better be.*" Because he promised he could, in spite of the fatigue and the worry and the cold, Marcus was.


WHEN PHILLIP'S first month was over and he had been installed semicomfortably (and a little bit symbolically) in Marcus's room as his new roommate, Adrian told Marcus that he'd never come so close to killing a newborn vampire in his entire second life.

"Jesus fucking Christ and his entire manly kit, mate!" Adrian complained in Phillip's second week. "That wank git has the sex drive of… of… I don't even *know* if there's an animal that fucks that much! And he's a *bossy* fucker for a guy who won't stick his dick anywhere but the crease in your thigh. 'Up, down, sideways, goddammit, get your cock out of my stomach!' Are you *sure* he was worth saving?"

One of the reasons Marcus had liked teaching school was the same reason Marcus got along so well at Green's hill: he liked having a natural order of things and a hierarchy and an obvious chain of command and everything in its place. It was extremely difficult for him to contradict Adrian in anything—except this.

"Absolutely," he said without any hesitation at all. "Look, Adrian, I know you don't usually… you know, let us have the same dinner twice when we're like this, but… do you think I could give it a go? He might trust me."

Adrian frowned—and on Adrian, with that amazingly pretty playboy face, the expression looked good.

"You know there's a reason we do that, right? Rotate people out of there?"

Marcus hadn't wondered when he'd been going through it, but now, facing the idea of going back in there again with Phillip after he'd been helpless, rutting, and feeding in Marcus's arms the last time, he had an idea.

"So we don't get attached," he replied softly.

Adrian nodded, that ever-present gentleness at the fore. "It happened with you, you know. That first bloke, Joshua? He had it bad."

Marcus closed his eyes painfully. Joshua had been killed by hunters two years before in his wolf form, but Marcus remembered him as a laughing man with a wicked sense of humor, and as the fragile-seeming boy in his bed that first time Adrian had taught him to feed without savagery.

"I didn't know." God, he hadn't. And he imagined Adrian had only told him in order for him to see how painful it could be. Well, lesson learned, he thought with a quaver to his jaw.

"There was nothing you could do," Adrian told him now. "You weren't interested in blokes after your change. Sensual and consensual, mate—you know that's our only rule."

Marcus nodded and gave the kind of grin he liked to think he'd learned from Adrian. "Well, I can't promise it'll be sensual, buddy, but I can promise that we'll both be willing."

Marcus went in to feed Phillip next.

"Oh joy!" Phillip snarled, his feeding face very much in evidence. "You again. God knows, I owe you so goddamned much, I just need you to rub my face in—"

"Jesus, shut up!" Marcus never told people to shut up, not even fractious students. "Do you want to be dead? Because I'm telling you, we can change your state right fucking quick, asshole!"

"Well, don't expect me to be grateful!" Phillip snapped. "I'm locked up here like a prisoner—"

"Well, you *were* a *corpse*!" Marcus couldn't help but remember him, eyes not even closed but glazing over quickly with death as he vomited blood. That gave him fear and a little bit of anger, and a determination not to take any of the guy's shit until he saw reason. "Do you want to be one again?"

"I want to be *free*!"

"Then you need to learn to feed like a person and not like a savage!"

"I'm not a person anymore—"

"You're not *human*, asshole. That doesn't mean you can't be a person. Those people who've been coming in here and taking your shit, you think they haven't been through this? You think becoming a shape-shifter or a vampire is a picnic for *anybody*? They picked this life because it was better than the alternative—"

"Yeah, well, lucky them, to get a choice!"

"You think I got a choice?" Marcus yelled. By now they were both yelling and circling the room, feeding faces on, claws flexed, fangs extended. The vault, which had been nicely furnished when Marcus had lived there, was now a litter of broken chairs from Phillip's rages when he was left alone, and the bed frame was cracked and splintered, leaving a bare mattress in the middle. The two of them kept the mattress between them as they faced off, and Marcus scented the air.

He could smell Phillip's arousal from across the room.

Green often said that a creature's two instincts when they turned were to fight it or fuck it. Good. At least Phillip was showing some interest in option B.

"You didn't?" Phillip was suddenly still. For the first time in two weeks, his eyes stopped glowing, and Marcus saw them in the light from the bare bulb in the ceiling.

They were brown.

"No," Marcus growled, still keeping his guard up. "I was an accident, like you. My car tumbled down a hill, and Gina remembered me and convinced Adrian to bring me over. Don't you see? I was a risk; they didn't know I'd love it here. They just didn't want to see me dead."

Phillip's body was still vibrating, but his feeding face had almost completely receded—only the lengthened canines remained.

"I'm always hungry," he said, his voice as small as a child's. "I'm never out of control, and I can't control my hunger. I can't live like this."

Marcus dropped his voice but not his guard. "Keep your teeth out," he commanded, and Phillip didn't look startled at all as he complied.

Marcus sank to his knees on the bed, a big California-sized king, and knee-walked awkwardly to the middle of the bare mattress. He held his wrist out in front of him, like an offering from a stern master.

Phillip dropped to his knees in a surprising goddamned hurry and took it.

He was delicate with his teeth, and the pain was… exquisite. Marcus tilted his head back and remembered to breathe, breathe, breathe even though he didn't need to breathe, not at all, and that oxygen was making his blood rush, and *everything* tingled, and his cock… damn… it was swelling, aching, pushing against the button fly of his jeans.

Phillip stopped suckling for a moment and looked at him. Marcus met his eyes and realized that he was almost somnolent with bloodlust satiation and dreamy with passion. "You like this," Phillip breathed.

"It's good," Marcus said simply. "If you're gentle, careful, most creatures here like it. Just don't be an asshole, you know?"

Black blood welled sluggishly through the holes as he spoke, and Phillip kept his eyes locked with Marcus's as he bent his head and suckled tamely from it.

Marcus's hips jerked, and Phillip looked at him sharply. "Lap at my wounds," Marcus hissed, "and they will close."

Phillip did as he asked and watched in wonder as it worked.

"That happens for everyone, not just vampires," Marcus said, in his element. "Now take off your pants."

Abruptly Phillip's eyes were red again. "I'm not a fag!"

"That's not even a word here!" Marcus snapped. "What you do in bed like this—do you *want* to do it to a woman? Do you?"

"I'm not a monster!" That almost sounded hurt, and Marcus risked getting close enough to touch Phillip's hair with his broad peasant's hand. It had grown out since that night on the slopes and wasn't as chicly cut anymore.

"We want you to keep thinking that," he said gently. "The women can take it, you know. They do—when their bodies snap back like they do after the change, they can take it as rough as we do. But we can't take it. Adrian only brings good people here. Good men. There's a thing inside us that would break if we hurt a woman like that. But men, even if we weren't attracted in the first place, it feels less—less violent when we're with a man."

"Do they send women in to the women?" Phillip asked, pushing unconsciously against Marcus's hand, and Marcus had to smile. He was very curious, and very smart. He really would be good company when this was over.

"Yes," Marcus told him, grinning a little.

Phillip took a completely unnecessary breath and shivered all over. "That's really hot," he said, slowly unbuttoning his fly.

Marcus nodded, because he'd gotten to see some of that, and damn if it wasn't. "Oh yeah…." He shuddered.

"What should I do now?" Phillip had unbuttoned his jeans and pushed them off his lean hips. He knelt there in his bloodstained white T-shirt and nothing else. Marcus blinked. He almost said, "Whatever you want to," but he hesitated too long, and Phillip said, almost desperately, "I'm still hungry. My stomach is full, but I feel so empty. God, Marcus, I might not be such an asshole if I was just… I don't know. Full!"

And Marcus had a revelation. Phillip had always topped, invaded, thrust—all of the vampires seemed to need to do that. It reassured them to be in control. But Phillip wasn't in control now, when he was apparently in control in his natural state. He needed to know there were boundaries, limits, a place for him. He needed someone *else* to be in control. He was frightened and starving and confused, and he maybe just simply needed.

"Come here."

Phillip moved closer, and Marcus gathered the hem of his T-shirt in his hands. He pulled the thing off and started to touch the other man. Just touch him. It was sexual, of course, because there had been feeding, but the touch was giving, not needing. Marcus gave reassurance, pleasure, gentleness, and… control.

Phillip groaned under his hands, and Marcus moved behind him, kissing his shoulders, palming the curve of his lower back. He applied a little bit of pressure, to see if there would be resistance, and there was none. None at all. Phillip went over willingly, a naked, muscular man facedown on the mattress, waiting, trusting that Marcus, who wasn't a leader at all, would make it all better, would lead him to safety.

Marcus did his best. He kissed the back of Phillip's neck, his ears, down his spine, and although he'd never done this before—deliberately seduced another man—he found that the cues a male lover gave were the same as with women. When Phillip groaned, Marcus was doing it right. When he writhed, Marcus was *really* doing it right.

Marcus reached beneath that taut, muscular body and pulled Phillip up to his hands and knees. He had better access there to interesting toys— Phillip's nipples, which made him groan, the flat plane of his stomach, which made him gasp, and then, there it was, every boy's favorite playground.

Phillip's cock was amazing, long, and thick, with a curve and a flared head, and Marcus wanted it. Not like he had in the ravenous days when he'd last done this, but in a very personal way. *God* did he want to touch that with his mouth.

"Roll over," he commanded roughly, and Phillip said, "No."

"What?"

"I can't…." He couldn't finish the sentence, and Marcus's heart sank a little. Phillip wanted it, but apparently he didn't want to face it. Well, sensual and consensual, right?

"Okay," Marcus conceded, and he reached around, grabbed Phillip's cock, and squeezed hard. Phillip groaned and buried his face in the mattress, so Marcus did it again.

"God!"

"You want my fist but not my mouth?" Marcus taunted. "Stupid asshole."

"*God!*" Phillip groaned again, and Marcus rather enjoyed torturing him. Hey, changeling or not, the guy had been making the lives of everyone in the hill just fucking miserable. A little turnabout—even in play—was just all that was fair.

Marcus opened his mouth over the tight, flexing muscles of Phillip's ass cheek and suckled hard, letting his fangs graze the tender skin while Phillip groaned underneath him and thrust into his hand.

"God, please!" he begged.

Marcus pulled one last time and released him with a pop, knowing he was leaving a hickey on vampire-white skin and not caring. (It would be gone in a second, for one.)

"Goddess, no," he said, feeling childishly pleased.

"*God, I'm fucking begging you!*" Phillip snarled, and Marcus gave that diamond-hard ass a light swat before releasing Phillip's cock and parting the clenching cheeks.

"And I'm telling you you're not ready," Marcus retorted. He licked his finger and started rubbing at Phillip's entrance, massaging gently until the tight little knot of it relaxed.

"Who cares about ready?" Phillip whined, and Marcus took pity on him and started to explain, making sure his breath dusted Phillip's very exposed, very intimate parts as he continued to massage.

"I do, idiot. Think it's any fun for me if you're dry?" He licked his finger again and massaged some more. Phillip relaxed enough for that finger to just… slip… right on in, and Phillip keened as Marcus wriggled farther.

"Don't care," Phillip graveled, and Marcus twisted his finger a little harder.

"Too bad. You wanted to use and abuse me. You had your chance—I even greased myself up for you, just so you could fuck me raw." It was true, and Marcus still had lube running down his crease, teasing and, quite frankly, imbuing every moment of foreplay with some serious wriggle-your-ass-right-out-of-your-jeans tension.

Phillip's body tensed, like he was going to argue, and Marcus added a second finger, relaxing when he felt the man go boneless and willing and pliant.

"I'm hungry," he begged pitifully, and Marcus knew, *knew* that he was talking about feeling empty, lost, afraid, and that having someone inside him, steering, taking care of him, was what he craved, *had* craved since his awakening. No one wanted to do this to a new vampire, especially one who hadn't come over consensually, but Marcus had known Phillip, no matter how briefly, before he'd died. Marcus was the only one with a feeling for how his heart had beat before, and only Marcus could do this.

"I'll fill you," he promised darkly, scissoring his two fingers until Phillip howled and grunted into the mattress. "I'll fill you, but I'm not going to hurt you, you hear me?"

"Auuughhh!"

"You hear me, right?"

"Yes! God, yes!"

Marcus got up on his knees and shoved his jeans down, almost whimpering himself with the relief of the pressure. He took a gentle moment and stroked Phillip's back, his flanks, the backs of his thighs. His cock was aching and dripping, and Phillip was screaming and begging, and Marcus wanted to savor this moment—he wasn't sure if he and Phillip would ever get another one like it.

He positioned himself and thrust slowly home—or that was his intention. Phillip threw himself backward, slamming his ass into Marcus's hips and making him see stars, even as Phillip screamed, "*Yeeeeessssss!*" into the bedding.

"*Fuck!*" Marcus growled, throwing his hips forward. Phillip grunted, and Marcus placed a heavy hand in the center of his shoulders while he piston-thrust his pelvis in a blur of irritation and lust. "Fucking try and take it from me? Don't think so, asshole, don't think so, goddammit. You gave it to me, you wiggled your hot little ass, and it's mine, and it's mine and don't fucking move. Do you hear me? *Don't fucking move!*"

Marcus was ranting and fucking with his feeding face on. His blood was up, and for the first time since he'd changed into a vampire, he was fucking without deliberate gentleness or any consciousness of his improved strength or stamina. Dammit, the guy had begged for it, and he'd goddamned well just lie there and fucking take it, and fucking take it and take it and take it until Marcus saw him spurting his toenails out his cock onto the fucking mattress!

Marcus grabbed Phillip's hips, gave a particularly vicious thrust, and heard Phillip grunt beneath him. Then he realized that while he'd been ranting, Phillip had been babbling too, and he shut up and kept fucking and listened, because Phillip's gibbering and begging just made him hotter.

"God, yes, please… oh please… that's right… fuck me harder… so tight… it's so tight and it burns… burns good… please don't stop… filling me up… please don't stop… need… need… please… God please… fuck me, just keep, don't stop, Marcus, please, I'm gonna fucking come just whatever you do just *don't stop fucking me! Auuughhh!*"

That last was because Marcus was too close to coming to listen to that anymore, so he reached around, grabbed Phillip's cock, and yanked, yanked hard and squeezed, and did it again and again while he kept thrusting. Phillip suddenly stiffened and quivered, convulsing around Marcus's cock as he screamed and came in icy ropes over his stomach and Marcus's tightened fist and forearm.

Marcus pulled his hand away and smacked Phillip smartly across the ass before pumping in once, twice, then raising his hand to taste Phillip's spend, which exploded across his tongue like ambrosia, and listening to his begging, almost incoherent, sobbing cries some more and….

Coming. Coming so hard his eyes rolled back and his toes curled and he saw spots and stars and those other things that humans saw when they forgot to breathe, but he saw because it felt like he was about to spurt his balls out his cock along with everything in them.

Phillip howled beneath him and collapsed in a twitching mass of sobbing moans, and Marcus fell on top of him, still buried in his body. They stayed there, twitching and calming, until Marcus began to shrink, and he fell limply out of Phillip. He rolled slightly, and Phillip made perhaps the saddest sound of protest Marcus had ever heard.

He'd dominated the man in bed, but he wouldn't make him beg now—not now, not after they'd been naked and raw with each other to the point of vulnerability and pain.

"C'mere," he muttered and stretched out his arm beneath his head while rolling to the side, all the better to pull Phillip toward him. Phillip scooted with a little sigh, and Marcus rooted on the ground next to the mattress and found a rumpled blanket that he threw over their cool, still bodies as they stopped shivering in the aftermath. They wouldn't get cold, no, but blankets never stopped being comfort.

Phillip stayed facing away from him, and Marcus wanted to sigh, but he didn't. What did he expect? The guy had obviously been the same as Marcus—rabidly and rigidly straight—until his life took a turn for the undeath. Marcus wasn't going to force affection that Phillip didn't feel. Instead, he played the grown-up again and stroked Phillip's coarse, straight, dark hair tenderly, the way Adrian or Green would, and breathed softly into the hollow of his neck and shoulder.

"If you just tell us what you need," he said quietly, "we'll give it to you. I swear, Phillip, you can be happy here. There are people who want to make you happy here, including me. We just need to know what you want. I'm sorry you lost your life—all the parts of it you miss. But that doesn't mean what you have here now can't be good too, okay?"

There had been a service for the four people lost in the avalanche who hadn't been recovered. Phillip had been among those named, and Green and Adrian had been relieved. Just as predators had supposedly made off with Marcus's carcass, Mother Nature's own viciousness seemed to have taken care of Phillip's death as well. But Marcus knew the loneliness of seeing your family move on without you when you were still there on the planet, still holding them there in your heart.

"Stay with me," Phillip said unexpectedly. "Stay with me through this. We don't have to fuck all the time, and I'll feed from whoever you want, but…. Never mind."

He'd firmed up his voice with the last, and Marcus's heart hurt a little.

"Of course," he said softly. "I'll stay with you. Let's get up and start cleaning up, okay? The next time a shape-shifter comes in, it doesn't have to be so brutal, okay?"

Marcus could actually hear Phillip swallow. Goddess, did the humanness ever really leave them?

"Good," Phillip agreed. "In a minute. We'll get up in a minute."

In a minute would be dawn, Marcus realized, feeling the terrible weakness rushing in on him. *"Adrian?"*

*"You going to live, mate?"*

*"Yeah—could we get some cleanup in here when the sun comes up, while we sleep? I think he's ready to be civilized about this."*

*"Think you're right. Good job, mate."*

*"You know what the bad news is, don't you?"* It was only fair he be honest about it.

*"I knew before you went in,"* Adrian replied gently. *"It's okay. We'll be here to pick up the pieces, right?"*

*"Right. Thanks, Adrian."*

*"Anytime."*

Marcus kept stroking Phillip's hair until the dawn claimed them both.

# ROOMIES

PHILLIP NEVER did tell Marcus about his interview with Green. But just like with Marcus, shortly after it happened, Phillip woke up ensconced in Marcus's bedroom in the other king-size bed.

And proceeded to fuck anything with*out* a cock that lived under the hill.

"They'll do *anything!*" Phillip marveled one night, after two werekitties (sort of a shape-shifting giant tabby cat) left the room all but purring in their human forms. "I mean, when I was human, I had to do some fast talking to get two girls into my bed—and into each other— but these girls? Man… just *suggest* something, and if it's not physically possible for *them*, they'll find something here that has the equipment for it or can make it out of oak trees and spit and polish!"

Well, maybe not exactly, but since most everything that lived under the hill was allergic to latex, he was damned close.

"Well, sensual and consensual *is* the rule," Marcus said dryly. Dawn was fast approaching, and he'd returned to his bed in the darkling for the same reason humans went to their beds at night—it was a comfortable place to lie down for a while.

"Why do they all leave before dawn?" Phillip asked on a yawn. He'd been out of the vault for about two weeks, and already he was comfortable enough to sleep naked. They didn't really get cold unless they were in a snow cave and it was below freezing, so he was turned over on his side, his lean body perfect and marble in the dark.

"Our souls go somewhere," Marcus told him, just as Adrian had told *him* nearly ten years before. "If we're with someone living when the sun comes up, and our souls leave us, it's possible we could pass through them and mark them. It's sort of a frightening thing for a mortal, and it gives the living power over us, so that's not good either." Marcus sighed and swallowed. "And we freak people out, you know? I mean, we're *dead.* Anyway, it's just safer that way, you know?"

"Mmm…." Phillip nodded. Dawn must have been close, because that still-as-death lethargy was upon them both. "What happens if vampires are close together?"

Marcus didn't quite have the energy to shrug. "Probably nothing. I think the closest we have to that is the maker's bond. But you've got that with Adrian—"

"And you," Phillip yawned, and although Marcus knew perfectly well that Phillip hadn't connected with Marcus that way, the sun picked that moment to rise, so he was unable to say so.

But apparently Phillip wasn't done with the conversation. They were still lying exactly where they had been when Marcus's eyes popped open with the sunset and Phillip said, "Why aren't *you* having sex?"

Marcus blinked and turned and then blinked again, because Phillip had moved in that time and was kneeling by his bed, still naked, and was peering at Marcus curiously now that they were both awake and ready to face the darkness.

"I've had sex," Marcus said dryly. "I've had lots of sex. I'm just between girlfriends right now."

"Scoot over," Phillip grumbled, "and let me get under the covers."

Marcus blinked again. "We're doing this now?" he asked, a little befuddled. "I thought you hated having a roommate."

Phillip had bitched copiously the minute he found he wasn't in the room alone, and Marcus had grimly explained about Green's power protecting the hill to make sure no one came and bothered the vampires while they were sleeping, and that the weather stayed in the range that suited the sidhe, and that the shape-shifters weren't vulnerable to the hunters who were still all over the area at the time.

"There's just not enough room for us all to have our own place. At least the darkling is underground, okay? Even if the sun takes you in the hallway, as long as you're in the darkling, you're safe."

Phillip had subsided and had seemed to enjoy Marcus's company when he wasn't out and about chatting up girls or flying straight up as far as he could just to look at the world from that high.

But now he was crawling into Marcus's bed as if it was the most natural thing in the world, and Marcus was a little annoyed.

He'd gotten used to the idea that he and Phillip would never be lovers again. It hurt. It hurt a *lot*. But he knew that risk, had *known* it would come to that, the minute he'd walked into the vault to calm the guy down. He'd been through the change. No one who had been through the change could be that straight, and Marcus already liked the guy, albeit reluctantly. Risking his heart was inevitable, like the dawn stealing his soul.

"I like having *you* as a roommate," Phillip confessed. "I just want to know why you're not getting any."

Marcus shrugged. "I told you—between girlfriends at the moment." He'd actually been seeing Gina yet again when they'd gone skiing, and Marcus had come home with a whole new emotional facet.

"You have *girlfriends*?" Phillip boggled, and Marcus shook his head.

"Just because a lot of people here *aren't* monogamous doesn't mean you *can't* be."

"Yeah, but why would you *want* to be?"

He was really sort of adorable. "For the same reason you would want to be as a human, Phillip. A body in a bed is just that. A partner—that's something else."

Phillip grunted. "I wasn't good at relationships as a human. My best relationships were with my coworkers or my clients." He'd confessed to being a stockbroker, and Green had enlisted his help with the collective's finances. Phillip was good at it, and he'd told Marcus that it made him feel useful. He liked that, and he also liked having all of Green's money to play with, as long as he did so safely. Which was why it was no surprise at all when he added, "I'm really sort of an asshole, you know?"

Marcus looked at him, his brown eyes taking on that unexpected shyness in the dark of the room. They had enhanced sight, so they left the lights off a lot, and Marcus liked the way Phillip's face looked in the dark—it was like they hid a secret part of him that only Marcus got to see.

"Well, we're sort of stuck with each other for a while," Marcus said now, letting some humor sneak into his voice. "I suggest you try not to be too much of an asshole, because our lives could be really fucking miserable if we get on each other's nerves too much."

Phillip's shy smile grew even shyer. "I like you. I'm not good with people—you all might have had to put me down if you hadn't walked in the vault, you know."

Marcus blushed and looked away. He didn't want to wear his heart on his sleeve. He didn't want to burden Phillip with this inappropriate crush. He just wanted Phillip to keep talking to him, keep being his friend.

"Well, if I hadn't liked you, you'd be dead," he admitted wryly, and he was rewarded with Phillip's loud guffaw. He turned his head and pillowed it on his arm, resigning himself to the intimacy of the situation, without the promise of even a kiss.

"What are you doing tonight?" Phillip asked unexpectedly.

"Going round the gas 'n' sips with Adrian. There are some werecreatures he wants to check on, make sure they're okay. I'm sort of his right-hand man for that."

Phillip grunted. "You're good with 'em," he said reluctantly. "Green doesn't have anything for me to do—"

"You could come with us." Marcus hoped his voice didn't sound as needy to Phillip's ears as it did to his own.

Phillip looked both hopeful and regretful. "I scare the shit out of them," he said hesitantly. He'd gone with them once before, but the werecreature they were going to visit had helped care for one of the men Phillip had savaged in his first two weeks, and one look at Phillip had sent the little werefox hauling tail through the underbrush in front of the gas station.

"Well, not in the last month!" Marcus looked at him through the same eyes that saw the hidden shyness, and the same heart that had heard that embarrassed confession of *I'm an asshole.* "Look, man, you want to hang out, I'm good with that. Come with us. Adrian's a good guy—you'll have fun."

Again that shy smile, and Marcus started thinking he'd walk through sunshine for it.

"Don't get so fucking needy," Phillip said, rolling his eyes. The smile remained, though. "Give me a minute, and I'll go shower."

Marcus frowned. "A minute? What do you need a minute for?"

"This!"

Without warning, Phillip lifted up and closed his mouth over Marcus's, and Marcus actually gasped.

And then he responded, and Phillip plundered, hard and strong, and invaded and took. Marcus gave without thought and without reservation, kissing back, following, allowing himself to be led. His whole body went on high alert. He'd gone to sleep in his jeans the night before. (Vampires did not "sleep." They died. There was no comfort consideration until the sun set the next day, and usually they were alert and ready to go. Pajamas weren't really necessary.) His cock was hard and ready underneath the button fly, and he was helpless in Phillip's arms.

Phillip pulled back, hauling air through lungs that didn't need it, and looked at him in surprise. "It was a test," he mumbled, arching his hips unconsciously under the comforter. Marcus could feel his hard-on through the covers, against his thigh. "I wondered if I could kiss a man, if I had changed enough and…. Goddess—God—whoever…." He passed his hand in front of his lean, kiss-swollen lips in an unconsciously vulnerable gesture, and Marcus had to swallow hard on his own hurt.

Marcus pulled back abruptly and popped off the bed. "Sensual and consensual," he rasped. "Toying with someone as an experiment is just cruel!"

Phillip looked at him—puzzled, still, and in a state of wonder. "I had no idea it would be that way," he muttered, and Marcus couldn't look at him anymore. He ran for the shower, clasping his aching cock in the onslaught of hot water and squeezing until white cascaded through his vision and spat out over his fist.

Phillip's surprised wonder was behind his eyes the entire time.

Phillip had apparently skipped his own shower and was dressed (black slacks, a V-neck sweater—very sharp) when he got out, and Marcus very studiously ignored him as he pulled his jeans and sweater (plain brown crewneck) on, along with plain boxers. They had an allowance—more than any of them used, actually—and he could afford anything he liked. He liked worn jeans, he thought resentfully. Phillip could keep his slick stockbroker's shit. He looked good in it.

He looked wonderful in it.

"That girl, Beverly, one of the werekitties—she's coming back this morning," Phillip said into the strained quiet.

"Good for her."

"We'll probably go out for a while, have sex, be a couple. I've noticed that it works to have a shape-shifter in your bed."

"It does," Marcus said neutrally. It was true. Gourmet food and uninhibited, sensual sex, all in one package. He'd dated his fair share of fragile-seeming, tough-bodied shape-shifters as well.

"When that runs its course, I think I may want to kiss you again."

Marcus looked at him, puzzled. "When it runs its course?"

"Hey—I was a serial monogamist when I was breathing. Don't ask me to change that now!"

Marcus laughed and shook his head, unable at this point to do anything else.

"Well, for all you know, I'll be dating someone else by then too, so don't do me any favors."

Phillip grunted, as though he hadn't thought of that. "Well, we've got time, I guess."

Time for this inconvenient, horrible, aching crush to stop pressing against his chest?

"Fucking awesome."

IT NEVER went away. They did the rounds with Adrian that night, and after that, *every* night. Phillip continued to help Green with the finances, and Marcus would spend that time tutoring the young shape-shifters or vampires so they could gain skills that would help the collective, but they always, girl or no girl, other errands or no other errands, spent at least a couple of hours a night in each other's company.

It started to feel like sunset to Marcus. It was the time he was truly alive.

True to his word, Phillip kept dating little Beverly, and Marcus took up with Gina again. Marcus wasn't sure how Beverly felt, but in her room one early morning, Gina looked at him as their bodies lay still on the sheets and said, "Who the hell are you pining for, Marcus? Because the only thing engaged in what we just did was your dick."

Marcus tried a smile and kissed her cheek. "Sorry. I was distracted."

"No shit." Gina stood and stretched, comfortable in her nakedness, and threw on a T-shirt for form. When Marcus had known her alive, her hair had been hacked and spiked and dyed and a general disaster. In death, her hair was shoulder length, dark blonde, and curly. She didn't do anything to it—no dye, no spray—and Marcus liked that. He liked the smell of her skin just after she'd fed. He liked that she cared for the new vampires and shape-shifters like he did, and that together, they were Adrian's backup line when he was bringing new ones over.

He liked many things about her—enough to maybe be mated to her for many years.

But she wasn't Phillip, and that wasn't anything they could fix.

"I was…." He floundered for words. "Imprudent. I was imprudent, and I got… I don't know. Supernaturally attached."

"Bullshit," Gina said flatly.

"I'm sorry?" Gina was not usually that forthright. She'd been timid as a human and was quiet as a vampire.

"Adrian says he's got the maker's connection. The fact is, you were attached to the guy before he was changed. It's not 'supernatural attachment,' you moron—it's love!"

Marcus shook his head and shrugged. "It's going to go away," he insisted. "It's not…." He couldn't make himself say it.

Gina came and sat down next to him as he struggled to sit up in bed and find his jeans and boxers. "We're not the elves, you know," she said gently. "We're perfectly capable of lying, even to ourselves."

Marcus swallowed and for some reason remembered that moment outside his family's house, right after he'd been turned. How easy would it have been to tell himself that he just wanted to go visit them to say hello? That he wasn't dying to taste their lifeblood as it flowed hot over his mouth?

"Goddess," he swore, resting his forehead on his knees. "It *is* real."

"You guys are roommates," Gina told him unnecessarily. "Something is bound to happen. Don't lose hope, baby."

"What am I going to do in the meantime?"

Gina shrugged, the gesture surprisingly grown-up for someone who would never age past twenty-three. "Do what you've been doing. Date other people. Just not…." Her voice caught sharply, and Marcus looked up.

One crimson tear trickled down past her nose to hover on her lip. Her tongue darted out to taste it before it dropped, and he reached out a fingertip to wipe the track of it. He brought the fingertip to his lips and sucked gently.

"Just not you," he said, feeling like complete shit.

"If that would be okay, baby?" she said, her voice rough. "You—do you know I loved you back when you were my adult-ed teacher?"

Marcus shook his head. "I'm a man," he told her. "And I was human for a long time. We're not that bright, you know."

Gina nodded and stood up abruptly. "I'm gonna go shower. If you could, you know…."

"Yeah."

Marcus put on his jeans as soon as she disappeared, and was back in his own bed before dawn.

There was a *whoosh* from the doorway just as the sun rose, and when he awakened, he wasn't alone.

# Benefits

"Don't you have your own bed?" Marcus snapped, pretty much the minute his eyes jolted open.

"Yeah, but I didn't want to sleep in it," Phillip replied. He was all that was casual, there in his blue jeans and black sweater. God, the jeans were designer, and the sweater was cashmere. Did he do *nothing* that wasn't slicker than lube on a glass sex toy?

*Goddammit, Marcus, you have a literature minor. Find another fucking metaphor!*

"Sprite invasion?" It was a legitimate question. The tiniest of Green's faerie kingdom tended to set up shop in inexplicable places. Once, an entire dorm full of nyads had to relocate because the pixies, nixies, sprites, and brownies just showed up in every corner of their room and started fucking like lemmings for over two months. Green had no idea what had set them off, but the subsequent boom in nixies, pixies, sprites, and brownies practically doubled Green's power base and allowed Green's power over the weather to extend for a fifteen-mile radius surrounding the house. Everyone was pleased, and there was more construction in the hill. Maybe if there was a sprite invasion, Marcus wouldn't be stuck with a roommate who looked damned good in a designer cashmere sweater. It was a promising thought, but Marcus, looking at Phillip's perfectly made bed, was not optimistic.

Phillip's expression at the question, though, was priceless. "Where would they invade? And isn't that a little bit personal for a fey to venture without permission?"

It took Marcus a minute, but by the time he figured out what Phillip meant—that, coupled with the stray thought about lubricant—well, he was pretty much convulsing with laughter.

He calmed himself down a bit and looked up to find that Phillip was looking at him with an expression that Marcus could only term "soft."

"What?" he asked, and Phillip shrugged.

"You are one of the quietest people I've ever met. I had no idea you could laugh like that."

Marcus blinked at him, and the full weight of his crush came slamming down on his chest. In a moment, he didn't feel like laughing at all.

"I still don't know what you're doing here," he said.

Phillip looked away. "There's a woman named Grace downstairs in the vault. She was dying of cancer, and Adrian—he was all the way out in Redding, man, you know that?—and he sees her, sitting outside on her porch and he—the thing is, he had to talk her into it. She loved her husband so much she was willing to die, just to spend her last two months with him. And Adrian, he loved her so much, and not just as… I mean, man, she's not even pretty. But Adrian, the way he talked about her in my head as he was asking for help to go get her—"

"He didn't ask me!" Marcus was hurt. Getting the new vampires, helping the novices, wasn't that his job?

"He said you were doing something important," Phillip said, surprised.

The only important thing he'd been doing the night before had been… breaking up with Gina. Christ. Half the hill was telepathic, and three-quarters of it had supersonic ultraspifty hearing, but this was the first time in ten years Marcus had ever bemoaned the loss of his privacy quite so acutely.

"I was, sort of," Marcus muttered. Well, no matter who he slept with after this, the truth was he couldn't bullshit *anyone* about it anymore, could he? "So why does a new vampire mean you get to sleep in my bed, jerkoff? The last time you did this, you kissed me and then blithely announced that you were going to continue fucking someone else for a while."

Phillip shrugged, and damn him, it really *didn't* occur to him that he'd done anything wrong. "Well, you know. Fucking isn't kissing. What we did in the vault was one thing. I just wanted to, you know. Think about doing it outside the vault—"

"Didn't you do it with Green?"

Again that shrug. "Green's different, and you know it. Being with Green isn't fucking. It's like… like being rolled by the love god or something. He does that to everybody. It's like his job, and he's employee of the goddamned millennium."

Marcus blinked, still lying on his side because, in spite of his irritation and his rather wounded feeling of being Phillip's guinea pig, you could *not* have a conversation with someone lying side by side in bed that wasn't unequivocally intimate. Phillip's lean Dracula face looked almost boyish when he was lying there, and his eyes were half-hooded and sweet and not burning out with some sort of repressed fury. This was the face that Marcus saw when they were hanging out in their room, reading or listening to music or watching television. This was the face that you could catch a glimpse of right before or after he dared you to race, or after he won. (Now that they were both vampires, Phillip won any race, any contest of strength, any competition hands down. For Marcus, it was all about the experience. For Phillip, it was all about crowing like Peter Pan on steroids.)

"But you're not hearing me," Phillip was saying, pulling Marcus away from dwelling on his crush. "Adrian brought Grace back, and she was really in love. And she's got this whole mother thing going, so, like, it's going to be all girls in her room, all the time, because she's totally freaked out by Adrian—because, you know, he looks, like, sixteen—so he wants us available."

"Available?"

"We were in our thirties—"

"You still are!" He'd only been brought over six months ago!

"You know what I mean. We don't look twelve."

"You said he looked sixteen!"

"Why are you being suck a complete dick?"

They froze, and Phillip's fangs shot out. He used one of them to worry his lower lip, while what should have been a simple flub in his speech, half a spoonerism, really, hung between the two of them like the blow job of Damocles.

"Such," he said unnecessarily. "I meant 'such.'"

"I know," Marcus said, his mouth feeling like talcum powder and baking soda. "I'm sorry. I didn't mean to be a dick."

And there. It should have been gone between them, but it wasn't.

"Why were you?" Goddess. Nothing about Phillip invited confidences. He was slick, and he was cavalier about all the shit that Marcus really loved, and he was bold and confident when Marcus was laid-back and observant. How was Marcus supposed to tell him anything, when a kiss was a test and fucking didn't mean kissing either?

"You're in my bed," Marcus said, wondering if that would be enough of an explanation.

"You like me here."

If Marcus had fed recently, he would have blushed. As it was, he had to look away. "How would you know that?" he asked his dresser bureau. It was pretty, he realized, not for the first time. Green and some of the other sidhe tended to carve the furniture here. The furniture in this room was hand carved, hand finished with linseed oil, and generally felt like a living extension of the hill itself.

And it was a hell of a lot more comfortable to look at than Phillip's intense brown-eyed scrutiny.

The hand on his crotch was a surprise, and he was hard, swollen, and aroused against his jeans. He didn't have a shirt on, and that invading hand traveled confidently up his chest—which was pretty muscular, with all the working out he'd been doing since Phillip had moved in—and pinched his flat, rose-colored male nipple.

Marcus gasped, undulated his hips helplessly, and tried not to thrust his fangs through his lip with the twin emotions of shyness and irritability.

"What in the fuck are you doing?" he asked—but there was a whine in his voice, and when Phillip's hand went back to his cock, he thrust toward it and not away from it.

"Why don't you just—I don't know—do what you did in the vault? Grab me by the hair and… just…."

Marcus finished Phillip's thought with action. His hand knotted in Phillip's slicked-back hair, and he pushed. Phillip didn't even put up a show of reluctance. Phillip's hands were fumbling with Marcus's fly almost before Marcus had a good grip, and Marcus almost came in his jeans right there. He growled instead, irritated, aroused, and strangely hurt.

This was okay, as long as Marcus made him want it. It wasn't how Marcus had imagined love with either sex. But his jeans were unbuttoned and his boxers pushed down, and he was aware that Phillip was breathing, on purpose—knowing his rough, forced air was brushing Marcus's cock as it throbbed and quivered against his lower belly.

"You gonna just sit there?" Marcus snarled.

"You gonna make me do more?" Phillip snarled back. It sounded a lot like begging.

"Lick me, dammit, base to crown. Open your mouth and…. Ahhhhhhh, good. Like that."

Phillip was inexpert, but he was trying. When he opened his mouth and popped the crown of Marcus's cock inside, he wrapped his lips around it carefully, fangs too, and pulled in his cheeks. Then, with hardly more than guidance from Marcus's hand cupping the back of his skull, he took Marcus all the way down to the back of his throat.

Marcus almost came—again. His hand clenched in Phillip's hair, and he made an effort to get himself together. "Phillip, I'm going to give you a choice. I can either come in your mouth or come in your ass…. Fuck!" Phillip had swallowed convulsively, and he knew he spurted a little into the back of Phillip's mouth. His whole body was shaking, buzzing, high and tingly with the need to *just fucking come*….

Then Phillip stopped for a second and whined, obviously in an agony of indecision. Marcus closed his eyes, thought past the damned painful aching throb of his groin, and said, "Look, man. If you want to suck me until I come, I won't leave you high and dry, okay? I'll take care of—"

Phillip growled, swallowed some more, and grasped Marcus's base with a strong, cruel fist, and every nerve ending Marcus had went flying out his skin—and spurting through the base of his cock and into Phillip's gulping throat.

The sounds Phillip made as he guzzled Marcus's spend were sexy enough to make Marcus hard again, but by then he was tender. When he couldn't stand the tenderness anymore, he dragged Phillip's head away from his groin and pulled him back up so they were face-to-face. Phillip's eyes were whirling and his fangs were *very* prominent, and Marcus had a moment to count himself lucky before he hauled that sexy, lean, come-covered mouth to his own and devoured. If he was going to be in control, Goddess fuck it all, he wanted a goddamned kiss!

Phillip whimpered and opened his mouth, allowed Marcus in, and… *Oh*…. Marcus had forgotten, from his vault days, what a man's come tasted like to a vampire. It was steak and strawberries and champagne and chocolate and…. Goddess…. He shuddered and plundered some more, and Phillip groaned, grinding up against Marcus's hip, reminding Marcus that his friend was in need.

He licked one more time at Phillip's tongue and pulled away.

"I promised," he whispered. "Now let me take care of you."

The jeans were gone in short order, and he already knew that Phillip didn't wear underwear. For the first time that knowledge was good to have and didn't make him ache and pine and yearn. Phillip's cock leaped out, straining against Marcus's palm. It was longer than Marcus's, not quite as thick, but with that sexy curve near the top, and Marcus took a moment to stroke it firmly while Phillip, arms still at his sides, went quietly berserk above him.

The end of Phillip's cock was thick and wider than the rest, and it started drooling thin white precome over the fat purple head, and Marcus couldn't torture him for long.

The first taste of that spend on Marcus's tongue almost made him come, when he'd assumed the second erection was just for show.

He groaned, shoved Phillip's cock to the back of his throat, and devoured, and when Phillip apparently forgot that he wanted Marcus in control and grabbed his hair and pulled, Marcus chuckled, staying resolutely forward and swallowing, letting his throat work on the head of that lovely purple cock.

"Auuuughhhhh!" It was a snarl, a cry, a howl, and a plea, and Marcus loved him. He'd do anything he possibly could to make Phillip happy.

He suckled hard and then very gently allowed his fang to graze the length of cock in his mouth. Phillip made that sound again, that tortured, sexual pleading. Marcus chuckled, and Phillip made it again.

Marcus tucked his teeth in then and sucked some more, stroking with his hand, swirling his tongue, and every now and then allowing the most delicate touch of fang. He'd been imagining what this act would be like since that first night in the vault, when Phillip hadn't wanted anything to do with it, and he was going to make Phillip crave it. The next time Phillip was with a girl or even Green, Marcus wanted him to remember the feel of Marcus's mouth on his cock and think that maybe Marcus could do this better.

Phillip made that sound again, and Marcus was suddenly so hard he hurt. He pulled back enough to talk, smacking his cheeks lightly with that drooling cock as he spoke. "I'm hard again. You know what that means?"

"Yes… please…."

"Please what?"

"Make me come…. God, Marcus. Please make me come…."

"Is that all you want?" He punctuated that with a thrust of his head and a pull into his mouth and moved his hand to Phillip's cleft, playing with his entrance in the sloppy mess that was pooling there.

"Please… please, Marcus. Please…."

As much as Phillip liked him to be in control, the truth was, Marcus could deny him nothing.

He thrust his fingers into Phillip's backside and swallowed Phillip's cock to the back of his throat. Phillip let out a cry that could probably be heard all the way through the hill and spurted come. Marcus let it coat his tongue before swallowing, because oh *shit* did it taste good. It was like blood but better. Like elf blood maybe, or shapeshifter blood with a chocolate chaser. And Phillip's hands clenching in his hair were an aphrodisiac, making him want, making him yearn… making him hot.

Marcus cleaned Phillip off with a gentle slurp and thrust his hips into the bed. He rolled over and tried to exert that command that worked with no one else but this man.

"You think we're done here?" he growled.

"Please no," Phillip whispered, and before Marcus could even issue an order, he'd pulled his jeans completely off and rolled over to his hands and knees.

He was already prepped and ready, and as Marcus positioned himself behind Phillip and got ready to thrust home and lose his mind, he had a second to think that maybe, if they did this again, they could do it face-to-face.

It was the last sane thought he had for quite a while.

Phillip was a screamer, and Marcus made him *scream,* loud enough to shake the floorboards in an agony of ecstasy, and Marcus growled behind him. Phillip collapsed, flat against the bedding, groaning and laughing in aftermath.

Marcus collapsed on top of him, smoothing his hair back from his high widow's peak, kissing the back of his neck, and wishing he was human enough to sweat. Phillip moved into the caress, and Marcus was relieved. He could touch him now with sweetness. The weight of his crush seemed a little less, a little easier to bear.

Then Phillip said, "Now *this* is the way to spend time between girls!" and the weight crushed Marcus against his lover's back, pushed his face hard into Phillip's neck, and crushed faint crimson trickles from his eyes, which he wiped on the comforter before he turned to his side again.

Phillip stayed turned away, even though he snuggled into Marcus's spoon.

"This is nice," he said softly. "I like this with you. I don't usually like it. Maybe it's because I know we're roommates. You don't really break up with your roommate, do you, not in this place?"

"No," Marcus promised. "No breaking up. Not here."

No monogamy either. No pledges. No undying devotion. But no breaking up. Marcus could exist with that, right?

It was a crush, right?

# The Rhythm of Years

YEAH, SURE it was a crush. It was a crush that lasted twenty ageless goddamned years!

Grace the vampire became, unexpectedly, Adrian's second. Marcus and Phillip weren't sure how it happened. One minute, they were Adrian's two most trusted men—something about the way they had come over, their self-assurance in their human roles, their maturity, made them good bets as vampires. They were stable, when those who came over because they were too lost to make it as humans often were not.

But if Marcus and Phillip had been stable as bachelors, then Grace—the stay-at-home mom with the lifelong lover/husband, the trucker's mouth, the wicked sense of humor, and the passion for cooking even when she couldn't eat what she cooked—was the solid granite that made up the bedrock of Green's hill.

The first time Marcus met her had been outside the vault, about a week after Phillip had blithely cemented their relationship as backup fuck buddies once and for all. (Grace had set a record—a week in the vault and then three days in Green's bedroom, pouring her heart out, talking books, movies, and politics, and very probably learning about making love as a sacrament in the place of things like cooking and cleaning and keeping a good home. Adrian sent in shape-shifters to keep her fed, and she was so gentle—and so unconsciously sensual, without demanding anything in the way of sex—that Grace became the first vampire to send the newly changed shape-shifters to as well.)

But that night Marcus had been both cautiously optimistic and incredibly despondent. They were fucking each other's brains out—it was *awesome*. But Phillip also kept reminding him that he was looking for a girl. In fact, he'd even expressed some hope that he could hook up with Grace.

Marcus had taken one look at her and known she wasn't Phillip's type, but she might have been *his* type back when they were alive.

She'd been cooking, ordering sprites and other fey about with the ease of natural leadership, and the two of them came wandering out of their bedroom in the darkling after Marcus had made Phillip scream once again. She'd taken one look at them, Phillip suave and cool,

Marcus undemanding and casual, looked at Marcus again sharply, and said, "Have you thought of gagging him? It would do wonders for your privacy in there!"

Phillip had widened his eyes and retorted, "I'm sure you've done your share of screaming, sweetheart!"

Marcus smacked him upside the head like a little kid. "Mind your manners," he said sharply. "She's a lady."

Grace had smiled, her freckled cheeks scrunching up into a fabulous, charming smile, and Phillip looked at his toes, dazzled and abashed.

"I'm sorry," he mumbled. "I was embarrassed."

Grace shrugged. "Are you shitting me? In this place? If you don't know everyone's business, you're not paying attention. I'm sure you guys know all about *me*, am I right?"

And Marcus, feeling like maybe Phillip needed a little bit of defending and a gentle lesson at the same time, said, "I know you stay outside the hill long past when it's safe."

Grace looked away. "That's very astute, young man," she said, and if she had been alive, she would have blushed.

Marcus looked at Phillip's face and saw a hunger there, the same aching loneliness that Grace faced daily—that, had he known it, Marcus had existed with since he'd first awakened at Green's hill.

"It gets better," Marcus said. "We find friends. We get used to people. It won't just be Adrian and Green—you'll start to feel at home."

Phillip hazarded a glance at Marcus's face, and Marcus made sure his eyes were there to meet Phillip's. "He's right," Phillip agreed, and Marcus smiled, pleased.

Grace nodded. "That's a real nice welcome," she said graciously. "Adrian told me to have you give him a buzz—" She tapped her temple. "—when you came out. He wanted to visit the places the new shifters hang out. He's got some kids he's thinking about bringing over and wanted your opinions."

Phillip shrugged. "I don't know why he asks me. Marcus has the better eye."

Marcus looked at him in honest admiration. "You can be more ruthless than I can. It's a good thing—you're looking out for Adrian when you do that. We need it."

Phillip rolled his eyes. "You're killing me with all this gushy shit." He gave Marcus a casual smack in the arm. "Here—I'm going to go to the shifter's room and see who's up for feeding. Talk to Adrian and then come get me."

Marcus nodded. Apparently his need to say a few words to Grace was practically radiating out his pores. "Could you scare someone up for me?" he asked. "I'm *starving*."

Phillip waggled his eyebrows and said, "A good workout will do that to you!" before disappearing.

He rounded the corner down the hall, and Marcus turned his still-smiling face to their new recruit—and apparently their new second-in-command, based on her easy way of distributing Adrian's orders and general authority. He was going to ask if Adrian had said something else or if Green was available—because *fuck* did he need to talk to someone about this steady, terrible weight pushing on his shoulders, and Green and Adrian did that for their people—but Grace beat him to the punch.

"He's not ready to know yet," she said with some confidence. Then she looked over at one of the dryads, who was dumping something into the pot, and said, "I know you don't like the chicken flavor, sweetheart, but I already made vegetable stock for you guys. This is for the shifters, and they need their soup to taste like meat, okay?"

"He's not ready to know what?" Marcus asked, but he didn't need to get in her head and do the universal vampire mind meld to know what she was talking about.

She caught his eyes and pulled one side of her wide, generous mouth up in a sympathetic smile. "He doesn't need to know it's more than a lust thing. The whole hill can hear you two, but you don't make that much noise when your heart's involved. He starts being quiet, you can start talking to him like it's real."

Marcus just regarded her through eyes he knew were liquid brown with hurt.

She gave a sympathetic grimace. "I'm always open to talk," she said, and he nodded.

"Me too. In case, you know, you get tempted to stay out too long."

Grace shrugged. "Can't stay out too long now! I've got children again."

Marcus was confused, even as he wandered down to the shape-shifter room. (It was actually modeled like a human dive bar—it was one of the most boisterous places in the hill!) Then he saw Phillip.

Phillip was in the corner chatting up one of the newer shape-shifters. She was in her early twenties and softly beautiful, and it looked very much like they were going to go in a corner and feed very soon.

Marcus watched as Phillip smiled lazily at her and dragged a knuckle down her cheekbone, and his enhanced, supersonic vampire hearing picked up, "And if you like being dinner, sweetheart, maybe when we get back before dawn, you can be dessert!"

Of course. Marcus's heart crashed to his knees. Then Phillip looked up at him and gave a wholly triumphant, boyish grin, inviting Marcus to share in his victory over the female species.

Marcus summoned up a real smile somewhere from the shards of his heart and gave his buddy the thumbs-up. Adrian's voice buzzed suddenly in his head.

*"Sorry, boyo. He's not ready yet. You know he's not ready yet."*

*"It's just a crush."* Even Marcus was getting tired of the sound of that lie, but Adrian loved him unconditionally.

*"Of course it is, mate. It'll get better. You know it."*

Wasn't it love, to lie boldly in the rubble of your friend's dreams?

And then Marcus found a laugh welling up in his throat, hot and bitter, but it would sustain him for the next twenty years. Of *course* Grace had children to look after now. He and Phillip were playing the oldest schoolyard game in the book....

Catch me if you can.


THEY PLAYED that game successfully for nearly twenty years.

Every time, they got a little bit closer to the permanent snare, and every time, Phillip darted away at the last fucking gasp. They would see other people for a while, it would end, and then there Phillip would be, in Marcus's bed, begging for that thing they had, only them, the thing that let Phillip be tender and giving, that thing that let Phillip trust and that bound Marcus tighter to him with every kiss.

After ten years, Phillip let Marcus inside him when they were face-to-face, kissing, nuzzling, closing his eyes, whimpering instead of screaming, and turning toward Marcus in the aftermath, stroking his skin as he calmed down from what was turning into a greater, stronger, more terrifying sexual peak.

That was almost worse than when he had turned away, but Marcus treasured every touch when it came, so he couldn't quibble or argue.

They found an equilibrium, of sorts, in their painful game. Marcus had a few girls who were always up for the ride when Phillip went chatting up another girl, and who were willing to break up on command when Phillip was between women.

They were the ones who gave Marcus the most hope.

Girls talk—boys don't. The girls told Marcus that Phillip was starting to pick fights, spurious fights, silly fights, to break up over.

"It's like he misses you," said Leah. Leah was an *awesome* fuck buddy. She slept with *everyone,* had no pretenses to monogamy, but didn't mind hooking up with Marcus and putting on a good show, just because he was kind to her.

"I doubt it," Marcus said dryly. As long as they'd been doing this dance, he'd learned some humor about it—and some honesty. It wasn't a crush anymore; it was dumb-fucking unrequited love. He could live with it, or he could move out of his room, or he could meet the dawn, but he wasn't going to make the world miserable because he was a fool.

"No," Leah said seriously, rolling over in her bed and kissing his chest. "Really. And it's not even an 'Oh my God! We're getting too close!' sort of thing. It's more. He'll tell a joke that you would have gotten or start a sentence that you would have finished, and when the girl doesn't get it or doesn't finish the sentence or doesn't meet his eyes at the right moment, he'll get this—I don't know. You know how proud he is, right? And how he'll sneer at anything or pop off at the mouth just to avoid seeming close to human?"

Marcus nodded. He'd seen it. Not firsthand, not since that first time they'd been together outside of the vault, but he'd seen Phillip do it to other people.

"Well, he'll get this look on his face that's almost—I don't know. Wounded. It's like he's been hurt to the center of him. And then he'll be a complete asshole, and, well, finis. Relationship over."

Marcus couldn't help it. He was cheered up. The behavior of his lover was deplorable, and the surge of happiness certainly didn't speak well of Marcus, but it was a sign of hope. He'd thought he'd be locked in this weird emotional limbo for a hundred years—at which time he'd been prepared to give up, just because one hundred was a big round number, and it sounded like a long time.

Twenty years sounded like a long time too, but in Phillip's company, they'd sort of flown right by.

"So that news makes you happy?" Leah asked, grinning unrepentantly in the face of his extended canines.

"Does that make me a bad person?" Marcus asked innocently, and her grin widened.

"Not if you're willing to go down on me again, baby—you do it sooo… mmmm… yeah… my God… oh fuck… oh…. *Jesus, Marcus, fuck me through the goddamned floor!*"

Leah was a screamer too, and Marcus didn't mind—not this time. Not one bit.

And so things continued, and might have continued to that one-hundred-year mark, but then Adrian brought Cory home and their lives were turned upside down—and run through a meat grinder, resized, reapportioned, and served up raw.

That Adrian brought a human home was no big deal—he did so all the time, especially when he was recruiting and worried about the recruit (the people Adrian tended to recruit were often living dangerously). He brought them home and let them wander the hill and find the place they fit best. He did *not* make love to them in the hill—and he didn't make them exclusively his.

Cory looked like a standard recruit—five zillion piercings, dyed black hair, so much makeup you could barely tell her gender.

But something was different about her, and it was clearly apparent from the first night Adrian brought her home. Phillip and Marcus had watched from around a corner as he all but spirited her into his room, his tongue so far down the girl's throat that it was a wonder she could breathe.

"Oh good," Renny said softly, rounding the corner and ignoring the fact that the two of them were trying to look invisible. "He finally talked her into it."

"Talked her into what?" Marcus asked. Renny was a little werekitty, brought over by her mate. Renny weighed about ninety pounds soaking wet. She could curl up in a corner as a kitten *or* as a girl, and right now, Renny seemed to be the one person who could answer any questions about Cory and would talk. Marcus had tried asking Adrian's best friend, Bracken, one of Green's elves, the week before. Bracken—characteristically—told him to fuck off and then shoved Phillip toward him and told *Phillip* to fuck him off.

"We don't work that way!" Phillip snapped with wounded dignity, and Bracken nodded in satisfaction.

"And I don't bear tales." With that, the grumpy fucker stalked off, and Phillip had been left looking after him in admiration. It was true. Adrian, for all his sweetness, was best friends with a guy who made Phillip look like Dr. Seuss.

"He talked her into coming here," Renny said now, looking at the two of them like they were stupid. "He's been courting her for months."

"*Courting!*" Marcus exclaimed—in a fierce whisper, of course. "What about Green?"

Renny shrugged. "I'm sure they'll all end up together somehow. You have to know Cory. She's...." Renny gazed off into space for a minute, her demeanor as distracted as her flyaway, static-charged, fine brown hair. Marcus and Phillip looked at each other, wondering whether to prompt her or not, when suddenly Renny shook herself and said, "Bright," as though that pause had never happened. "I knew her in school. She was bright—so bright, people would refuse to look at her. She's so bright, she can't see the darkness around her for the brightness. You'll see. Green will see it too. It's really amazing."

With that, Renny spotted Mitch at the end of the hall and trotted away.

Marcus and Phillip looked at each other dubiously.

"Really amazing?" Phillip muttered. "I'll have to see that for myself—holy *Goddess*! What in the *hell*?"

There was... a force. A terrible, wonderful, blood-saturated magic force being unleashed in the hill. Phillip reached out both hands to Marcus's shirt and *clung*, simply whimpering, and Marcus leaned up against the wall. Both of them had come in their jeans, just from that one sweep of sex magic, and their crotches mashed wetly together as they held each other and shuddered.

The next wave was starting to roll; they could feel it.

Marcus was the one with the presence of mind to haul Phillip to their room, and after that, about all they could be sure of was that Marcus topped, because he always topped, and that they frequently didn't have room to do more than bite each other and scream before the wave of magic rolled through the room and they were coming again, coming and coming and still hard.

Eventually it ended. It had to end. And when it did, they lay tangled in their blood-and-come-soaked sheets and shivered, and that was where they were, wondering what in the fuck had happened, when the dawn came.

And that was their first introduction to Cory.


THEY'D GIVEN Adrian hell the next night—taking a virgin sorceress in a hill already saturated with blood and sex magic? Lunacy, incredible lunacy. Adrian had been embarrassed, until Marcus had stepped forward, literally, and stood in front of their leader like he was protecting someone innocent.

"You guys—have you seen her?"

Grace joined him and nodded for him to continue, and he figured that *she* at least knew where he was going.

"She dresses like she's got nothing to lose. He couldn't read her mind, right?"

"Right!" Adrian spoke up and moved out from behind Marcus, flashing a wry smile. "And she doesn't know what she is, either. *I* don't know the whole of it. But I know I've tasted human, shape-shifter, and fey for a hundred and fifty years, and she's an entirely different breed of bird. And…." He made the last word meaningful and suddenly looked as stern as any of them had ever seen him. "She's off-limits, you hear? She's mine."

They all looked at him uneasily. None of them wanted to ask how this would affect that tender, timeless bond that Adrian had with Green, but no one wanted it to end either.

The next few weeks were fraught with terrible unease among the vampires: shape-shifters were being murdered, including poor Renny's mate, Mitch; there was an enemy stalking Adrian's people, and Cory was a target. But she fought off the enemy well enough on her own on a few occasions, and although her pale, freckled skin gained a few scars, she gained an absolute beauty in the eyes of Adrian's people and the shape-shifters.

One night, Cory and Adrian made love, except bigger, down on the front lawn in full view of anyone who cared to watch. (It was Green's hill—they *all* cared to watch.) Phillip sank to his knees in front of Marcus and took him inside his wet mouth, right there at the hall window, while Marcus fought to stay standing.

After Marcus had clenched his hands in Phillip's hair and spent everything, including his soul, Phillip came up and kissed him, a totally unsolicited, tender kiss, and then turned his attention to the two lovers out on the lawn. He leaned back into Marcus's arms, and together they watched a sort of magic happen that they'd only ever seen in Green's bed.

"She's healing him," Marcus muttered. He couldn't explain it—what she was doing really was magic—but there had always been a cloud, a pain, a well of aching melancholy in Adrian's heart, and Cory was filling it, making him whole.

Phillip grunted and snuggled into his arms, and Marcus closed his eyes and savored. There must have been some spare magic from all that healing out on the lawn, because it had given them this moment, this sweet, unforced moment, when Phillip wasn't trying to find someone else and was simply, quietly, right where he belonged.

Marcus would have died for Cory for that moment alone.

It really was such an odd time—there was the enemy and the fear, and at the same time, there was the amazing love. The night that Green joined Cory in Adrian's bed was another moment that Marcus wouldn't forget. Luminous, beautiful, the wave of sensuality that washed the hill spawned an entire generation of lower fey and drove the vampires into a lovely, sexual, sensual frenzy that they would use as a watermark for relationships for years to come.

Phillip spent it with his girlfriend. Marcus spent it alone, in the next bed, aching—right up until he felt Phillip's girlfriend's mouth on his cock.

Marcus had no choice but to fall into the threesome, the woman in the middle, just like the one that was happening in Green's room. It was sweet and wonderful, and Marcus didn't know when his heart had ever hurt with quite so much passion and pain.

Phillip was in his bed, but he thought having someone else there with them was the way it should be.

The night afterward, he went up alone into the garden to see what Cory had wrought in the throes of sex and sorcery.

It was amazing. Fully grown trees had erupted from the earth—thornless oak trees, and lime trees—all of them grown and twisted into the shapes of the three lovers who had coupled and tripled in the hill the night before.

His throat grew tight with the beauty of it. Erotic, yes, but… but lovely. Loved. He saw Adrian, in all of his haunted beauty; Green, in all of his kindness; and this new person, this teenaged child, as a powerful force of nature. Marcus had spoken to Adrian's lover before this, but he'd never really thought of connecting that vital, aggressive little person with the woman who could love two immortal beings at once.

*It's such a grand sort of lover to do that. All I've really ever wanted was one lover who would love me alone.*

The thought made standing in that garden intolerable. He had just turned on his heel to go back down the stairs and join Phillip in the vampire common room to plan what they were doing that night, when he ran into the little person in the flesh.

"Jesus," he swore, darting backward with such preternatural speed that he hit the tree behind him.

The grand lady of the manor, the woman with two vampire marks, and the lover of Lord Green and his consort Adrian, burst into giggles.

"Crap!" she swore. "For crying out loud, I didn't mean to scare you!" She giggled some more, and his vampire senses picked up the scent of blood under her skin.

"You're blushing!" he accused, and she turned her head around, taking in the erotic pictures of the grove with one jerk of her chin.

"Wouldn't you?"

Marcus remembered all those years Phillip screamed fit to bring down the rafters. "I have," he said dryly, and she stopped looking embarrassed and grinned at him. His stomach clenched a little, and he realized that she was a younger version of Grace and a human version of a geode—plain and dusty on the outside but with a beautiful, precious center—and stronger than she looked.

"Phillip?" she inquired delicately, and he rolled his eyes.

"God—even you know, and you just got here!"

"What *is* the deal with you guys?"

Marcus looked away. "We're... us," he said after a minute. "He wants us to be...." He gestured vaguely. "He wants us to be *this*. But we're not. We're us. But only when he's between girls."

"Ouch," she said softly. "It's hard, I think, when your beloved doesn't know how you feel."

A part of him flared to anger. She should talk. The whole world knew how Bracken looked at her, and she never saw. But then, he thought, as she looked at him with compassionate eyes, that it was not entirely her fault. Bracken wouldn't reach for Adrian's beloved for all the lovers in the world.

"I like that word," Marcus said softly.

"What word?" she asked curiously.

"Beloved," he told her. "It's a good word."

She smiled a little, looking embarrassed all over again. "It's Green's word. It's one of the things you have to learn, being here, you know?"

He nodded. Yeah. All sorts of ins and outs to this place, that was for certain. This little girl was doing better than he had, and that was also a fact.

"I was just on my way down to Phillip," he said after an awkward silence, and she stepped to the side as though to let him pass.

"I was just on my way to look at the stars and pray for clarity," she said dryly. He stopped on his way past her to ruffle her hair, and the sound of her throaty laughter followed him down the stairs.

"What kept you?" Phillip asked as Marcus walked into the vampire common room. This was the only place in the hill with leather couches, most of them black, hardwood floors without carpeting, the better for cleanup, and the biggest television available in any given year. Most of the vampires were gathered, along with the shape-shifters who were good for feeding duty. Phillip was feeding from his girlfriend, but he pulled away from Tina's throat as he spoke and caught her body as it fell limply against him in ecstasy. His face was covered in blood, and as Tina practically purred (she was a werepanther), he wiped his palm across his mouth and flickered his tongue over it to catch the last drop.

"Nice table manners, dickhead," Marcus snapped, and Phillip rolled his eyes.

"I'm dining casual." He shrugged. "Wait a sec—gotta clean up. Look at me, darlin'. We've got somewhere to be." Tina met his eyes with a vapid, somnolent gaze of her own, and with one mighty swing of his vampire will, he whammied her into sleep.

Phillip set her down indifferently in the corner of the black leather couch, pulled a handkerchief from his jacket pocket and cleaned his face up, then threw on the leather jacket and turned around. He looped an arm over Marcus's shoulders as they walked.

"Seriously, man, where the fuck have you been? She's not big on conversation, and I was a half a swallow from having to take her to bed."

"And wouldn't that be a tragedy?" Marcus fell in step with him, their bodies syncing perfectly. They'd been walking together like this, in perfect compatibility, since Phillip had emerged from the vault.

"Jesus, don't be a dick. Where were you?"

Marcus shrugged. "I went up to look at the garden—it's pretty fucking spectacular. Have you seen it?"

Phillip rolled his eyes. "It's trees. What's to see? And that took you so long?"

"I met with the lady of the house. We had a chat."

"Well, isn't that cozy? Is she still plain as a potato?"

Marcus turned aggressively to him, thrusting forward with his shoulders until Phillip was backed up against the wall of the hallway looking surprised and turned on at the same time.

"Don't talk about her that way," he growled. "She's perfect, Phillip, and we need to treat her with respect, you hear?"

Phillip sighed and surprised Marcus with his sadness—and his remorse. "She's like Grace," he muttered, and Marcus nodded, letting his sarcasm show.

"You think?"

Phillip looked away, and Marcus was suddenly aware that they were in a darkened corridor that led from the bottom part of the darkling to the upper level. They were alone and their bodies were pressed together. Phillip arched his hips against Marcus, and in addition to being embarrassed, he was very, very aroused.

"You're good at that," Phillip whispered. "So good at knowing the goodness in people. You sure you want to keep taking me along for those recruiting missions?"

Marcus swallowed and pressed his groin forward. "I don't want anyone else by my side." It was the truth, in all ways, incontrovertible and absolute.

Phillip let a little smile slip through that pouty, disdainful façade he usually wore and thrust his face forward. His eyes closed, and Marcus was stunned to realize that he was asking for a kiss.

Marcus had never been able to deny him anything he wanted. Phillip's lips parted and Marcus's tongue entered, tasting the shapeshifter Phillip had sampled for dinner. And *that* was when Adrian's voice sounded in both their heads.

*"Family meeting, boys. All vampires, front lawn."*

Marcus groaned and deepened the kiss for a moment. Dammit. Damn Adrian. How many chances would he get where Phillip was willing and soft and admiring one of the few things Marcus could actually do better than he could?

How many chances would he get where he could think the word *beloved* and expect that someday it might be returned?

# Tragedy and Hope

It had been such a lovely night, a night of such promise of peace, of such lovely things to come. It had fooled them all, lulled them into complacency and into a belief that all would be well, simply because the leaders they loved to follow also loved to love. It left them totally unprepared for the night that destroyed their hearts—everybody's hearts—and Phillip and Marcus had a front-row seat.

The enemy responsible for the unsettling shape-shifter deaths had finally revealed himself. He'd been after Adrian, poor, tortured Adrian, the whole time. They'd established a meeting to parlay—and to fight. No one fooled themselves that there wasn't going to be bloodshed, but Goddess… the terrible things they lost! As long as Marcus was sentient, he would never forget the jumble of images from that night.

They had awoken, angry and ready for battle, and Adrian had given a fierce smile as they launched themselves off the top of the hill. They had flown out over Gold Country, then over Folsom Lake toward the gravel pits where the enemy—a half elf from Adrian's tortured past— had decided to confront Adrian once and for all.

Adrian was so… so *full* that night. He was full of his beloveds, Green and Cory; full of his friends; and full of his people, the vampires. He was full to bursting with a complex, brilliant mixture of fear for them, pride, and that intense, charismatic spark of leadership that he had always been capable of but had never let burst forth.

Until Cory, until his healing in the garden, he had never believed in himself enough to lead his people into battle. Now he did.

Marcus had hovered, waiting for his orders, as Adrian descended for a moment to talk to a shape-shifter who had been there and get the lay of the land. Beyond the rise where they hid, Marcus could hear Cory herself bandying words with the enemy, and he smiled with fangs. She was fierce and sarcastic and bloodthirsty—all the things Green and Adrian were not—and he loved her for it, just like the rest of the hill.

He was not prepared to watch Adrian leap into the sky in a moment of panic that every vampire in his head could feel. He was certainly not prepared to watch Adrian, their gentle Adrian, fly into a magic trap and….

Disappear. Explode. Disintegrate like a popped balloon. His blood covered the upturned faces of Cory and Green as they watched the vampire they both loved more than life explode in a tragic burst of sorcery before they even realized he was coming to save their lives.

Marcus kept thinking, *She's barely nineteen*, as Adrian's beloved, soaked in the gentle rain of her first lover's blood, started sucking in power for a terrible scream.

Marcus knew what she was doing. They'd all watched her learning what her sorcerous power was and what she could do with her will and emotion. Her emotion now was terrible, terrible destructive grief, and a cold, rational part of him expected her to destroy.

Marcus felt the loss—in his chest, in his head—of the man who made him, of the friend who had succored him, of the vampire who had created his beloved because of Marcus's desperate plea. In Marcus's despair, he wanted Adrian's beloved to destroy *him,* so Marcus wouldn't have to wake up to a bed without a lover and a life without a leader and a heart without a purpose.

Green called out in a mighty voice, "My people, *move!*" and Marcus did not. It was Phillip, swooping down from the sky and knocking him practically into the next town, who saved him from that destruction. It was Phillip who pinned him to the side of a tractor with main force as the little girl with the punk haircut and the piercings and the power and the broken heart killed every enemy on the battlefield with the power of her heartbroken sunshine scream.

It was Phillip who yelled into his face, "If you won't live for yourself, goddammit, then live for me, asshole! Live for *me!*"

Marcus forgot pride then, and shame, and who it was that was supposed to lead the two of them when they were together. Instead he broke, weeping in his lover's arms until they had to either fly from that place or die by the sun.

They learned something about grief after that night, watching Cory and Green grieve.

Adrian had given Cory the third vampire mark as he'd died, and with it came the maker's bond to the entire kiss of vampires. Every vampire in Green's hill felt the power exchange, and every vampire in Green's hill refused to talk to her about it, not even to hint to her that their leader, their heart of the hill, didn't even realize she was MIA.

It was hard enough watching her grieve herself to death.

She'd been such a solid little person when Adrian had first spirited her into his room. Her hips had been wide and her thighs chunky, and her semiperpetual scowl had been fortified by a plain, wide-cheekboned face, and she'd seemed invincible.

After Adrian's death, she had become almost transparent with pain, and as lovely and fragile as a blown-glass sculpture of a warrior with sharp and tiny spires and clear and deadly swords.

Green held her together, and together they held the hill together as the entire hill drifted about in a white-fog sea of shock.

When Green sent her away to school, in the hopes that living in a place where not every heart beat with the same grief might give her a chance to recover, there was a certain relief, coupled with a frightening despair. Maybe, maybe their leader would become stronger with a break from the wall of grief the hill had become. Maybe, maybe the vampires could keep it together.

It was at this time that the "blood/sex/magic room" became more and more necessary to survive.

Adrian had been the one to name it and probably the one to make sure it was built. Marcus had asked him about it once, and Adrian, creator of vampires, beautiful boy and demigod in bed, had blushed.

"They had one in the kiss where I was brought over," he mumbled. "It… it just feels like part of a healthy kiss to me, mate—but not something I'm comfortable talking about, to tell the truth."

Adrian had rarely gone into the blood/sex/magic room.

It consisted of a giant bed, and someone must have changed the sail-sized sheets during the day, but Marcus had never seen them. It was, quite simply, the site of an ongoing vampire blood orgy, and a night spent in the room was a night of shifting, groaning bodies biting, licking, sucking, fucking, feeding, and rolling about in the excesses of sex and blood and come.

It was the vampires' equivalent of the full-moon dog run of the shape-shifters, and although most vampires did not spend a lot of time in that room, *all* of them spent *some* time there.

As Adrian had said to Marcus shortly after he'd been brought over, when he was nearly despondent at the idea that he'd never again see the sun, it was impossible to despair after the full-throttle release of sex and bloodlust in a room where no one could hurt or be hurt by anything you did.

The term "endorphins" had not been in vogue then, but it was now, and that room had become the sanctuary for the vampires to get high off their own blood/sex endorphins; and when Cory left the hill, there wasn't a vampire in its environs who didn't spend a night a week there.

Marcus resisted at first.

Phillip had slept in Marcus's bed since the night Adrian died. There had been no sex between them at first, no making love, just a simple body-contact desire—cold or not, there was someone there to anchor them both in reality, to keep them from simply staying out on the front lawn and physically disintegrating with the sunrise.

After the first week, Marcus couldn't take it anymore. He awoke with Phillip in his bed, looking at Marcus with expectant, frightened eyes, that lean mouth flat and grim, and his body reacted. He took that mouth in a punishing kiss, and Phillip groaned, then growled, and Marcus had him flat on his stomach and was pounding into him with fury and despair within moments.

Afterward, Phillip did an unexpected thing—he held Marcus to his chest and whispered nothing, simple comfort words, into Marcus's hair as Marcus broke and wept blood all over his bare chest.

There was sex in their bed after that—lots of wordless, intense comfort sex—that helped ease the loss of Adrian but did nothing to assure Marcus that he would not be mourning Phillip the next time a pretty shape-shifter walked by.

After Cory had been gone for a month, coming back from school on weekends for stressed, unsatisfying visits, Marcus rose one evening to find Phillip standing naked at the side of his bed.

"Where are we going?" he asked muzzily, wondering how the guy could have been awake long enough to get naked.

Phillip took his hand—an unusual gesture in itself—and pulled him up out of bed. Marcus was… rumpled. He looked down at himself next to Phillip's pale beauty and realized he hadn't showered in several days and hadn't changed clothes either.

"Look, man. I don't know what you and me are, but you're fucking falling apart, and I can't watch and not do anything."

Marcus looked back at him, mute agony vibrating from every still vessel in his body. "You don't know what we are?" he asked, a second away from hysterical, vicious laughter.

Phillip shrugged. "Look—whatever relationships are here, we've got one. And just like you wouldn't let them kill me, I'm not going to let you die of grief, okay? Now come *on*. You hate going here, but it's better with a big crowd, and there's a full moon tonight, and half the hill is going to be there, and I think Green will be too."

Goddess. Green? Marcus had needed Green's healing for so long. He hadn't wanted to ask. He hadn't wanted to bother. Marcus was the stable one, right? The one who could keep the young ones anchored, the one who kept Phillip from flying beyond the pale. Marcus was the one Grace depended on, and the whole world needed Green, and why would Marcus need him more than anyone else?

"Green?" he asked hoarsely, and Phillip stroked his hand. The gesture was self-conscious, but Phillip's high brow was wrinkled, and he looked sad beyond measure.

"I know I'm not enough," he admitted.

"You're waiting for someone else," Marcus said gently. He didn't even let his voice get bitter when he added, "Someone real."

"You're real to me now," Phillip said decisively, still frowning and stroking his hand. "Do you think some random woman could mean more to me than you do right now? Come on, brother—let's go heal."

Maybe it was the promise of Green, and maybe it was just enough that Phillip cared, that he acknowledged he cared, but Marcus felt a sudden, bright, ripping slash of hope through his miasmic armor, and he clung to the red pain of it. Goddess—if there was hope, he would suffer the pain of healing.

He didn't like to think of those hours in that big bed, with the smooth limbs and voracious orifices of the other vampires there with him. But he did remember that first night, because his initial disappointment that Green wasn't there was acute, and he felt cheated. Then Phillip took his mouth in that mass of bodies, and then he was penetrated by slick fingers, and then, oh Goddess, Phillip was inside him while others kissed him and suckled from him, fingered him, and stroked. Those other mouths, breasts, cocks, hands—those were not what mattered. What mattered was that Phillip looked at him, truly looked at him, while moving inside his body. Under the cover of the orgy, Phillip seemed to see him as a lover in need for the first time in twenty years.

Phillip heaved and spent, and the moment was over. Someone was licking Phillip's spend from his thighs, and Phillip was licking Marcus's spend from his stomach, and Marcus simply closed his eyes and allowed himself to be rolled from body to mouth to body and joined the writhing, heaving, groaning orgy of communal vampire bodies trying to fill the void their leader had left when he left them.

They went back to that room a couple of times before Cory came back from school. She came back at the end of the semester, both triumphant and weakened. She had truly grieved herself almost to death, and then she had been attacked when her mourning was the most acute. Marcus and Phillip had gone down to the Bay Area to help when she'd been healing, and Marcus remembered the moment she had looked up and seen them both and realized that they were her people.

He'd been so terrified that she'd reject them, his hands had been shaking. She hadn't, though. She'd smiled, the expression huge in her peaked, pale face, and nodded a little, accepting the faith and worship they had both given Adrian but was now hers by right. Before they'd left the Bay Area and come back up the to the hill, she and Green had claimed that power, blowing their combined mark through everyone who owed them blood fealty, and Marcus and Phillip had looked at the magic tattoos that had sprung up on their left and right wrists and felt hope. (The tats were inked so that when they clasped hands, the tattoos mingled. Marcus noticed this. He was not sure Phillip did.)

So Cory returned to her kiss and started making the small ritual blood exchanges that marked the vampires as hers. Her sorcery—and her own special person—made this exchange amazing. She seemed to have the ability to taste the things each vampire had cherished in life. Marcus tasted of "dry-erase marker and coffee," and Phillip was "computer paper and hot chocolate." In the end, they had loved similarly, and it gave him hope of a different sort.

But Cory wasn't just bound to the kiss of vampires. Through accident, divine fuckup, and Bracken's intense possessiveness as a lover, she ended up ritually bound to two other lovers besides Green—Bracken and a shape-shifter she did not love, who had been bound by accident. Bracken seemed able to deal with the situation, but Nicky, the other lover, was having a hell of a time fitting in.

She returned at Christmas, and so six months after Adrian's death, Cory and the vampires had begun to find a balance. To the intense amusement (and sometimes discomfort) of the entire hill, she spent the next six months after that trying to find a balance with the lovers in her bed as well.

The big bed, the one with the red lights and the crimson sheets, was a place that Marcus and Phillip visited less and less often, and for a moment, a brief moment, Marcus began to feel even more hope. He began a quietly optimistic friendship with Cory and came to love her as much as he'd loved Adrian. Some of it may have been sexual—she had that plainly pretty thing going that had always made him search for the beauty underneath, and the hill's little Goddess had it in spades. She was strong enough to survive heartbreak, smart enough to be the best student he'd ever had, and kind enough not to laugh when his infatuation made some of the moments between them heavy enough to cause blushes.

She was also off-limits, because she was in love with two men, one of them Green, and even Marcus, with all of his Phillip-doesn't-love-me bullshit, wouldn't put that weight on her shoulders. Perhaps the off-limits thing made it easier to love her—there would be no complications if he just thought of her from afar, right?

By February, Phillip had begun to bring girls to Marcus's bed, one at a time, in an obvious, unspoken attempt to find a third lover to bind them together, and all of that peace disa-fucking-peared.

# ULTIMATUM

"WHAT THE *hell*, Marcus?" Phillip was puzzled and pissed off, and Marcus didn't care, fuck it all, not this time.

"She giggled like a hyena!" Marcus snapped, fighting the urge to kick his bed. Their bed. The bed they kept sharing with women who did nothing for him but showed Phillip's increasing desperation to have one in their bed. Phillip's bed hadn't been fucked in for *months*, but Marcus's bed? No. *That* bed got the sheets changed every day.

"She giggled like a hyena," he repeated, because the noise had made his teeth grind. "She had no sense of humor, she was dumb as a rock, and she gave the worst blow jobs in history!"

Phillip shrugged. "To *you*, maybe."

"To *anyone*, Phillip. It's hard to give a decent BJ when you keep talking while you've got the guy's cock down your throat."

Phillip fought off a smirk. "Well… yeah. That was sort of annoying."

"It was *really* annoying, and I'm not sure how Nicky decided to recruit that woman, but I think some village is missing its idiot, okay?" Nicky, Cory's third and accidental lover, was still struggling to find his place at the hill. He'd become, by default, a shape-shifter recruiter who was, possibly, the worst judge of character *ever.*

Or that could just be Marcus's opinion after Madison "Call Me Dissy" had *bitten his prick* while Phillip had been banging her from behind.

Marcus sank down to the bed, which was covered in a new black and burgundy quilt that Grace had made him for Christmas. He loved it a lot—and he also noticed that Phillip's quilt was store-bought. Grace had made Phillip an Aran sweater for Christmas, but Marcus's bed had been blessed by their head-mama vampire herself. Of course Phillip didn't get it, in the same way he didn't get the tattoos or the fact that the girls Marcus liked were too serious for Phillip and the girls Phillip liked were too… too… too *goddamned stupid to live*!

"Jesus, Marcus, when did you get to be such an asshole?"

Marcus glared at him. "When you decided to make being a threesome a pet project! Dammit, does there have to be a woman in here?"

"You *like* women!" Phillip reminded him snottily. "I *like* women! We *both* get off with women! What's so bad about having one here? I mean… shit, Marcus. You keep acting like we're human or something! You took care of *that* little problem twenty years ago—why can't we party a little?"

"Because I don't want a party! I just want you!"

A year. Almost a fucking year. Here it was, nearly Thanksgiving again—Adrian had been dead for a year and a half, and their little Goddess had been married to three lovers for almost six months, and Marcus and Phillip?

Well, they were in the same place they'd always been. Marcus was longing, and Phillip was futzing around because he thought love came around every goddamned day!

Phillip stopped and looked at him. "Since when?" he asked honestly, and twenty years of romantic backlog effectively shorted out every brain cell in Marcus's head.

"Since when?" Marcus echoed blankly.

"Well, yeah. You never said you just wanted me. Since when was that an option?"

"Since when?"

"I woke up in here in another bed. I assumed you didn't do guys."

"Since when?"

"Well, you've only ever done *me*. I mean, I've never seen you sleep with Green!"

"And you take that to mean…?" Marcus was truly drawing a blank here—he could not seem to fathom the big thing that Phillip didn't know. The thing Marcus wasn't going to tell him, because the man wasn't *ready* to know. Twenty years had gone by, and Phillip didn't know?

Phillip shrugged. "I don't know, man. It's not like you're in love with me or something."

"Auuuuuggghhhhhh!"

He pulled back his fist and planted it in Phillip's surprised face. Phillip had been a stockbroker—even as a fighter he tended to swoop and dive and tear with his teeth. He'd never broken up a fistfight or watched the werecreatures' fracas in their common room, but Marcus had. When Phillip pulled back his arm to try to hit Marcus, Marcus caught his balled-up fist and pushed Phillip away.

"What in the *hell*, you jerkwad! Jesus, try and get a guy laid…."

"*Auuughhh!* You *fucking* idiot! *Jesus* fucking *Christ*, how can you *possibly* think this is about getting *laid*?"

Marcus's fists bunched in Phillip's shirt, and suddenly the two of them were crashing through the door to their room in a melee that Marcus couldn't seem to stop. Phillip would block a punch, and Marcus would swing again and connect, and Phillip would swing and miss, and the whole time, Marcus was just *willing* him to come to his senses and figure it out.

And that was when someone grabbed him and Marcus by the shirt collars and shook them like misbehaving dogs.

"What in the *fuck*, you idiot fuckheads?"

Marcus looked down at his dangling toes and held very still. "Sorry, Green," he whispered. He looked from the corner of his eye and saw that Phillip was doing the same thing. Green was six feet seven inches tall, and although he didn't advertise the fact, stronger than human. And apparently the two of them had gotten on his last nerve.

"Do you have any idea how tense we are here, mate? We've got two new shape-shifters on deck. You know that, right? Stronger than hell, and in the middle of some emotional bullshit that would curl your toes." Teague and his partner in business (and apparently in everything), Jack, had joined the hill the day before. By all accounts Teague was skittish as hell, and Jack was hostile to everyone who wasn't Teague. Marcus had a moment to think sourly that he was glad he and Phillip weren't the only ones on the hill with heterosexuality issues, because it made him feel a whole lot less foolish about…. shit. Had they shattered their *door*?

"I'm sorry, Green," Marcus said again and was rewarded by another shake from the back of his neck, this one gentler.

"And we've got some fucked-up werewolf business going down. You know that too, right? Tomorrow night you're going on a run with Cory and Bracken—I need to know you two idiots are up to the job! They're counting on you!"

Marcus grimaced. He and Phillip were Cory's right-hand men out on the field. Whenever there was a supernatural threat that Cory felt needed her personal attention (and her formidable weapons), she and Bracken put together a team and investigated. They'd gotten pretty good at it—and since she and Green had widened their power base, there had been enough problems to keep Green and Bracken's beloved pretty busy. Marcus and Phillip were always on her team, and Marcus liked it like that. He hated the thought, but he was pretty sure that if Cory had been on the hill just a little bit longer, had perhaps had a little more confidence in battle, that with all of her sorcerous gifts Adrian might not have had to die on that hillside in a burst of gentle blood rain. One thing was certain—she might not have been a vampire, but Cory took care of Adrian's people like they were her own children. If she was yelling at someone, it was usually because that someone put his life thoughtlessly in danger, and for Cory, there were *no* acceptable losses.

It was that thought that finally made Marcus relax. He wriggled a little and was gently put down on the ground, Phillip with him.

"We're fine," Phillip said sourly, straightening his casual dress clothes. "He just decided to lose his temper for the first goddamned time in twenty years. We'll figure it out."

"Well, I hope so, mate. If you two can't get this figured, maybe it's time for a new living arrangement. There are at least three new empty rooms in the darkling—maybe one of you needs to move out!"

Marcus gasped, the sound reverberating around the hall like a rifle shot, and he turned stunned, hurt eyes toward the man who was father, big brother, best friend, best lover, and hero for the entire hill, all wrapped up in one.

"You'd do that?" he asked, his voice so laden with shock and hurt that Green moved his hand up to the back of Marcus's neck again—but this time to massage and comfort.

Green lowered his head so they were temple to temple and said, "Only if you make me," very softly. Then he turned those sensual lips to Marcus's ear and said, "Tell him, Marcus. He doesn't know where you're coming from, and he needs to."

Marcus looked at Green miserably, remembering that long-ago conversation with Grace, where she'd told him that Phillip wasn't ready yet. But then, how long ago was that? For the first time, the weight of twenty years hit him—truly hit him. Twenty years they had been growing closer together with every sunset. Maybe, if Phillip wasn't ready after twenty years, he never would be. If nothing else, the weight of this "crush" was beginning to remind Marcus with every passing second that he could never truly breathe.

"We'll make it right," he said numbly, and Green gave him a kiss on the temple before summoning something—Marcus thought it might have been a wood troll—that popped out of thin air to start working on their shattered door. Green ruffled Marcus's hair, and then Phillip's, and disappeared around the bend in the corridor, leaving Marcus and Phillip looking at each other in silence.

Marcus couldn't do it—not now. Not in this tense moment of aftershock.

"I'm going to go flying," he said abruptly and turned on his heel and left.

He knew he wasn't alone about half a second after he walked outside and leaped into the air. For a moment he thought about ignoring Phillip, but then the thought crashed into his chest that maybe he and Phillip wouldn't be a team forever. Maybe, in spite of all the time they should have had, all of the promises immortality had to offer, this would be the last time they went flying together.

He looked at Phillip, the man he'd loved for over a third of his existence, and gave a broken grin. The roaring of the wind was almost too loud in his ears to talk, so he went mind to mind, recalling those words from two guys on the top of a snow-covered hill a little more than twenty years earlier.

*"Wanna race?"*

Phillip let his glee show over their contact, and Marcus leveled out flat and told his spectacularly gifted vampire body to go *zoom*. Phillip was right there with him. They had no specific path—it was only speed and the joy of flying together that held them to each other's sides.

They soared, the blackness of the sparsely populated mountains at their feet, the glittering stars of an unlit night at their backs, nothing to lose, and nothing but the dawn to hold them back. Marcus might have just continued forever, straight into the gray twilight of dawn, if Phillip hadn't been at his side. As it was, Marcus was the one who remembered to turn back, and their trip back to the hill—a bright and misty fairy ring to their preternatural eyes—was straight-on speed. No dodging, turning, cutting each other off, or soaring higher to avoid a collision—simple speed. When they touched down in the garden, they were both laughing with exhilaration.

The top of the hill had been renamed the Goddess Grove, and it was as beautiful and sacred now as it had been the night Adrian had helped make it. For Christmas the year before, Green had installed a granite bench in the clearing by the trapdoor (also magically created) that emerged from inside the hill. Adrian's likeness was carved on the side.

Marcus and Phillip touched down right in front of the bench just as the sky went a lighter gray. Marcus raised his face up toward the waning darkness and closed his eyes. Green's ultimatum—and advice—weighed him down as soon as his feet hit the ground.

"I know you loved him," Phillip said softly. "I mean, I was always sorry I couldn't be him."

Marcus looked at him in some confusion. "Who?"

"Adrian."

*Adrian?* "We all loved him," Marcus said, because it was true. In the end, even the elves had loved Adrian—and a lot of them, older than Moses, had sticks up their asses as far as the vampires were concerned.

"Yeah," Phillip said quietly, "but you *loved* him, loved him. You know. Like...."

Marcus looked at him, blinking in confusion and feeling hollowed out like the center of Green's hill would be if the people he loved hadn't been there.

"Like what?"

"Like you loved Cory," Phillip said, looking away. "And don't deny it—you loved her. Right up until the wedding, when you stopped looking at her all cow-eyed."

Marcus shrugged bitterly. "It was a crush, asshole. Trust me—by now I know the difference between a crush and real love." The words made him want to rip someone's head off. He could, too. If nothing else, the past year battling at Cory's side had taught him that he could be a true vampire, bloodthirsty and ruthless when the violence presented itself. Around Cory, well, it tended to present itself.

"And Adrian?"

*What-the-fuck-ever.* "I never loved Adrian," Marcus grunted. "Not like I love you."

And with that, he couldn't stand this conversation anymore. He flew down the granite stairway, knowing Phillip would be behind him. Phillip would never be so foolish as to wish the dawn would take him to ease the pain of a broken heart.

HE ROSE the next night trying to tell himself it was for the best. Phillip had made it downstairs and to their room, but he'd spent the night in his unused king-size bed.

They'd been so late coming down that Marcus hadn't even had time to cry before the sun rose, and for ten or so hours of daylight, he'd rested in peace.

He woke up the next evening and heard Phillip zoom out of the room. *Well, fuck. Fuck fuck fuck fuck fuck fuck fuck.* Vaguely he thought that Cory had a run the next night—they were hunting a rogue shape-shifter and bringing the new werewolf alpha with them to see if he'd fit with their crew. Marcus would have to tell her, he thought dully. One of them would have to stay back. It would probably be him—the thought hurt, but there was no denying it. Phillip's customary fearlessness made him perfect for the job.

Awesome. Well, this was why human couples stayed together when they fell out of love—you didn't just split from your spouse, you split from your friends and your children and even your job. Phillip was the most useful—Marcus would have to hand him over and lose Cory in the divorce.

He stood up and started pulling the stuff out of his bureau to take to another room. He heard a crash behind him, and when he turned around, he was surprised to see Phillip there with Bracken. Bracken was, characteristically, being a complete jerkwad.

"Look, dickweed—just because you want this out of your room doesn't mean you can rip it apart, okay? *Green* built this!"

Phillip snorted. "Well, by all means let us dip it in wax and set it up in a fucking shrine. Green doesn't give a shit. If he gave a shit, he wouldn't have put it in a room with a guy who went through three beds when he was down in the fucking vault! I just want it gone!"

"You don't have to move," Marcus said, staring resolutely at the pile of T-shirts in his arms. Phillip had started giving him the good ones—tight fit, with the ring collar and the nice fabrics—for Christmas. *Well, hell.* All his clothes were from Phillip. He probably even had some of the bastard's socks in his pile. The only thing he wouldn't have was Phillip's underwear—because Phillip didn't wear any.

"I'm not!" Phillip snapped. "Dammit, Bracken, take the fucking mattress first!"

"I'm married to a woman who could cook you for fun and laugh while you sizzle—you know that, right?" Bracken growled, but as Marcus cast a puzzled look over his shoulder, he saw that the big elf and Phillip had managed the mattress. It was unwieldy, but they were both preternaturally strong, so away it went. What was left was a frame that was handily jointed in the middle, all the better to disconnect and fit through the door.

"Cory adores Marcus," Phillip said smugly, coming back in the room and grabbing his end of one of the frame halves. "She won't cook me, because she knows that will fuck him up royally. So stop making threats and help me get this fucking thing out of here."

Marcus turned away from his clothes and looked at Phillip in complete and total annoyance. "You're *leaving* me, and you're using me as leverage? Jesus—what an asshole!"

"I'm not leaving you," Phillip snapped from the hallway. "And you're not leaving me. So shut up, sit down, and wait until I get this fucking bed out into the hall, okay?"

"Awesome!" Marcus snapped. "Whatever you say, Phillip. You're the lord of all you survey, Phillip. I live for your command, my fucking liege!"

"Oh Jesus, shut up!" Bracken and Phillip snapped in tandem, and Marcus scowled at both of them. He plonked his ass down, as ordered, onto *his* bed, the one with the handmade quilt, and stewed until Phillip slammed the door, shouting, "Thank you, dickwad! I'll remember your cheerful assistance!" down the hall as Bracken thumped away.

Marcus turned to him in disbelief. "Did you just make him haul that down to one of the vacant rooms by himself? Jesus, Phillip—that guy is going to have your back tomorrow. How badly do you want to piss him off?"

Phillip rolled his eyes and looked bored. "Shut up," he snarled, walking around to face Marcus, and for the first time in their acquaintance, looking well and truly pissed at *Marcus* and not at the world in general. "Cory's in the hall, doing some sort of levitation bubble—calls it practice. Whatever. She's got it, and you and I need to have an actual conversation instead of you shutting up and being all fucking noble and shit!"

"That wasn't what I was doing—"

"*Bullshit*! I know you, Marcus."

"That's a pile of crap!"

"I do! Now shut up and listen, or we'll still be hashing this out at dawn!" It was November, and the sun had scarcely gone down an hour before. It was a long time until dawn. "You think I don't, but I know you. You want to be the good guy. You don't want to be the bloodthirsty vampire. You want to be the good guy, so you… you're *in love with me* for some insane amount of time I don't even want to add up, and you just… what? Conveniently neglect to mention the fact? We've been living together for twenty years—we play chess, cribbage, Scrabble, and Trivial Pursuit and fuck like bunnies, and the whole 'I love you more than Adrian' thing doesn't come up? Not even once? You go out into the world, and you try to recruit lost teenagers and save their poor little souls, and you drag me along when I suck at it, and you do this why?"

Phillip shook his head, and the look he sent Marcus was stark and sad. "I'm an asshole, Marcus. I should have known. Maybe I've always known. You do all that shit because you love me. You've always loved me. And when it takes me by surprise, you assume it's all your fault."

"I shouldn't have," Marcus said to no one in particular. "I… I shouldn't have gone into the vault with you—I mean, I did it because we were going to have to put you down, and I fell, and I fell hard, and I just… I've been hoping you could love me too."

To his surprise, Phillip sank to his knees in front of him and grabbed one of his hands.

"Don't give up on me, asshole," he rasped. "Just don't. You're going all tragic, like the magic window's passed. Don't you see? This whole twenty years—it's been the magic window, and I've been falling through."

Marcus rolled his eyes. "You just moved out of our room—how far could you possibly have fallen?"

"God, you're dense! That fucking bed was the problem in the first place, you know that?"

Marcus narrowed his eyes. "I thought the problem in the first place was that you slept with anything that moved and I was your backup fuck buddy!"

Even on his knees, Phillip could look imperious. "But don't you see? I woke up after being in the vault, and I was in your room but in another bed. I thought… I thought you didn't want me. That what we did in the vault, that was just… vampire training. I kept crawling into your bed, and you never objected, and I thought, well, maybe he's okay with it. Maybe he'll let me stay."

Marcus squinted at him, completely at a loss. "I *always* wanted you to stay. *You* were the one who kept chatting up women left and right. And I can't do that anymore, okay? I can't! It just—"

"Hurts too much," Phillip said hoarsely, propping his chin on Marcus's knee and looking into his eyes soulfully. "I know. It hurt every time I did it."

Marcus couldn't help himself. He framed that narrow face with his hands and ran his thumbs over Phillip's cheekbones. It had been fifteen years before Phillip would let Marcus touch his face like this. Marcus was going to savor every opportunity—even the last one—to do so.

"Then why did you?" he asked, his voice gruff.

"Because I thought it was something from the change—you know, you fuck nothing but guys for a month, and you walk away a little bent. And then I thought I had the maker's mark with you, because what I felt for you was a little like what I felt for Adrian, but…." Phillip trailed off and leaned his cheek against Marcus's palm. "Adrian died, and what I felt for you was even bigger and a lot different and still there."

"Why all the threesomes?"

Phillip grimaced. "I was trying to make us… you know. Permanent. Cory, Green, and Adrian—that was permanent. Our new werewolves? They're going to be a threesome, and that's going to be permanent. It's like no one gets a one-on-one here—I just wanted something forever with you."

Abruptly Marcus pulled his hand from Phillip's cheek and pressed the heel of his palm against one eye after the other. It came away stained in crimson. Phillip grabbed his hand and planted a tender kiss in the center, lapping at the palm.

"I love you, asshole. Isn't that enough of forever for you?"

Phillip took one more swipe with his tongue. "Well, yeah," he whispered. "And that's why I had Bracken get rid of the bed."

Marcus pulled at his hand again, because his vision had gone red again, and he was surprised when Phillip whispered, "Let me." Suddenly Marcus was the one with his face framed by Phillip's long-fingered hands, and Phillip's thumbs brushed at his cheekbones, coming away scarlet. Phillip popped a thumb in Marcus's mouth—only to vampires did tears taste sweet.

Marcus suckled and swallowed, then said, "I need to hear you say it."

"I know you do," Phillip muttered. "You've been waiting for twenty years—you deserve it."

Marcus had to concede that he was right. "Damned straight."

"I love you, asshole. I've loved you since that first downhill race. I've loved you since you looked at me on the ski lift like I was a complete dick, and you still smiled at me. I may have been straight before the change, but if I had met you when we were alive, we would have been best friends until we died, and you still would have been the one person I loved best in the world."

Marcus managed a grin, one that had Adrian and Green in it, and even a little bit of Cory's fierce scowl. "Does this mean I still get to top?"

Phillip smiled back. "Can I try it once in a while? Now that I know you love me, I think you'd forgive me if I'm awful at it."

Marcus found a little bit of a laugh forced from his tight, aching chest. "God, I wish you would. Twenty years—you know, it would be *great* to try something different."

Phillip laughed too and rested his cheek on Marcus's knees. "God, I love you."

"I love you too, dickwad."

"Asshole."

Marcus's voice dropped, and the hill's sacred word, the one Adrian had used for Green and Cory, sounded loudly in the quite room. "Beloved."

"Beloved."

It echoed there as they sat, Marcus running his fingers through Phillip's hair, for a very long time.

wanting more, and then broke away. "Now keep up with me, 'kay?" he said, before launching into the air.

Phillip did, of course.

*"Last one there fucks the other into the bed,"* he crowed in Marcus's head.

*"As long as it's our bed, I don't give a shit!"*

*"No losers in love?"*

*"Not ours."*

And the hell of it, the best blessing of all of it, was that it was all true. They loved each other. It was their bed. And breaking up was not an option.

As far as Marcus could figure, it was the third time for them that the end was only the beginning.

Later, after separate showers to wash away the grit and gore and river water, Phillip took Marcus to bed and seduced him.

It shouldn't have mattered—Marcus had loved him for twenty years. Marcus was a sure thing, and he fully expected quick and dirty sex, but that wasn't what happened.

What happened was long slow kisses, whispers across his jaw, hot words in his ear, nibbles down his neck. What happened was that Phillip spooned him from behind, nuzzled the back of his neck, rubbed his chest, and played with his hot spots from his nipples down to the flutter of his clenching stomach, palming his upper thighs and touching all of him with a tenderness that Marcus had only glimpsed.

Marcus had to breathe. He *had* to. His chest beat up and down as he gasped for something, anything, to ground him, make him catch that elusive, terrifying will-o'-the-wisp of orgasm at the peak of this terrifying slow burn of arousal.

"You want me, right?" Phillip whispered, and Marcus half whimpered, half howled.

"Don't be an asshole...."

"Not my asshole we're worried about," Phillip whispered. He thrust two fingers into Marcus's mouth, and Marcus sucked on them, hard, making them slick and smooth.

Those treacherous fingers made their way down an obvious path. Marcus shuddered when the first one breached him, softening, probing, stretching....

"*Yesss….*" It had been so long since those few days of rolling in the group bed, and even then, that had been hallucinatory, grief ridden, and far away. Marcus had wanted to be wanted, wanted to be taken, wanted Phillip to love him for so long….

"*Auuughhhh….*" Two fingers, scissoring, stretching, burning….

"You like that? How long have you been waiting for that?"

"Too long!"

"You want some more?"

"Please?"

"You sure?"

"God, Phillip, *please….*"

"I like it when you beg." Phillip's canines tickled his neck, and he moved his invading fingers long enough to haul Marcus's thigh up. Marcus kept his leg propped, and Phillip positioned himself, thrust a little, felt the resistance, retreated….

His fangs did the same thing, and Marcus was delirious with need.

"Phillip, please…. Phillip…. God. *Fuck me….*"

And Phillip thrust inside, wrapped his arms around Marcus's shoulders, and anchored him as Marcus howled in joy.

"Like that?"

"Yes…."

"Want more?"

"Yes…."

"Love me?"

"Goddess, yes!"

"I love you too."

Phillip thrust harder, faster, as quickly as he could, and Marcus hunched down and met him, thrust for thrust, and still Phillip continued to whisper.

"I can't reach it from here…. Grab it."

"Phillip!"

"Grab it—I want to see you stroke it."

"Ah, God…." It was so deliciously dirty, so amazingly hot to grab his cock and stroke, pull on it, harsh and fast and…. "*Phillip!*"

But Phillip beat him to it, coming cold and slick in his ass at the same time those fangs punctured the skin of his neck, and he sucked hard as he came. Oh God… the pain, the exquisite pain, the heady draining in his neck and the feel of Phillip's spend sliding between his ass cheeks and down his thighs was all he needed. Marcus shot, coating his chest, stomach, and abdomen in a chilly spatter of semen. Phillip shuddered again and again, finally licking the puncture wounds in his neck as Marcus's eyes rolled back in his head and the final spurt hit his skin.

Dawn hit just then, their bodies still locked together, their sex still sliding on their skin, and when the sun fell behind the horizon, Marcus awoke with Phillip hard inside his body and they did it again.

They showered after that and fell into bed, just because that was where they wanted to be. Phillip propped his chin on Marcus's stomach, and Marcus played with his hair. Like real lovers. Like forever.

"We could have been doing that for twenty years," he said moodily after a moment, and Marcus shook his head.

"No, man. I think it took us twenty years to be able to do that."

Phillip rolled his eyes. "God, you're a girl."

"God, you're an asshole!"

"You love me, though, right?"

And for a moment, his eyes were worried. Marcus smiled a little.

"Yes, asshole, I really love you."

Twenty years? Twenty years was nothing. Twenty years was that breath before a first kiss. Twenty years was the stroke of a knuckle down a cheek. This moment, together, all of the moments that followed, no matter how many there were?

That was forever.

GUARDING THE VAMPIRE'S GHOST

AMY LANE

# PROLOGUE

# A BRIEF WINDOW INTO THE GREAT QUARREL

*THE ROW that allowed Adrian, vampire prince and consort to Green, Lord of Green's hill, in Foresthill, California, to be allowed into the Realm of Heaven caused two major earthquakes and a tsunami. Nobody in the Realm of Heaven was sure how it happened—it violated all of the laws that had been set down since the split of the God and the Goddess (or She Who Would Not Be Named), and it was just flat-out wrong.*

*Vampires were not supposed to end up in heaven. They were the Goddess's creatures, along with the elves, sorceresses, were-folk, and the sons of man and the other. These folk should end up with the Goddess in their afterlife—that was the rule. But Adrian had gone out in a shower of blood defending the people he loved best—two lovers and a brother of the heart among them—and suddenly the Goddess was there petitioning for him to be allowed where vampires should not be.*

*More specifically, she was petitioning for him to be allowed in the antechamber.*

*"His lovers need him," she'd sniffled. "You know they're important to me—and they might not make it without some assurance that his spirit continues."*

*Of course, God had put up a front about faith and belief, and the resulting crack across his face had resulted in one of the earthquakes and the destruction of a mini-mall that night, and that particular line of reasoning had been dropped right quick.*

*But in the end, it didn't matter. The Great Quarrel (as the angels called it) could only be resolved by the Goddess's plan, which involved Adrian's lovers and his best friend, and this meant that she had God over a barrel. The deity hadn't had his Goddess by his side in over two thousand years, and the state of the world showed that he was hurting. He'd give her almost anything to help her plan come to fruition—a vampire in the anteroom to heaven was really no big deal.*

*So the details didn't matter. What mattered was that an accident of divine politics put a vampire in the anteroom to heaven, and now he was the angels' problem.*

*And the angels really didn't know what to do with him.*

# Part I

# Failing

Shepherd, Angel of Penitence, looked at Saint Peter unhappily.

"Us, really? Me and Jefi? We're the best people for the job?"

Saint Peter looked Shepherd blandly in his angel-hazel eyes.

"All of the host of heaven are more than qualified," he said dryly, and Shepherd gave him a pointed look. They both knew what he wasn't saying, and damned if Shepherd was going to let it slide.

"Yeah, but you usually give this assignment to people you're trying to get rid of. The Angel of Chickens? Seriously? You think we didn't notice that he—"

"*She*—she chose a gender when she fell—"

"Yeah, when she fell with the Angel of Oak Trees!" Who was now an actual "he" and not just the gender neutral sort of "he" that sounded more definitive than the sexless "it."

Saint Peter shrugged. "Some angels are simply ready to fall. It's not permanent exile, you know. They can restore their grace whenever they repent."

But they didn't. And neither had the two angels after them or the *three* angels after them! There was something about this assignment that seemed to send angels tumbling down to earth like baby birds out of the nest. The last three angels had landed in Las Vegas, and they were currently organizing a brothel. Shepherd was understandably upset.

"But… but, Peter… it's *Jefischa!*"

And that was the crux of the matter right there. Jefischa was the Angel of the Fourth Hour of the Night. It was sort of an unstable time—and Jefi was just like it. He could be quiet and big-eyed, all contemplation and expectation, or he could be playful, like a child escaping before bedtime. He could be melancholy and sad, like a mother after hearing a poignant story before sleep, or raucous and rowdy, like a young man on his last beer. He could be all of these things at once. Shepherd knew, because they'd been partnered since forever. Literally. The fourth hour of the night was an excellent time for repentance. Shepherd got a lot of calls in Jefischa's company, and the dour, placid Shepherd was grateful for the one angel in heaven who didn't roll his eyes and groan when Shepherd walked into the room.

"Jefischa is perfectly capable of maintaining the integrity of his own soul," Peter said mildly, and Shepherd glared at him.

"Jefischa," he said fiercely, "is an innocent—"

"So whatever unholy wiles the vampire is working on him should not have any effect at all." Peter's voice was firm and growing firmer, and Shepherd usually would have stood down, but... Jefischa! Sweet, mercurial, melancholy, playful Jefischa. He needed to be protected, even from himself.

"So he's more easily led astray!" Shepherd countermanded, and Peter glowered at him until Shepherd finally did stand down.

"Have a little faith in your partner, Shep," Peter told him, gentleness in his voice. "Lord knows, being his partner is something you've not once had to repent."

Peter disappeared, and Shep glared at the white fuzzy halo where the archangel used to be. "Ha-ha," he grumbled, but then Jefischa appeared at his side. It was serene, "retiring for bed" Jefischa, and he smiled at Shepherd and asked him what was wrong.

"We're guarding the vampire," Shep said, keeping it short. Maybe if he didn't give Jefi the details, he wouldn't find out anything that could make him fall.

"Ohhh...." Jefi was suddenly all big eyes and child-at-a-bedtime-story. The fourth hour after dark, indeed. "We get to guard him? Wow! Do you think we'll find out why all those people fell? Why do you think they fell, Shep? I mean, I knew Anpiel—she was the sweetest thing. And she and Zerachiel—they were always fighting! I have no idea how they ended up down on earth together." Jefi gave a mock shudder. "Weird."

Shepherd raised a sour eyebrow. "Yeah. Weird. Look, Jefi. You've got to promise to follow me on this one. No...." If Shepherd hadn't been a vague form of personified energy, his hands would have waved in the air. "You know how you get. No acting human, okay?"

Jefi bobbed his head and then stopped, puzzled. "Do I act human, Shepherd?"

Shepherd looked at him, feeling helpless. "You act... compassionate, Jefi. Empathetic. You... you forget, sometimes, that our job is to be a beacon of guidance for them. You seem to want to be their friend."

Jefi's energy—his "wings"—turned an unbearable color. It was a murky sort of brown-orange-green, and Shepherd hated it. He suddenly found that he would say anything, *do* anything, to make that color go away.

"You… you don't like me when I do that, Shep?"

"No! No… no, I like you fine. It's one of the things that makes you— well, um, you, Jefi! No. Don't change that. Just, I don't know… keep it in check this time, okay? There's something about this guy. We're falling like mortals around him, Jefi. I don't want anything to happen to you."

Jefi's wings brightened up a little, but they were still a troubled brown-green. "Okay, I guess. You'd… you'd let me fall alone, Shep?" There was a moment of absolute shock, and then Jefi covered his eyes. "Ouch, Shep… that color *hurts*. Make it stop—whatever you're thinking, make it stop!"

Shep was thinking of Jefischa alone on the cruel, barbaric surface of the planet below. He was thinking of him being abused and suckered into the worst of what humanity had to offer—the drug hells, the brothels, the places where humans routinely threw away their lives, their souls, their humanity. He had no idea what his *wings* looked like, but the painful terror of Jefi left alone was enough to paralyze his very being for a moment.

"No," he said roughly, after a moment of getting himself under control. "I'd never let you fall alone, Jefi. No worries. That's why we need to be careful on this one. We like it up here, right?"

Jefi smiled, his wings going bright and iridescent, and Shepherd knew his own appearance brightened up considerably. "Absolutely, Shep. Anything you say. Besides, what do we have to worry about? He's not a human. He's a vampire. I'm sure he'll be *very* different."

The two of them appeared over the entryway to the anteroom and paused. It was, after all, the gateway from a soul's seat on earth to its destination in heaven.

"Shep, what're the ropes for?" Jefi asked. He was naturally curious; the fourth hour of darkness was often a time for digging into secrets or children pattering down a darkened hallway.

Shepherd stared at the golden cords and frowned. "I have no idea." The cords seemed to be attached to all of the souls drifting about. They were brighter on the side near heaven and growing dimmer by the moment on the side near earth, and neither of the angels had any information on what those cords were supposed to be.

Their puzzlement was greeted with soft laughter from a person coming *out* of the anteroom. There were plenty of people drifting *in* to the anteroom, and usually there was someone to greet them. That was the purpose of the anteroom: it was like an airport greeting area. Most of the people going through were in transit, and most of them had people waiting for them. Those that didn't, well, they had angels to help them through the transition—Yahudia and Zaranpuryu being the main two, but they often recruited help. Either way, the anteroom was mostly an exclusively one-way proposition. Except for the young human with the white-blond hair and the sky-spangled eyes, weaving his way gracefully between oblivious souls.

He was so solid in appearance, so full of flesh and vibrancy, that he was nearly blinding.

"Hey there… wait a minute!" Jefi said. His energy vibrated; his wax-perfect human shape all but bounced on its pale bare toes. "You're not supposed to be coming out of there!"

The young man laughed. "Yeah, mate, I am. I was a little out of it, but I swear even *I* heard the row that got me my weekend-pass privileges set in stone. Check with your boss, duckies, but do it on your own time. I've got somewhere I've got to be."

Shepherd didn't really have a mouth, but he knew that what looked like his jaw was swinging on its hinges. The young man faded out of the walkway to the anteroom, leaving Shep and Jefi staring at his narrow, retreating back.

"Was he wearing a black motorcycle jacket?" Jefi asked out of the dark of the night.

"Yes, Jefi. Yes, he was." And ripped jeans and a white T-shirt. He'd looked like James Dean—only better. The pale hair was in a layered, curly halo around his face, and the blue eyes had been open and guileless, inviting people in as opposed to smoldering and warning people way.

"He was very beautiful," Jefi said in an admiring way. "By human standards, he would have been very coveted."

Shepherd blinked his eyes, feeling very stupid. "Oh, for the sake of heaven…." His angel form washed the color of softest rose. They weren't supposed to swear. "That was Adrian, Jefi. Who else could it be? Weekend pass, inhuman beauty… dammit. We just let the vampire escape."

Jefi was silent for a moment, considering. "Well, technically he's got a pass. We didn't really let him escape."

Shep looked at him. Just looked at him. Jefi smiled charmingly, and Shepherd blew out a great chuff of air and threw his ass on a cloud with enough force to dislodge that sucker so it could float free. Jefi put his angelic "hands" on the cloud—it was about chest high—and instead of levitating or sweeping his mighty wings to and fro, he heaved himself up and clambered into a sitting position next to Shepherd like a toddler getting into bed with his big brother. Shepherd watched him silently, and when Jefi smiled that great, open grin into his face, Shep had no choice but to return it with a little smile of his own. You couldn't stay mad at Jefi. This quality wasn't one of his gifts as an angel. It wasn't in his realm of power—it was just Jefischa. He was probably the only reason the fourth hour of darkness had so much possibility—because the fifth hour of darkness was dark, brooding, and violent. Drunks got mean in the fifth hour of darkness, when they were happy and sloppy in hour number four. Shep was pretty sure that was because Patrozhin was a dour, unsympathetic bastard who should have been made the angel of misers with pancreatitis.

"You're right," Shepherd said, just to reassure Jefi that all his goodwill wasn't for naught. "He's got carte blanche. I don't know why, but it's out of our hands."

"Mmm...." Jefi sounded distracted. "I still don't know what those ropes are for." Jefischa put out his hands and made stroking motions. "They look... soft... and warm... and sweet to touch. I want to touch one...."

"No," Shepherd said uncertainly. "I.... Jefi, there's something very... mortal about those. Look. They're a direct link to earth. And did you see the size and the thickness of the vampire's? It was...." He flailed for a comparison.

"As big around as the vampire's wrist!" Jefi said excitedly. "Yes! And the cord leading to heaven, it was much finer than those of these people here. You're right, those *are* mortal things." Jefi turned a look of pure adoration toward Shepherd. "It's a good thing you spotted that! I would have just run right in!"

Shepherd ducked his head and looked away. "Just looking out for us, that's all." And then, irritably, "You know, I really wish Peter had given us more of a heads-up about this place. It's really complex!"

"That's because you're not filtering out the white noise!" Peter tutted from behind them. Shepherd rolled his eyes. Saint Peter liked to just pop in unannounced when someone was on assignment. The humans had a word for it, but one did not call the right hand to the Lord of Heaven an "officious asshole."

Still, Shepherd and Jefi took Peter's advice. They filtered out everyone who did *not* have access to the planet below. There was still the occasional soul—serene and filled with purpose—being drawn back to earth with those thick, almost pulsing cords of gold, but once the influx of souls was filtered out, it was an okay place. Shepherd heard a change of music—there'd been Mozart permeating the air earlier—and he raised his eyes toward Jefi with a wince.

"Isn't that a little contemporary?"

"I like Death Cab for Cutie."

Shepherd felt more than saw Peter's rolled eyes, so he grinned and said, "You know, I think it's a good choice myself!"

"Very cute," Peter said through clenched teeth. "Look, he's down on the planet, so I know you've already met. And he'll seem very nice and very personable. Just don't get personal with him, okay? That's where the others slipped up. Don't make that mistake."

"We hear you!" Jefi turned that open smile to Peter, whose jaw relaxed in spite of what Shep assumed were the man's best intentions. "Are you going to tell us what the gold things are?"

"Just don't touch them!" Peter called, fading from their vicinity rapidly. Well, he was the head honcho here, off to do big important things.

Jefi stuck his tongue out at the empty place where Peter had been, and Shep choked back a laugh. "Very mature, Jefi."

An actual circle of gold appeared over Jefi's figurative head. "I *am* an angel, you know."

Shep let the laugh escape, and Jefi preened.

After Peter left, though, the gig was pretty tame. Shepherd called up a great work of literature to read between calls of penitence, and Jefi lay on his stomach, peering at the world below, scanning for more music as the fourth hour of dark swept the globe. They could (and had been known to) spend months at a time sitting doing just that, but they hadn't been settled for more than a few hours when their boy showed up.

"Hullo. Glad to see you're still here!"

Jefi looked up, grinning. "Did you have a nice time?" he asked politely, and Shepherd glared at him. "I was only asking. I mean, *we* don't get day passes out of here. I thought it would be nice to go somewhere and visit friends."

"Yeah, mate. It was positively smashing. Here, I'll go and get out of your hair." There was something about Adrian's tone that told them both that a great deal of pain was involved in his "smashing time."

Shepherd and Jefischa met unhappy glances. They were angels. Part of their job description was to alleviate pain.

"I'm sorry, Adrian," Jefi said, sympathy written in angelic lines across his form. "Why do you go if it hurts you?"

Adrian shrugged, and something about his face told them that he'd rather not talk about it. "They need me. I'd go if it was torture, because they need me. It's not torture—makes the afterlife bearable, if you must know the truth. I've got to tell you two, it hurts them the same as it hurts me. But we need it."

Shepherd and Jefischa watched, at a loss as Adrian moved slowly back to the anteroom. The thick living cord of gold that seemed to bind him to the surface of the world was faded now and not quite as thick as it had been when he'd left earlier, but still it seemed to slow him down, make his footsteps sluggish as he disappeared through the veil of mists that marked the entrance.

"Well," Shepherd said fitfully, "that was disappointing. He doesn't even look like a vampire, really."

"I saw a little fang," Jefi added helpfully, and Shep smiled at him to let him know it was appreciated. "Shep, your wings are gray."

"Yeah." Shepherd sighed. "Well, the sky feels like a sad ocean after that, doesn't it?"

Jefi closed in behind him. It wasn't a physical touch, not the way humans did it, but Jefischa managed to comfort Shepherd in his glow. "Why do you suppose he gets visiting privileges if they don't make anyone happy?"

"Maybe sadness is as sweet as it gets if you're a vampire's ghost, Jefi. Sometimes not even heaven gives happy ever after, right?"

"Shep, that's blasphemy!"

Shepherd sighed. "You don't hear them down there. Everybody begging forgiveness, and the ones who really need it won't acknowledge they've done anything wrong. It seems like penitence is… it's like a novelty you can buy, a pretty bauble. You say something mean, you blurt out an 'I'm sorry' and think penitence is served. But that thing you say…

it's around forever, long after your penitence has been discarded and the next awful thing comes out of your mouth." Shepherd cast a covert glance in the direction where Adrian had disappeared. "But not that one. Now that we've spoken again, I remember him. That one, penitence was deep and it was real. Maybe sadness is really a treat for that one. Maybe that's why he gets to visit."

Jefi's energy felt… well, it felt contemplative at Shepherd's back. "You like him."

Shepherd shrugged and pulled out another book—Dostoyevsky, a personal favorite. "Let's just say I'm on a first-name basis with his demons, and they're worthy. When he was on earth, I never knew he was a vampire."

Jefischa's energy blinked. "How could you not know?"

Shepherd sighed and situated himself, sprawling like a particularly large, long-legged human male might, had he not been an angel and wearing a form for the sake of the entering mortals. "He didn't repent the things he did as a vampire. I mean, they're supposed to have a mantra, right? 'No shame.' But nobody can do that for real, right? Most vampires, they slip up—they kill somebody they didn't intend to, they turn someone who goes rogue. Even the ones who become vampires just to be evil—to kill indiscriminately—even *they* feel shame. But not Adrian. If he hadn't made his livelihood in sex and blood, I'd swear he was a saint."

Jefischa was quiet for a moment. "You liked him, when he was on earth."

"It was nice. A good man's penitence is a rare and precious thing. I was grateful when he was relieved of it, though. He bore the burden too long."

"Shepherd?"

"Yes?"

"All you know of humanity are the things they regret."

There was a dark silence then, and Shepherd didn't know how to make it lighter. "Yeah, Jefi. That's about right."

"Have you ever heard them, right before they go to sleep before a big, exciting day?"

"No."

There was a subtle fluttering near where Shepherd's shoulder would be if he'd had one. "You should. It feels like flying."

Shepherd had a sudden, irrational wish. He wished that he had real hands and not just constructs of energy. He wished that he could ruffle Jefi's hair—if he had any. He pushed the wish aside but managed to lighten his wings up to an open gray-blue. "I'll be sure to try that, Jefi. But for now, let's give him a day or two to himself and then go visit. I can feel his penance now, and he shouldn't be alone for too long."

"Why? What's he regret?"

"Dying and leaving his loved ones alone."

Jefischa made a suspicious sound, and Shepherd extended an energy-construct arm. Jefi draped himself across Shepherd's "body" and made himself comfortable. From the way he was bobbing his head, Shep figured he was listening to music. "C'mon, Jefi," Shepherd said after a moment. "You know it's no use grieving for that one. Mortals have a short time, that's all."

"Yeah. But Shep, he wasn't mortal."

Well, yeah. A vampire in love probably assumed he really did have worlds enough and time, didn't he?

"We're all susceptible to ending, Jefi. Even you, and even me."

"I don't believe that, Shep. Falling isn't ending. I think there will always be a Shep and a Jefi. The world wouldn't spin right without us."

"And we'll always be together, right?"

An affronted silence. "Otherwise we wouldn't be Shep and Jefi!"

"Oh. Of course." Shepherd was usually a restless, brooding sort of presence—unless Jefischa was this close, purring over him. So the reassurance actually made him happy. For a moment, a mere moment, he felt an anticipation of something unknown like Jefi had described, but it was immediately lost in the blissful hum of eternity ever after.

They gave Adrian a couple of turns of the sun and then went in during Jefi's hour. Adrian was draped on a couch, playing some sort of electronic game on a big screen with a recently departed teenager who had messy brown hair, jeans, and the rapidly fading marks of a fatal motorcycle crash. They were busy making lights and sounds for a moment, and then the teenager—who hadn't heard the two angels come in—said, "Are you sure no one cares if we're playing *Grand Theft Auto IV*? Because my mom kept telling me this game would fuck up my morals."

Adrian caught Shepherd's eyes and winked. "Well, mate, I think if you've ended up here, you've probably got nothing to worry about."

There was a sad and quiet silence. On the "television" in front of them, a character took a clip in the gut, vomited cartoon blood, and died. "Yeah. Do you think she knows that?" The kid's leather jacket repaired itself as he spoke, and what looked to be a fatal head injury knitted itself up as well. "I…. You know. We were fighting a lot when I ended up here."

Adrian pressed pause on the game—something about the movement suggested he'd had conversations like this many times before. "Mate, most mothers love their sons. If she was bitching at you to clean up your act, it's because she loved you. She's going to miss you, no two ways about it. But she'll look at your pictures and cry, and then she'll let you go, because she knows someday she'll see her little boy again."

There was a thoughtful silence. "Will I know?" the boy said. "Will I know when she's coming?"

Adrian smiled at him with an insouciant, fuck-me sort of grin, and he fingered the cord emerging from his chest. "You'll feel it here, mate. You can come meet her when it's time."

The boy felt at the cord as though he'd only now noticed it, and even Shepherd realized that you couldn't really see them unless you were looking. Suddenly the expression on the boy's narrow, apple-cheeked face became dreamy… hooded… sultry.

"My girlfriend misses me too," the boy said, and Adrian smiled sympathetically. The boy began to caress the cord, bathing his hand in its energy. His head fell back against the couch, and his body—or what he imagined to be his body—began to bulge at the crotch of the newly repaired jeans.

Adrian stood from what looked to be a beanbag chair made out of cloud and unobtrusively exited the room, closing a "door" behind him.

"Well, he'll need to be alone for a while. Was there anything you blokes wanted, or did you want to do the voyeur thing some more?"

Shepherd wasn't sure about Jefi, but he knew why it took *him* a while to answer. "I… we weren't aware that humans… uhm… souls… could still do that here."

Adrian raised a mocking eyebrow. "He was feeling his connection to the human world, mate. He was seventeen when he died. You could probably populate Mars out of what's pumping through that gold cord."

Jefi giggled. Shep glared at him and he subsided, but Jefi's hand was set solidly over his mouth, and his dancing angelic eyes showed that he was still amused. "It makes sense," Shep said at last, slowly, and then Jefi moved his hand and interrupted.

"Do *you* do that, Adrian?"

Adrian's smile was both devilish and kind at the same time. "Boyo, I wasn't even human. I was vampire. We fuck like lemmings on speed. I can *still* do that. And I often do!"

If Shepherd had actually been breathing, his breath would have absolutely stalled in his chest. As it was, Jefischa made a sucking, whooshing sound and almost choked on his own spit, which was pretty damned hard since angels didn't have any.

Adrian laughed loud and long, holding his middle and whooping until he was wiping his cheeks for tears that weren't there and gasping for breath, and Shep tried to pull himself together. Before he could get a handle on his shock—or his terrible curiosity—Jefi said guilelessly, "Oh, I get it. You were *kidding*!" and that set Adrian off again. While he was rolling on the pale cloudy floor of heaven, Shepherd and Jefi looked at each other in mortification.

"Not kidding," Shep said, feeling an odd temperature fluctuation. Jefi must have been feeling it too. His wax-perfect features were starting to turn a little pink.

"Thinking not," Jefi answered back in a small voice. Adrian was starting to subside now, but he was still giggling a little to himself as he stood gracefully and swept imaginary dust off his blue jeans. He wiped another imaginary crimson tear from a razor-blade cheek and reached out and clapped Jefischa on the back. Jefi and Shep exchanged shocked glances when the slapping sound rebounded and echoed off the vaults of heaven's anteroom, but Adrian seemed unperturbed.

"That was priceless, you two. Thanks for that!"

"We didn't do anything, did we, Shep?" Jefi sounded so sad, so insecure. Shep wrapped his arm around Jefi's shoulders and squeezed reassuringly. He knew it was only his energy, but it felt more solid than usual. But that didn't matter.

"No, Jefi. I think Adrian was just surprised, that's all." Shep glared at Adrian, daring the vampire's ghost to contradict him. To his surprise, Adrian was instantly contrite and instantly kind.

"Yeah. No worries, Jefi."

"Jefischa!" Shepherd growled, surprising them all.

"Jefischa," Adrian corrected smoothly. "No worries. I was not aware that you were not aware, that's all."

"We thought… you know… that…."

"Sex gets left behind with the meat sack?" Adrian filled in, and he rolled his eyes when Shepherd and Jefi both started to look shocked again. "Well, physically, yes. Sex is a physical thing. But… but it's also a connection. When you do it right, it's all energy, just like the two of you."

Shepherd grew very still. "I don't hear about that kind in my travels," he said softly, and Jefi squeezed his hand reassuringly. Shepherd squeezed back before he realized they didn't really have hands. "We've heard about it in general," Shepherd admitted, "but… those people are very often happy when they get here. Not a lot of time for…."

"Serene souls, content to wait on their mates?" Adrian supplied with some irony, and Shepherd nodded. His throat felt dry, and in sheer irritability he conjured a glass of water, which he raised to his lips with shaking hands. Jefischa, who was clearly capable of conjuring his own glass of water, took Shepherd's glass from him and finished it off.

"Well, I'm not one of those," Adrian said sharply. Then, looking at them, he seemed to take pity on them. He crouched down and rubbed at the frosted froth of the floor like he was wiping a dirty window with his hand.

"Here, look at this, would you?"

Shep and Jefi both knelt on the floor of heaven and looked at the clear window Adrian had made for them.

"How do you know how to do this?" Jefi asked, and Adrian shot him a scornful look.

"I've been here for over two years, humanwise. Do you know how many nights that is, longing for a look at them? Now here: I'm about to share some serious shit with you gits, and you'd best not blow it off."

"You don't have to," Shepherd said seriously. He was almost afraid to learn more about Adrian. In a few moments of conversation, the man… vampire… whatever! had managed to completely discomfit the two of them, and they were a pretty serene duo, all things considered.

"No, you have to guard me. You'll have to deal with me. And the first thing to understand is that *I'm not human*. I haven't been for over a hundred and fifty years, but it's okay. Because until about six weeks before I got blown into a powder, I thought the human race was pretty fucking overrated, if you want to know the truth. Now look at them. *Look at them*!"

They looked. Shep saw three… well, people, for lack of a better word. Two of them weren't really human. "They're elves," he said to Jefi, who peered at them curiously.

"You don't see a lot of elves, do you, Shep?"

"Elves don't really have anything to repent," Shepherd said honestly. "And if they do, they're not talking to us. In fact…." Shep squinted through the little window. "That entire place—I know that place. There's over a thousand souls there, but it's like a penitence vacuum. Hardly anyone there has any true regret."

"It's a faerie hill," Adrian agreed soberly. "Except it's got more than just the fey. It's got vampires, were-folk… and her."

"Wait a minute," Shepherd said, his eyes widening. "I know what they're doing together. Do you know how many people I've had repent *that* particular position right there?"

Adrian chuckled, the sound oddly gentle. "These three have never been your penitents, Shepherd. And certainly not for what they're doing right now."

Jefi cocked his head to the side, and then his eyes got wide. "*Whoa….*"

Shep smacked him lightly on the back of the head, and Jefi recovered himself and remembered his job. "Is that your lover?" he asked with respect. "She's…." He faltered. And well he might, Shep thought with surprise. She wasn't beautiful. Adrian—well, Adrian sort of oozed human sex and human beauty, but this woman was plain as a potato. And she was young. Even by human standards.

But Shep was an angel, and he was used to looking at the heart of humans. "She's lovely," he said, and his voice was reverent, because she was. Seeing that, he looked beyond the inhuman (almost angelic, if he'd admitted it) loveliness of her two companions in the garden by the light of a waning summer sun.

"They're all beautiful," he whispered. "They're… bright. Even the one with the dark energy, it's intense and grounded, practically growing granite roots." He looked up at Adrian. "These were all your lovers?"

"'Lovers' is an easy word. I was lovers with most of the hill," Adrian admitted without even a blush. "Two of them were my beloveds. The third, Fuckface there"—the dark energy—"he was my friend."

"But now you hate him?" Jefi asked, appalled, and a flicker of a smile passed over Adrian's pouting, pretty, palely pink mouth.

Shep wondered if Jefi longed for that pouting mouth to be open and laughing again.

"Still love him—just not like I love Green or Cory, my beloveds. Not any less, mind you. Just different. Do you see them? All of them down there?"

Shep and Jefi nodded.

"Now you—Shepherd—that's the angel of penitence, right? You can listen to people's hearts. Now listen. What do you hear from them? What's the one sin that they repent?"

Shepherd swallowed and wished for another glass of water, but he didn't conjure one. "They repent that they let you die."

Adrian nodded. "Yeah, mate. That's right. So there they are, and at night, when their longing for me gets too awful, when they can't stand one more minute of knowing they can never touch me again, they reach out with their souls and let themselves miss me." Adrian's hands grasped the cord at his chest. It was thick and almost hurtfully bright. "You see that? That's low ebb, people. They try… oh *Goddess*, I can feel them trying. They know it hurts me. They know it leaves me weak. Hell, they probably know that this is bad—and I mean just plain *bad*—for all of us. So they stomp on it, and they love each other, and they forge a life together and go on. But sometimes… I can't even blame them. It's agony. It's bloody, excruciating agony… but I live for it, you hear me? I'd give anything—the weakness, the pain in my chest that feels like claws, the knowing time is passing and I'm not even there to share—I'd give it all and take it all right in the pie hole, just to be near them again."

His voice was shaking, and Jefi—Jefi was always so compassionate. "Well, they won't be there for long," he said, and Adrian turned a vicious smile at him. Jefi quailed, and even Shep shut his eyes.

"They're elves, Jefi," Shep rasped, embarrassed. "They live forever, or they fade away. They don't get to come up here. That's part of the great quarrel. The God's people and the Goddess's people are apart in eternity." Shepherd couldn't imagine why Adrian would have agreed to this terrible half life in the anteroom, and he was going to ask when Jefi just had to try to make it better.

"But the girl… at least *she*…."

Adrian shook his head bitterly and dashed at his cheeks, where black-scarlet tears were dripping in a horrible death mask on the face of a man who had died twice. "She tried, Goddess knows. I've had two face-to-face talks with her already, because she's reckless and foolhardy and brave. But… don't you get it? The whole reason I'm here, mates—this entire perversion of life and death—it's all to keep them on the face of the planet. They almost died when I died. One of them goes, the other two topple like dominoes. I was crap under my beloveds' heels, or I should have been, but my death alone, and the entire works goes. You're so fucking sharp, mate"—he gestured at Shepherd—"what happens to the power in that hill when those three people go? What happens to the sanctuary, the peace—hell, the fucking weather?"

Shepherd's breath caught—he was getting used to it. The energy signatures of the three of them were woven into the soil, into the blood, into the souls of every creature on the hill… and beyond.

"Your people will die," Shepherd whispered. "They will scatter to the winds, naked and alone. That place, their power, it protects every soul in the hill."

"But the girl," Jefi protested, devastated by this much pain.

"You heard the row same as I did," Adrian said flatly. "Her High and Mighty-ness has some plan for my beloved. She's not coming here. She's *never* coming here. No matter how brave she is, the Royal Bitch isn't going to let her die."

"That's…." Shep met Adrian's eyes with naked sympathy. Even an angel, with no concept of human feelings, knew the absolute pain of Adrian's dilemma. "I'm so sorry, Adrian."

"I don't want your pity, mate. I'm good." The first part was the truth. The second part was a blatant lie. "And I'm sorry I made your bloke here feel bad." And that rang with sincerity. "But here's the thing. If something makes me laugh, I'm gonna fucking laugh. And if I want to sit in my little illusion of a room there and toss off until my wanker bleeds, you two don't have a fucking thing to say about it, you hear me?"

Jefi let out a little moan, and Shep held his hand and stroked it. Poor Jefi. He liked bedtime stories, and those always ended so much happier than this one. But Shep never dropped Adrian's gaze. "I hear you, but you remember something too."

"What's that?"

"We minister to everybody, even you. If you want anything—even company—we're here."

"Bloody nice of you to offer," Adrian conceded. He ran an arm over his face and stained his white T-shirt with blood brine from his tears before he wandered off. Shepherd wondered how long it would be before Adrian—or the part of him that controlled his reality in this place—remembered that the body wasn't real. The blood-vampire tears weren't real. The white T-shirt wasn't real. They couldn't be. All that had been real about Adrian had died months ago, probably going up in flames when the sun rose. Everything, of course, except his pain. That alone would make the heavens weep, wouldn't it?

Jefischa was disconsolate, so Shepherd guided him to the nearest cloudbank and pulled him up carefully, wrapping an arm around him and pulling him against his chest.

"C'mon, Jefi. He can deal. He looks pretty, but damn, I think he was made to do this. Did you hear him laugh? It's like when he died the first time, only the best of humanity came back and walked his skin."

Jefi was an angel. He was supposed to cry prettily. Silver tears were supposed to track down unblemished golden skin and give an air of delicacy to an angel's inhuman beauty.

Jefi's nose was swollen and red, and his eyes were swollen and red, and his chin was wrinkled and quivering in an alarming way. Shepherd was appalled. Not at the unattractiveness, but that Jefi should be so distraught. He rubbed Jefi's back and dropped kisses in his hair. He noticed as he did that Jefi was starting to look… different. Not bad, and not solidly, but… but sometimes, he would see a sharper line at his jaw or his nose, or a different highlight in what was supposed to be chestnut hair. But when Jefi gave a little grunt, a new sound, Shepherd forgot all about what he looked like.

"Mmm…." Suddenly Jefi arched his spine, undulating into Shepherd's touch like a cat. "That feels different, Shep. Mmm…."

Shep stopped his gentle stroking and looked at his partner curiously. "What feels different about it?"

Jefi paused. "It…. My back tingles. Why does my back tingle?" Jefi frowned, some of the terrible grief easing from his face. He turned his head and then stood up and began turning circles like a cat with tape on its tail, and Shep had to laugh.

"Here—stop moving, dammit, and let me see!" He lifted Jefi's traditional "robe" from the hem, and Jefi giggled.

"You're looking at me naked, Shep."

Shep rolled his eyes. "It's not like angels have…" What was the current mortal word? "…'junk' to get in the way, Jefi."

"I wonder what that's like?"

Shep frowned at Jefi's back. "What what's like?" he asked absently. There was a handprint on Jefi's back. And it looked… solid. Real. Angels *looked* real. Inhuman beauty or no, they were supposed to look *real* for the humans. But this handprint…. Shep was staring at it curiously, splaying his own hand out to match it, when Jefi interrupted his thoughts.

"What it's like to have external genitals?"

It was a common topic in the heavens, actually, and Shep shrugged. "How do you know you wouldn't have breasts instead?"

"You mean, like his female lover? There… touch… there…." Jefi wiggled, and Shep kept touching him just because it made Jefi happy.

"Yes, Jefi. Women traditionally have breasts. Men traditionally have external genitalia. Which one would you want?"

Jefi shrugged, making his skin, his angel skin and the disconcerting, hand-sized patch in the middle, ripple. "I don't want breasts. I think they'd get in the way."

"Well, genitalia certainly give a man a weakness," Shepherd observed. He'd seen it often enough. Nothing made a man repent quicker than a solidly placed blow to the gonads.

"Does that mean you'd want breasts?" Jefi asked, shocked enough to turn around. It left his robe all rucked up around his plain, smooth lower body, and Shepherd shook his head in certainty.

"No, Jefischa. I'm pretty certain I'd be a man. I wouldn't worry about the breasts getting in the way, but I don't deal well in the 'acceptance and reformation' department. I don't think my personality is equipped to come with a vagina, if you must know the truth. Testes, scrotum, and a penis are probably the way to go."

Jefischa succeeded in turning all the way around and looked Shep in the eye. His eyes were lighter, Shep thought randomly. They were supposed to be an all-purpose hazel, but they weren't anymore. Jefi's eyes were gray, and they were rounder than they used to be.

"Adrian was lovers with a man."

Shep smiled a little. "Yes, Jefi. I know. Lots of them. Women too."

"Which would we be? Would we be like… Fuckface and Adrian, or would we be like…." Jefi frowned to remember the name. "Green and Adrian? Would we be friends, or would we be beloveds?"

Shep swallowed then and swallowed again and wished desperately for some more theoretical water but couldn't remember how to conjure it to save himself. "I don't think I could ever call you 'Fuckface,' Jefi, so I guess we'd have to be beloveds."

The anxious look eased a little, and the lines of tension around Jefi's newly gray eyes relaxed. Shepherd put his hand out to rub Jefi's back some more, but Jefi shrugged away.

"I thought you liked that." Shepherd felt inexplicably hurt.

"I do," Jefi said, swallowing too. He looked so sad. "It feels like humans do, when they go to sleep and something really big is going to happen in the morning."

Shepherd raised a tentative hand and rested it on Jefi's shoulder. "Then why don't you want me to keep doing it?"

"Because we don't sleep up here, Shepherd, and the morning won't be any different for us than it has been since the world began."

With that, Jefi threw himself on the misty ground and rubbed a clear space to watch the people below. Shepherd didn't have to check over his shoulder to know Jefi was looking at Adrian's friends and trying to fit himself into the mysterious, complicated patterns of love that still bound Adrian into their midst. He'd wanted to keep Jefi from the frightening possibilities that this vampire had held from the very beginning. He'd known Adrian was dangerous even when all they'd known about him was that he seemed to make angels want to free-fall into gravity and humanity like the humans themselves liked to free-fall from airplanes with only silk and cords for safety.

As it turned out, the vampire's biggest evil was that he was more human than most of the humans who came to heaven. Who knew that being human would make a vampire such a danger to the two of them?

It didn't matter.

What mattered was that Shep had set out to keep Jefi from getting hurt. What really mattered was that he'd already failed.

# PART II

# FALLING

As IT turned out, Adrian liked to play chess. In fact, he was better at it than most angels. He was so good at it that it took Shepherd a while to figure out that he was *letting* Jefi win.

When the vampire asked the two of them if they'd like to play, it was almost like he was offering *them* something, throwing them a bone. *Well, these two blokes don't seem too inept, maybe I'll go play with them and make them feel better.* The really pathetic thing was, Shep and Jefi just sort of jumped at the chance, waggling their tails and turning their puppy-smiling muzzles up to him in supplication.

It sure beat making him cry, that was for damned sure.

He talked to them as they were playing, and they learned more and more of the complicated life that made up Adrian's past. They learned that his passionate love affair with the little human girl (who was not so human, he assured them) had lasted a terribly short time before he'd died. They learned that he and Green had been lovers for nearing two centuries and that he and Bracken *had* been lovers but had never really meant to be forever that way. They learned that the beginning of his life as a vampire had marked the end of his life as a victim and the beginning of his time as sort of a supernatural social worker. He often brought the humans who were floundering in their world into the realm of the Goddess as either vampires or shape-shifters. They thrived there, it seemed, and he confirmed Shep's silent leanings toward the Goddess's side of The Great Quarrel. Shep heard a lot of people in pain; it was nice to know that someone out there was working to alleviate worldly pain instead of letting heaven be an all-purpose panacea, like a carrot on a stick.

And it seemed as though Adrian's hobbies translated into the afterlife as well.

While Shepherd and Jefischa watched, passively at first, Adrian would disappear for a time. They knew where he went—to the lower levels, the place in heaven reserved for people who hadn't quite come to peace, either with who they had been when alive or with the manners of their deaths. Shep and Jefi weren't allowed there. It took a special sort of angel to work that section, and Lucifer and Gabriel pretty much had it locked. But Adrian would go (although he scornfully pronounced Lucifer "a git wank of the first order" and announced that Gabriel would be "a great bloke without the pretty blue stick up his arse") and return, usually with a smuggled refugee on his arm.

It was Jefischa who pointed out that the cord anchoring the refugees to earth was often a mix of pale gold and rabid, angry vermillion.

It was Shepherd who first noticed that Adrian seemed to be having unlawful heavenly relations with the refugees as soon as he closed off his "room."

And both noticed that the more time the souls spent in Adrian's company, the less angry the red—until finally, all that was left was the gold.

"What do you suppose he's doing in there?" Jefischa asked one day, after Adrian had given one of those insouciant, inviting grins and disappeared into his room with a very plain girl and her beautiful boyfriend on either arm.

Shepherd managed a droll look. "Playing cribbage."

"Ha-ha—I *see* humans having sex, Shepherd. I have a pretty good idea of what he's doing physically, or imaginary physically, or whatever. I just want to know what he's—you know—*doing* with them, to make them so much less angry and so much more able to accept the love that will make them happy here."

Shepherd had wondered that himself. In fact, he'd wondered enough to listen in to their hearts, and he'd been surprised. "He's turned penance into an act of love," he said at last, not wanting to explain any further. Fortunately, he was friends with Jefi for many reasons. One of the principal reasons was that Jefi sometimes got exactly what he meant and didn't make him say any more. Jefi's (pouty, round) mouth made a little O and he nodded. He got it, and the conversation was tabled for the moment.

But not forever.

"What I don't understand," Shep said later, while Adrian was there, "is why you don't feel unfaithful. You *have* lovers. Even if you're waiting—"

"A millennium or so," Adrian supplied dryly.

"But still! Won't it make them jealous?" Shepherd knew it would make *him* jealous. *He'd* be furious if Jefi was with anyone else. Jefi was *Shepherd's*. It was a solid, irrevocable, permanent forever. Four millennia in each other's company gave him dibs, dammit—he would *never* share nicely.

"Now, mate, you know as well as I do that the quickest way to lose a friend is to talk politics, right?"

Shepherd blinked and nodded. It was true. The Goddess's children were often given permission not to adhere to absolute monogamy. It was almost written in their bylaws, if the Goddess had believed in order enough to have such a thing.

"I'm not talking politics," Shep argued weakly. "I'm just… you know… asking. Will they forgive you?"

Adrian smiled—his bittersweet smile, they had learned. The one that let them see into his true heart. "Mate, they would rather I be here, doing some good and making some friends, than caught in some terrible limbo with no touch at all. Wasn't it one of yours who said 'True love is not jealous'? We just take that literally, that's all."

Shep's face fell a little. What he felt for Jefi wasn't true? He'd been sure it was. Did that mean he'd have to share him, if they did fall? Suddenly Adrian was up close, smiling into his face and winking at Jefi, who seemed lost in the conversation.

"I'm not saying you have to share, mate. It's just what works for us. There's no reason to break up a team that's worked since time began just because the nature of the team has changed. You feel me?"

Shepherd was not sure what his expression was. He was trying to keep it neutral, because he didn't want either of his companions to know the true nature of his thoughts. It didn't matter, though; Adrian put a hand over his eyes, and Jefi looked at him in delighted shock.

"Shep, you're not supposed to *do* that in front of anybody but angels! You know that!"

Shepherd immediately put a damper on his glory, but it didn't stop a little voice from singing *Mine, mine, Jefi's all mine!* Eventually, he learned that he didn't want to.

Just like eventually they learned that mostly, Adrian was a hell of a nice guy. Vampire or not, he'd had the good fortune to love so deeply and to feel that love in return so assuredly that he really could wait a thousand years to see his beloveds and his beloved friend again. It was worth it.

They would watch as Adrian, in the middle of chess, in the middle of whatever he was doing in his room, was called away. The cord at his chest, the one that should be fading and becoming more a memory than a reality, would grow thick and fat, would begin to glow, would throb in time to a heart that hadn't beat in a hundred and fifty years… and then would pull him toward the living who loved him.

No matter how tired he was when he returned to heaven after each visit, he always looked happy to go.

Jefi watched him go one night as Shep moved up to take his place at the board.

"What do you think that's like?" Jefi asked softly. "That much mortal love. It's so intense, you know?"

Shep nodded and tried to figure out where Adrian was on the board—and whether he'd been planning to let Jefi win or lose. Aha! That knight was about ready to be sacrificed, and then the whole house of cards would fall down. Jefi was going to win this one.

"Yes, I do know," he answered, moving the knight and preparing to fall. Jefi ignored the offer and moved a pawn for no reason at all. Shepherd sighed and pretended to study the board again. "Mortals love very intensely. That's why angels fall when they love like mortals."

Jefi looked up, surprised, and Shep blushed. He'd been doing that lately, having human physical reactions to emotional stimuli. In this case, the emotional stimuli was the suggestion of what the other angels might have done to fall.

"Too much gravity in our skin?" Jefi asked with quietly dancing eyes.

Shepherd returned the look with his own gentle humor. "Too much gravity in our hearts." He returned to the chessboard and once again put Jefi in position to win. This time Jefi took him up on it. They played in happy silence for a little, and then Jefi suddenly glared at Shep and conceded his queen.

"It's no fun when you let me win, Shep."

Shep stared at him, shocked. "Four millennia, and you haven't said anything!" he protested, and Jefi's scowl had nothing to do with the fourth hour of the night and everything to do with Shep.

"I didn't notice until Adrian didn't beat me. I mean, I could buy that maybe *you're* not the best chess player, but I know *I* suck! Why do you do it? It can't be any fun to always play a guy you have to lose to!"

Jefi was offended but not outraged or seriously hurt, and Shep breathed a sigh of relief.

"It *is* fun," Shep said, hating the new accident of energy and faux flesh that made him blush. "It's fun because I get to talk to you and we can, you know, be Shep and Jefi." Weak. How was it that an angel couldn't find a better way to phrase something as commonplace as simply being with another angel?

"Well, then, why don't you just play me and win?" Jefi's voice rose, and Shepherd revised his opinion. He *was* hurt. Shep looked away. He'd never meant to hurt Jefi. In fact, quite the opposite.

"It's no fun being left behind. I don't ever want to do that to you. I figured, you know… I'd just stay equal with you. That's all." Shep smiled as appealingly as he could. He was used to scowling, to being the stern member of their duo, the saturnine bass to Jefi's sweet alto—but he couldn't stand that he'd hurt Jefischa's feelings.

Jefischa regarded him levelly. "How long have you been ready to fall, Shepherd?"

It was Shepherd's turn to cough on his spit. It had been a quiet thought, only in the deepest nights when he'd heard the ugliest secrets mankind had to offer. He'd never given voice to the idea that he didn't want to hear penitence anymore. He'd never even hinted that he wanted to live on earth and see if he could live, eat, run, laugh, fornicate without ever repenting a damned thing.

"What makes you think I am?" he asked bleakly, putting off the inevitable. Angels couldn't lie. It was in the contract. Jefi shrugged, looking down at the chess set. It was automatically resetting as he watched, all of the pieces shaping themselves into light clouds and dark clouds to look like marble, even if they didn't feel cold and rigid to the touch.

"You blush all the time now. You… your appearance has changed. Your hair really is auburn, not the color of a watercolor picture, and it's shaved close to your neck. Your eyes are deep dark brown, and you have wrinkles in the corner, like you scowl a lot. Your nose is a little big for your face, but it suits you, and your lips aren't full—they're lean, and they tilt up. And your face isn't round or oval—it's square, and so is your jaw. Saint Peter hasn't said anything. I don't think Adrian has noticed. But I have. You… you're becoming closer to human. When were you going to tell me?"

Shepherd swallowed. Another human trait—one, in fact, he'd learned from Adrian, who, damn him, wasn't supposed to be human at all. "I wasn't," he rasped. "You don't want to fall. I don't want you to fall. I don't want to leave you behind. And I'm not. And in case you haven't noticed, your eyes are round and gray, and your hair is the color of a sandy beach, and it's long and wispy, like those boys who sing onstage. And your lips are full. And your face is narrow, with high cheekbones. And your jaw is square and your chin is pointed. And nobody here seems to notice. Nobody but me."

They sat there in stark silence for a moment, staring at each other, recognizing that the other had changed, feeling the changes in themselves.

"I'd fall if you fell," Jefi said quietly, staring into his eyes like he had not another thing in the world to do. He didn't. Neither of them did.

"The world is an awful place, Jefi," Shep said, and he wondered when angel's tears started to burn in his eyes. "I don't want you there."

"Better there with you than here without you." Jefi's big gray eyes were as serious as Shep had ever seen them.

Shepherd nodded, as though resolved about something. "Well, then, the changes stop here. No more…." He was going to say *No more talking to Adrian,* but he couldn't. Adrian had done nothing, and they were his companions. They were, in fact, becoming friends. They couldn't go back to being Adrian's guardians; it would be cruel.

"No more changing," Shep finished weakly, and for once, Jefi was the sardonic one. He raised an eyebrow as though to say *Yeah, that can happen,* but Shepherd had no answer for him. It was the best he could do. For a heavenly being, it wasn't much.

Adrian returned, and for a change of pace Shepherd suggested cribbage. It turned out Jefi could hold his own on a cribbage board, and they played cribbage or Hand and Foot pretty much from there on out. So it might have continued indefinitely, if not for two things.

The first was unexpected and frightening—because as often as people on earth report that it happens, the truth is that the closest they usually get to seeing the afterlife is a brief glimpse through a long tunnel. It wasn't often that someone still alive just appeared in their midst.

They were playing cribbage, and Jefi was giving them a sampling of music. Adrian adored music—the two of them shared a passion for Linkin Park, and Shepherd had to admit the band was growing on him. Suddenly, in the middle of "What I've Done," Adrian's golden cord pulsed *hard* and turned scarlet.

Adrian shouted, "*Fuck*!" and he stood up, looking wildly around until she appeared.

It was his lover, the human sorceress, and she was mortally hurt. Blood was flowing down her throat, and Adrian took two anguished steps toward her before taking her hands in his own.

"You shouldn't be here!" he told her, and she nodded and whispered something, nestling into his arms. They spoke then, important things, terribly important things, but Shepherd and Jefischa refused to listen. They put up a clear wall and stood, watching the two lovers touch when it was forbidden and talk face-to-face when they shouldn't even have been occupying the same place.

They could both see when the girl was called back. Her face contorted in pain and she grasped Adrian's hands tighter, and then she flickered in and out and was gone. Jefischa and Shepherd were there with Adrian before she'd even disappeared. The cord at his chest was no longer red, but it was still shiny, bright with need, and bigger than a man's wrist. He raised a shaking hand, covered in the blood that had flowed from her wounds, and licked it off delicately, closing his eyes in pleasure and pain as he tasted his beloved in the most intimate of imaginary ways.

"I've got to go," Adrian muttered, touching his tongue to the corner of his mouth between words. "She barely made it. Green needs me. He doesn't know why she did it, and I've got to tell him… *Christ*!" he screamed, naked and angry and unapologetic about it. He turned a furious, blood-tear-stained face toward Shep and Jefi. "She takes such terrible risks! It would kill him, you understand? Kill him… kill us all if she died, and we wouldn't even be together. Goddess… sweet Goddess… I've got to make Green understand."

"Make him understand why she'd do that?" Shepherd asked, appalled. "*I* don't understand why she'd do that!"

Adrian scowled, impatient and upset. "*You* of *all* people should understand why she'd do it. A friend was in danger, and she was trying to save him. She knows enough about grief by now to know you don't let anyone fall alone if you can help it."

He disappeared then, leaving Shep and Jefi alone and shaken. They sat numbly in a cloud bank and clutched hands. They'd been doing that a lot lately, and Shep took a moment to note that more and more, they were actually holding *hands* in his mind, and less and less *touching energy*. That was when he realized Jefi was stroking the back of his hand softly.

"Why does this upset you so much?" Jefischa asked quietly into the silence, and Shepherd shrugged. He should have been embarrassed to say this, but he wasn't. And it was something Jefi needed to hear.

"Because even though she was just here, defying every law we have to shed blood in heaven, when I see her, I don't see his girl, standing there, covered in blood and begging for forgiveness," he said at last. "I see you. I think being mortal could hurt very, very much. I don't know if I'm strong enough for that much pain."

Jefi's hand began to shake in his. "Well, it's a good thing we've decided not to fall," he said, but there was something empty in his voice that made Shep look at him closely.

"Why is that?" Shepherd asked.

"It's not like you've set high standards for the quality of your love, or anything," he responded bitterly, and then he dropped Shep's hand and disappeared.

"Jefi? Jefi?" But Jefi was gone, disappearing into the ether. He'd done this before when they'd quarreled, flounced off and sulked somewhere alone while he kept watch. Shep had learned that he'd return, usually pretending nothing had happened. It was just that this time, Shep couldn't figure out what he'd done to provoke this fit of the sulks. Of course he set high standards for a proposed life in the human world. Would Jefischa deserve anything less?

Adrian returned, nearly transparent with energy depletion, and retreated into his little space by himself without a word. Shepherd brooded, alone and feeling stormy and gray, and wished that Jefischa would return.

"What did you say to him?" Adrian asked after he'd recouped a little of his strength. Shep looked up from where he was contemplating a brothel. If he wanted to work himself into a good brood, a brothel was the place to do it. They repented everything: leaving their parents, giving children up for adoption, not listening to the people who loved them, their last trick. Settling his soul into a brothel and soaking up the regret and remorse and the terrible pain was guaranteed to make Shep feel worse—and make the brothel close down. Once he sat there and saturated the place with forgiveness and blessing, the women who had a place to go usually went back to the people they felt they'd wronged, and made their lives better. The women who had no haven except the brothel itself at least seemed to feel some peace about how it was they made their living, and developed a belief that survival was not a sin.

Shepherd was left with all of their regret, but he got to see them find their way in life, and it seemed to be a good trade. He watched now as the healing that was his trademark began to work and looked up at Adrian with bleak eyes.

"I don't know," he said, and then he felt the tug of something painful. That was a lie. He *did* know, and now he was obligated to tell the truth. "I told him that I didn't want us to fall because I was afraid I couldn't protect him from the world."

Adrian raised his eyebrows. "Well, no wonder," he said shortly, and Shepherd frowned at him.

"Why? What's he doing?"

There was a sardonic snort. "He's attending every children's choir practice for every religion known to man. I would too. What you said, that's bloody insulting!"

"What did I say?" Shepherd wailed, but Adrian had stalked off by that time. He was still looking transparent and un-Adrian-like, and apparently he didn't want to deal with Shepherd's ignorance any longer. Shepherd was left alone again, healing another brothel, and now he was *really* wishing Jefi would come back.

Jefi did, eventually, right about the time Shep was thinking he should check on Adrian. Unlike the other times he'd flounced off over the millennia, this time Jefi didn't pretend that nothing had happened.

"Has it occurred to you," he asked, startling Shepherd by appearing next to him out of the clear blue, "that all I'd ask for if I fell would be you? Adrian and his lovers and his friend—they're heroes. It's obvious. They're the stuff of story and legend, and they're scary fearsome, but they don't have to be us. We're not leaders up here, or at least I'm not. They'd find a replacement for me soon enough. There's no reason I'd be any different down there. And I'd be happy with that!"

Shepherd was affronted. "Replace you? Jefischa, they couldn't *replace* you!"

There was nothing childlike or starry-eyed about Jefi's smile then. It was, in fact, frighteningly adult. "No, Shepherd. *You* couldn't replace me. Heaven will do just fine on its own."

"You don't fall for a second-rate human," Shepherd sniffed with dignity, and Jefi took his hand and kissed it. There was a mild tingling on the back, and Shepherd was acutely aware of Jefi's breath and lips on his skin.

"Why not?" Jefi asked softly. "You fell for a second-rate angel."

Shepherd scowled. "You're the best, Jefi. There is no better angel. You have the biggest heart and the biggest sense of wonder. You are what storybook angels should be."

"Michael's stronger."

"Michael's vain."

"Rafael is purer of purpose."

"He's dull as dirt."

"Lucifer is more dangerous." Jefi's eyes had started dancing, and Shepherd smiled into them, saying exactly what Jefischa wanted him to.

"I have it on good authority that Lucifer is a git wank," he finished with a quirk of his lips. He and Jefi were very, very near, their faces almost touching, their miraculously colored eyes close and mysterious to each other. There was something Shepherd wanted to do… something burning at his skin. He'd seen the humans do it, but he was pretty sure it would be the beginning of the end for them both.

Abruptly he pulled back, suddenly understanding the curse of the blush that had been haunting him since Adrian's arrival.

"I should go check on Adrian," he muttered, and Jefischa, whose gray eyes were big and round, nodded agreement and swallowed hard. Shepherd looked at his face, bereft and flushed, and swallowed too.

The act of walking away felt like an act of penance.

Shepherd presented himself at the door to Adrian's "place": his room, which had taken on the color and grace—or lack thereof—of any college dorm room on earth. Or any college dorm room that came with really nice leather couches and a king-size bed. Shepherd knocked casually and opened the door, and then stopped short, staring.

He hadn't been aware that Adrian had company—at least, he and Jefischa hadn't seen anybody go in. It took Shepherd a couple of moments to realize that the man in Adrian's bed wasn't someone who belonged in heaven. He was… a mirage. A memory. A physical manifestation of a memory. A ghost in heaven of someone living on earth.

It was Adrian's lover, the elf, Green.

He was beautiful, with long gold hair that rivaled an angel's, wide-set emerald eyes, and pointed ears. That's about all Shepherd got to see of him, because at the moment, he was kneeling between Adrian's splayed knees with Adrian's engorged cock in his wide mouth. He was bobbing his head and making vacuum-locked slurping noises around Adrian's flesh while Adrian lay back in the large bed, one arm flung over his closed eyes and the other hand reaching to clench in Green's long hair.

Shepherd's whole body tingled in that way he'd come to know was humanity overtaking his angelic form, and he must have made some sort of sound in his throat. Adrian looked up at him with half-hooded, knowing eyes and that devil-may-care grin.

"Stay," he mouthed. "Watch."

And Shepherd was powerless to move.

Green spent an eternity pulling Adrian's tender flesh into his mouth, and when he was done, he reached up and grabbed Adrian's hand, laced fingers with him briefly, and pulled that hand down to his cock. Adrian squeezed himself and pulled up, and Green grasped his bottom in both hands and shifted Adrian's hips up, separated his bottom, extended a pink tongue, and began to lick.

Adrian seemed to forget all about Shepherd frozen at his doorway, and Shepherd forgot all about pretending to breathe. Adrian's face contorted, and his hand began to move up and down, sinuously stroking. Green moved his tongue up to Adrian's scrotum and penetrated his body with long thumbs, and Adrian's stroking became faster and almost brutal. He started to gibber, "Please… oh God… damn…. Please, Green. Shit… need you… need…. *Please!*"

Green's face peered over Adrian's long body, and he grinned. "You want me?" The voice was far away and distorted, but Shepherd felt the joy, the humor of this act, of their bodies together.

"Fuck me now, you bloody git!" Adrian snapped.

Green's response was to delve deeper with his thumbs, and Adrian hissed and whined, and his hand tightened on his cock to the point where Shep could see it was purple and spend was starting to leak from the top. "*Please?*" he begged, and Green laughed softly.

"Since you asked, beloved."

Green moved up then and fitted himself against Adrian's entrance. Shepherd sucked in a breath just watching—Green was bigger than most mortals. His body was longer, his shoulders were wider, and his cock, marble pale and uncircumcised, was perfect and perfectly proportioned. He didn't see how it could….

Adrian howled, lifted his hips off the bed with a flex of his legs, and drove himself desperately, impaling his body *hard* on Green, who closed his eyes and thrust deeply.

"Hard, Green," Adrian whispered. "Fuck me hard."

Coarse words—earthy words, used in a purely carnal act.

But looking at their faces, Shepherd didn't see only carnal, physical sex—although there was that. Shepherd saw love. The things they were doing with their bodies were… painful. Awkward. But the love, the joy he saw as Green framed Adrian's face with his hands and Adrian sucked a finger into his mouth and then let it trail down his cheek, as Green's hips began to piston, as Green lowered his head to kiss his lover before he was moving too fast to make the gesture graceful….

All of it, all of it, made this an act of love.

Green threw back his head then, his gold hair falling like sunshine rain over his bare white body, and Adrian—whose hand had never stopped moving on his own cock, even when their stomachs were mashed together—screamed just as Green howled in arousal.

"Do it, mate," Green panted. "Do it now!"

Adrian came off the bed, clasped his lover to his chest, brought Green down with him, and….

Bit his neck.

Shepherd hauled in a breath—and it actually felt like he needed it. He hadn't even seen Adrian's fangs extend, but there they were, long and lethal, and they buried themselves in Green's slender neck and soft white skin. Scarlet ichor pumped up, and Adrian opened his mouth and suckled, and Green… Green kept fucking him, the keening in his voice amped high and desperate as terrible, excruciatingly pleasurable aftershocks rocked them both into quivering nerve endings, tender and sensitized and beyond replete. They collapsed onto the bed, and Shepherd thought for a moment he could actually smell them, the collective odor of body fluids—sweat, blood, and come—that made up sex with a vampire.

"You don't always like that," Adrian rumbled, nuzzling Green's pointed ear.

"Sometimes," Green mumbled back. His body was still deeply entrenched in Adrian's, and Shepherd had the feeling they might stay like that for hours, if the rules of physical contact could be bent to do something like it. "When I love you so much it feels like my heart is bursting through my skin."

"So every day, then?" Adrian joked with a slight but still familiar smile.

"Every goddamned night," Green affirmed.

"Love you too." They snuggled, and Shepherd might have broken the spell and retreated, but Adrian met his eyes and gave an almost imperceptible shake of the head. And then Green fell asleep in his arms, his body fading from their reality as he did so.

Adrian flung his arm over his eyes again, but this time not to hide a grimace of pleasure. He stayed there, panting, for a long time. When he finally spoke, Shep realized he'd been studying Adrian's sex-flushed, come-spattered body with interest and... hunger.

"Elves remember when they dream," Adrian said softly, pulling Shepherd's attention from his splayed thighs. "True memories. Sometimes, he lets himself dream of those moments... and then...."

Adrian's voice was choked, and Shepherd passed the back of his hand over his cheeks.

"That must be really awful," he said gruffly.

Adrian turned a blood-streaked face to him. "No, mate. It's really wonderful. You see? I *lived* that—I lived it, and it lives in my heart still, and sometimes Green visits and makes it real. It's a gift, and I'm forever grateful. That's why you spend time on earth. So you have memories like that in heaven."

Shepherd felt his heart slow down at the words, and his body, which hadn't stopped tingling, thumped sluggishly at his groin, and again, and then painfully. His groin swelled, engorged....

Shepherd sucked in a breath and, completely unconscious of how he looked, grabbed his crotch.

"Holy shit," he muttered. "I have balls."

Adrian swung his legs over the edge of the bed and wiped his face on the rumpled sheets. "Yeah, mate? Congratulations."

"Congratulations on what?" Jefi asked, and Shepherd almost groaned. Damn, Jefi. He must have gotten impatient.

"Nothing," Shepherd said miserably at the same time Adrian—still naked to their gaze, his body glistening and still slightly erect—walked over to Shepherd and put a hand on his shoulder.

"Well, mate, let's see. If you're going to fall, let's see what equipment you're going to fall with!"

"You're going to fall?" Jefi cried unhappily, and Shepherd turned to him, confused and beleaguered. "I wasn't planning to!" he snapped back. "Dammit, Jefi! I caught… I saw… and then my body… it just…."

Adrian glared at him seriously. "Own up, mate. It wasn't what you saw. That's not when it happened."

"When did it happen?" Jefi asked curiously.

Shepherd shook his head. "Look. Nothing's permanent. They can go away. I can make them go away—"

"C'mon, let's see!" Jefi took liberties. Well, if anyone was going to, it was Jefischa, right? He gathered the folds of Shepherd's heavenly robe and pulled it aside, and gasped.

"Oh my," Adrian said with a smirk, and Shepherd looked down at himself.

"They're… it's… sort of… um…."

"Jesus, mate, you're hung like a fucking bear!"

Complete with rust-colored pubic hair. Jefischa reached out a tentative hand, but Shepherd realized that Adrian was watching and flinched away. Jefi looked up, hurt. "I just wanted to see. Are they the same as Adrian's? I don't think so. Yours isn't completely human, yet— see, Shep? Adrian's has veins and—"

And Jefi reached out that questing hand to actually *touch* Adrian's lush playboy body. Shepherd forgot all about trying to stay in heaven for Jefi, and a single word roared through him.

"*Mine!*" he snarled, and he grasped Jefi's hand inches away from Adrian's most personal parts.

Both angels gasped and looked at their hands as Shep held Jefi's.

Their hands had been… well, anatomically correct, but smooth and featureless. As they watched, Shepherd's hand became broader, harder, his fingers blunt and no-nonsense. Cinnamon-colored hair sprinkled the back of his wrist and—very, very lightly—the backs of his knuckles, and his skin was slightly rough. Jefi's hand in his was long-boned, finer, narrow, with long, tapered fingers and blond hair on his wrist only. And the skin was much softer than Shepherd's.

Shepherd watched as his thumb—almost independent of his will— caressed the inside of Jefi's wrist. Jefi sucked in a breath, and his body gave a wiggle and a convulsive little hop, and he looked closely at Shepherd. "I've got them too," he whispered.

Shepherd closed his eyes then, and in a heartbeat, a wish, pulled his wings up around his shoulders and used them as a canopy over himself and Jefi. The wings pulsed around the two of them, wearing sort of a bright, embarrassed fuchsia color, but they still did their job: instant privacy.

The men stood absolutely still. Shep's robes swung back into place, but still the two of them were as naked as either of them had ever been in multiple millennia of existence. Shep raised the hand not holding Jefi's and caressed his beloved's cheek. His thumb, blunt and hard, with a slightly scratchy cuticle, painted a swath of blushing, fair skin under his touch, complete with a light sprinkling of freckles. Jefischa closed his eyes, as though the slight touch was too exquisite to bear. Shepherd raised his thumb again and traced Jefischa's closed eyelid, and then the other, and saw lashes appear, dark at the root and pale at the ends.

Jefischa opened his eyes. They were the same round and stormy gray eyes they had been in these past weeks, but now they were full of wonder.

"I never meant this for us," Shepherd whispered. "I would have stayed here forever, just for you."

"What made your body change?" Jefi asked, as though knowing this would make peace in Shepherd's heart.

"Adrian." Shepherd's half smile indicated how very many of their last few turbulent moments in heaven he attributed to Adrian. "He was living his lover's memory. He said, 'That's why you live memories like this on earth, so you have them in heaven.'" Shepherd breathed in harshly. "I want those memories, Jefischa. Holy God, Heavenly Father as my witness, I want them with you."

Jefi grinned, and some very nonangelic tears leaked from the corners of his eyes. "Amen," he said softly. Shep captured one of the tears as it slid down a newly made crinkle in the corner of Jefi's eye. He raised his thumb to his mouth and tasted.

"It's not bitter at all," he whispered.

Jefi raised his hand to cup Shep's cheek, and they stood cocooned for heartbeats—actual heartbeats in their chests that they could feel throbbing at their throats.

Shep swallowed, feeling the burn all the way down his gullet. "I need to talk to Adrian," he said after a moment. He grinned cheekily, hoping Jefischa would trust him. "Wait here, would you?"

Jefi wrapped his arms around Shepherd's waist, and Shep realized that they no longer adhered to standard angel sizing. Jefischa was a whole head shorter than he was and far more slightly built. Shep was reminded of Green and Adrian again, and his arms wrapped around Jefi's shoulders, mindful of the wings tucked snugly against his back. He settled his wings lower, at shoulder level, and looked out from their tiny world at the ghost of the man who had started it all.

Adrian had dressed in the time it had taken them to talk and was sitting on his bed, waiting patiently for them to come out of their huddle.

"So I take it I'll be getting some new guards in a bit."

Shepherd nodded, sober as an angel should be. "Was this how the others fell?"

Adrian grinned. "Honestly, mate? I have no idea. You two liked me. You were fairly special."

Shepherd nodded and looked at Jefi, oblivious in the privacy of Shepherd's wings. "I don't know how to do this," he said desperately. "How do I make this good for him?"

"Lubricant," Adrian answered without blinking. "Lots of lubricant. And baths. You need baths when you get to earth or things don't taste so good."

Shepherd opened his mouth and closed it again, then opened it, widened his eyes, closed his mouth, shook his head, and started again. "I meant living on earth," he said after an awkward pause, expecting Adrian to laugh again as he had before.

He didn't. "Come here," he said softly, "and let Jefischa out so I can talk to you both."

Shepherd pulled back his wings, and Adrian came up to them both and threw a casual, comforting hand on each of their shoulders. "Now, you two have seen me look at them enough. You've seen me watch my home, Green's hill. When the time comes, I need you to think about Green's hill for me, right? Just think about it. I'm pretty sure you'll end up there, and then—well, Shepherd. There are some places on earth that aren't frightening—they're not terrible. Now, it may be filled with vampires and werewolves, but my home is still one of them, right?"

Shepherd nodded, relieved in no small way. He'd watched Adrian's home. It wasn't perfect, but it wasn't walking the world alone either. Adrian cupped Shepherd's cheek with a cool hand, leaned in, and kissed his temple. Shepherd realized he was maybe an inch or two taller than the vampire, and Adrian wasn't short. "Now I want you to do me a favor," Adrian whispered close to Shep's ear. "I want you to give Green one of these and tell him 'hullo' for me. Can you do that, mate?"

Shep swallowed and nodded, and then Adrian gave Jefischa the same sort of treatment. "And you, little man, I want you to do the same thing for my girl, right? Kiss them both, just like I kissed you. Touch their cheeks and kiss their temples and tell them Adrian says 'hullo, luv.' Can you do that for me?"

"Yes, Adrian," Jefischa said soberly, and Adrian backed away and smiled so widely his fangs came out. Funny how Shep always forgot he had them, but he'd look strange and unfinished if they weren't there.

"And both of you—when he's not expecting it, give that fuckface wanker one of these for me, would you?" He gave them both a gentle smack on the back of their heads and then laughed at their earnest, albeit confused expressions as they nodded their promise to him. "Now you two blokes have other things to do. Safe journey, right?"

"Right." Shep nodded. Then, gravely, "Thank you, Adrian. Have some… have some peace, if you can."

Adrian's smile was… was sweeter than a real angel's. Shepherd would always remember it when he thought of heaven. "I'll do that. And you two have some fun. I'm sure I'll see you again eventually."

Shepherd smiled bravely. "Later than sooner."

"Later than sooner, my brothers."

And with that, they were outside of Adrian's room, wrapped in the cocooning quiet of their own bright, pale wings.

# PART III

# FLYING

THEIR HEARTBEATS were so loud, Shepherd wondered that they didn't fill heaven with the thunder of their sin.

Then he lowered his head to Jefi's, brushed pink, pouty lips with his own lean mouth, and sin ceased to exist.

Jefi moved his head and caught the corner of Shep's mouth, the end of his chin, his cheekbone. He stood on tiptoe and rubbed his cheek against Shep's, his skin like satin, and Shepherd groaned softly.

"Am I doing it wrong, Shep?"

"No, Jefi. Your touch makes me real."

Jefi exhaled softly and tipped his head back, and Shepherd kissed down his jaw line, down the hollow of his ear, and along his throat. He opened his mouth and laved the little divot where the clavicles met, and Jefi breathed, "Me too. You make me real, Shepherd. Touch me."

They did, slowly, and every touch was glory. Shep's lips on the inside of Jefi's arm revealed a miracle of soft, pale flesh with the occasional tiny mole or freckle. Jefi burrowed down the neck of Shepherd's robe, and his palms gliding down his chest, revealed thick, unyielding lumps of muscle under smooth skin. Kiss by brush by stroke of flesh, they painted humanity onto each other's skin with quivering, gentling, ravenous acts of touch.

Robes that had previously simply hung and swirled and swung now became tangled around their hands, hanging up on sharp things like elbows and shoulders and knees. And wings. Shepherd grew impatient when Jefi was trying to gain access to his chest. He gave a roar of irritation and ripped his own robe from his neck to the hem, and it fell in tatters at his feet. Jefischa gave the neck of his robe a few ineffectual yanks and almost succeeded in throttling himself. Shepherd rained tiny kisses on his forehead and eyelids before he seized the neck of the offensive thing and shredded Jefi's garment too.

Jefi was a marvel of engineering underneath.

"Wow, Jefi," Shep murmured. He circled around, palming the space between Jefi's wings. Adrian's handprint had faded into the rest of his skin, and now all that remained was the human flush that Shepherd's touch left on his beloved's body. Shepherd continued smoothing his hands along the backs of Jefi's shoulders and palming the sensitized quiver of his upper arms. He stood behind the smaller angel and placed gentle, reverent kisses down the perfectly assembled puzzle that was his spine, and ended with a tongue lave and a playful nibble at the divots that marked each bottom cheek. Jefi gave a high pitched, breathless squeak, and Shepherd moved to the backs of his knees, cupping the insides of his thighs with strong hands when he felt Jefi's legs tremble. Inside his head he heard Adrian's voice, *Lubricant—lots of lubricant,* but there were too many other marvels to discover before he went there.

They would only fall once. Shepherd wanted it to be the best, most glorious ride since the act of falling came into existence. He wanted Jefi to remember their fall with joy.

"What?" Jefi asked when he could get a breath. By now he was still standing, but Shepherd was on his knees in front of him. "Shep, what?"

Shepherd looked up his body—all planes, angles, and secret shadows since his angel façade had faded. "You are so beautiful," Shepherd breathed, and Jefi's sex, which had become engorged and stiff with excitement, flexed against his thigh.

Shepherd extended a tentative finger and traced a careful line down Jefi's cock. The skin—like all of Jefi's skin—became more real as he did so, the surface of the thing becoming defined and rough with veins and ripples of erect flesh. Jefi drew in a harsh breath and held it, and Shepherd drew that careful line again.

Jefi's foreskin had retracted a little, but it still hugged loosely around the crown, and Shepherd pulled it back just to hear Jefi hiss and moan a little in his throat. His other hand reached down to cup the heaviness of his testicles, and he was delighted with the almost transparent, coarse fur that covered them. "Look!" He very gingerly lifted Jefi's cock so he could kiss the shadowed little valley between them.

"Shep," Jefi whined, and Shepherd grinned wickedly. Jefi wanted more. Shepherd had just been given an explicit demonstration on how to give more. Very carefully, he stroked Jefi's length and squeezed, making sure the foreskin skated around the crown, making a thick, slurpy sound of flesh and flesh.

Jefi's thighs trembled. He tilted his head back and grunted, long and drawn out, and Shepherd was much encouraged.

Shepherd stroked him again and again and one more time, and then, tantalized by the size and the shape and the wonderful sensitivity, he put that little head of flesh into his mouth and swished his tongue around. Jefi grabbed his head and groaned.

"Your mouth is *hot*," he panted, and Shep grinned around him. Then Shepherd moved his lips down farther, until the end of the thing was uncomfortably in his throat—another new sensation but not a pleasant one, so Shep didn't linger over it—and then moved his head back. He'd seen humans do this. He'd just seen Green do this to Adrian. Watching up Jefi's body to see his eyes close tight and his jaw go slack was reason enough to do this and do it often. Feeling Jefi's hands clench uncontrollably in his hair was another reason. All of it—the texture, the scent, the… oh… oh damn… the taste of Jefi's skin—Shepherd pushed his head down past comfort just to have the taste of Jefi's skin fill his mouth completely.

Then there was another taste, a sweet and salty taste, and Jefi found his words. "You need to stop," he panted. "I feel like… I'm going to… I feel like I'm falling…. I can't fall without you, Shep…. Come up here, please…."

It was Jefi's choice of the word "fall" that made Shep stop. He didn't think that God would be cruel enough to send them spiraling down into the world separately just because their new bodies had an unsynchronized involuntary spasm, but he didn't want to take the risk. He wanted to be as close as possible, buried in Jefi's flesh, merged inside his skin, as close to being one person as two bodies could possibly get, just to avoid the frightening possibility of falling to earth and not knowing where Jefischa landed.

"Northern California," Shep said, releasing Jefi's body from his mouth and going into study mode immediately. "Foresthill, Green—you remember all that?"

Jefi reached down, and although his body stayed erect, he sheltered his wings over both of them and framed Shep's face with his hands. "I won't need to, Shep. You'll take me there."

Shep knew he had a heart now, because it stopped beating, then and there. What a terrible burden such trust was—but he wouldn't give it up or throw it off his shoulders for the world. He wrapped his arms up around Jefi's backside and rested his cheek against Jefi's thigh until his heart started beating again. Jefi's hands were stroking through his hair, and Shepherd looked up at him again, knowing that worship was in his lover's eyes and not sure if he'd take it out if he could.

"I won't let you down, Jefi. I swear."

He took Jefi's extended hand and stood. Jefi took his face in his slender, soft hands and pulled Shepherd down into a hard, confident kiss. Shep found his mouth opening, being invaded, and the taste of Jefischa's tongue in his own mouth was an intoxicating revelation.

He could kiss Jefischa *forever.*

But eventually Jefi broke off the kiss to go exploring on his own. He slid down Shep's blank stomach and touched his tongue to the center. Shep gasped as a navel appeared, and Jefi giggled into the tender skin of his tummy, making Shep smile and gasp and then grind himself helplessly against any part of Jefi he could reach.

Jefi laughed some more, the sound deep and throaty and rich. He sounded… older. Grown up. Fearless.

And then he fearlessly engulfed Shep's cock with his mouth, and Shepherd forgot all about the richness of Jefi's laugh. His vision went black with stars, and heaven became a mysterious place, the kind of place he could fall into just by tilting his head back and….

"Not yet," he rasped. "Not yet. Jefi… Jefi, we've got to…." Jefi bobbed his head again, and Shepherd found himself in command again. "Lie down, Jefi. Lie down and spread your legs."

The rush that flooded Shep's brand-new bloodstream when Jefischa complied was wonderfully painful. Shepherd gave him a moment to situate his wings, spread out on either side of his shoulders, before he covered Jefi's body with his own and kissed him again. Their new bodies were heated and sweating, and their movements were no longer slow and exploratory. Their hands, their mouths, their chests, their thighs… every part of their bodies that came in contact was moving roughly, demanding to touch more of the other….

"Shep," Jefi panted, grinding his cock against the crease of Shepherd's thigh, "Shep, my body is *hungry….*"

Shepherd kissed him hard on the lips and whispered, "Trust me," into Jefi's delicate ear. Then he dragged himself down that pale, slender, perfect, fine-boned, surprisingly strong body and positioned his head between Jefi's spread legs.

First he spent some more time at ground zero. Mmmm…. Jefi tasted so *good*! His thrusts in the back of Shep's throat made Shep's whole body writhe, but Shep was getting close, and his body and mind were playing a treacherous game of hurry-up-and-wait. His body wanted to hurry. His mind wanted to wait. His body was starting to win.

Jefi's hands were clenching in his hair, and Shepherd took one of them, laced their fingers tight together, and then moved, wrapping Jefi's hand around his own body and showing him how to stroke.

Jefi made a sound like "ooooohhh" and did just that, and Shep moved his tongue and fingers lower.

*Lubricant. Lots and lots of lubricant.* Shepherd only had one kind of lubricant at his disposal, and he used it liberally. He'd seen Green penetrating Adrian—he knew that Green had prepared Adrian's body, licked it, stretched it, made it slack and wet and ready to accept Green's large erection. Shepherd did the same thing, except it was better doing than watching. Jefi's taste was exciting. The sounds he made as Shepherd stimulated his nerve endings were *hot*, and the sight of Jefi's hand on his own cock was etching the word *sexy* into Shepherd's brain.

By the time Jefi's opening was lax and ready, Shepherd's own body had been leaking for some time. Shepherd pushed himself up and knelt between Jefi's wantonly spread legs.

"This may—I'm sort of big, Jefi," he said anxiously, but Jefi made a pleading noise, a begging noise, and Shepherd knew he couldn't stop now. There was nothing angelic about Jefi anymore. His eyes were glazed and half-lidded, his mouth was open, his pale blond hair was mussed around his head, and his cock was rampant, erect, purple, and glistening with spit and pre-ejaculate.

Shepherd's mind went blank as he pushed into his lover. He wanted. He needed. *They* needed possession. *MINE.*

The final thrust that seated him deep inside Jefischa made Jefi's eyes pop open widely and his lips quirk up.

"Ooooohhhhhhhhhhh…."

"Does it hurt?" Shepherd asked.

"It's goooooooooood," Jefi sighed. "Hurts goooooooooooood."

Shepherd chuckled and began to move slowly, holding his shoulders up with strong arms and sturdy muscles. Jefi let go of his cock and wrapped his hands around Shep's shoulders, urging him on physically even though he couldn't seem to make whole real words anymore.

"Shep… please… please… yes… yes… damn… Shep… please…."

Shepherd growled and started pounding his hips against Jefi's thighs, burying his body inside Jefi's with determination and passion, and then… then… Jefi cried out and wrapped his legs around Shep's hips, and Shepherd's vision went dark against his closed eyes, and for a moment, they were on a precipice, looking out at the night sky. For a moment, they hovered, the world at their feet and heaven gentle on their faces as Shep's body heaved and his lungs gasped and he supplicated…. *Please, God… please. Let me be enough. Let me take care of Jefi like he deserves.*

For a moment, they hesitated, and then Shepherd opened his eyes, and Jefi's wide gray eyes were fastened on him, drinking in the sight of his passion and his lust and his love.

Shepherd plunged one last time into his lover's flesh and then buried his face in Jefi's neck and roared as his body released, and then he and Jefi clung together, shaking in orgasm….

Stepped off the precipice.

And flew.

# PART IV

# LANDING

*ADRIAN KNELT on the floor of his room, gazing through the window he was allowed and onto the crown of his home, Green's hill.*

*"Do you see them yet?" Saint Peter asked over his shoulder, and Adrian shushed him.*

*"Wait... wait.... There they are. See?"*

*Saint Peter knelt, right there on the floor of the vampire's room, and peered down to the earth below. In a lovely garden—with exceedingly interesting trees—two naked men huddled under a canopy of feathered wings, touching each other's faces in wonder.*

*"They'll be all right there?" Peter asked anxiously. "They fell with their wings intact. None of the others did—they can all pass for human."*

*Adrian looked up at Peter, troubled lines written across his eternally young human face. "These two were purer than the others. Why did you set them to guard me?"*

*Peter blew out a breath and sighed. "Shepherd would have soured, Adrian. The only thing keeping his soul clean was Jefischa. I... I just wanted them to have a vacation, that's all. Shepherd's stubborn about things like duty and obligation. If you hadn't"—Peter waved his hands vaguely—"you know, done whatever you do, he never would have chosen to fall." Peter shook his head. "You're a master, you know. How do you get them to fall so fast?"*

*Adrian shrugged. "It's not something I do on purpose, guv'nor. I really didn't even have to talk to the others. They just sort of fell on their own. But not these two." He looked down again and saw Green emerging from the trapdoor that led to the garden. He looked shocked by the new residents of his hill, but when it appeared they were too wrapped in each other to notice him, he sat on a marble bench, pulled out a book, and patiently waited.*

*"Was it worth it?" Peter asked curiously after they had spent some time just looking at the happy couple, feeling the sort of pride a set of parents must feel when seeing their children married off.*

*"Always," Adrian answered soberly. "Was what worth it?"*

*Peter looked disconcerted for a moment and then continued. "The time you spent with them—the extra effort. Was it worth it?"*

*"They were friends." Adrian shrugged. "Anything to help friends, right?"*

*"But Adrian, it must have hurt, opening your soul like that...."*

*"Hush, dammit. Wait. The best part's coming."*

IF HEAVEN was in Jefischa's arms, a better heaven was in Jefischa's arms on the top of Green's hill.

When their hearts had quieted down and their breath was no longer deafening in their ears, they realized they had landed. Shepherd rolled to the side and pulled his wings up to shelter the two of them, and they lay staring at each other under a feather canopy.

Gradually they became aware of small things. The grass below them smelled wonderful and real, but it was starting to itch. The smell of flowers in the sun was borne to them on the breeze, but it was a little cool—almost uncomfortably so—in the shade. The sun itself slanted longways. It was autumn, probably early autumn, and early evening as well. Humans probably didn't wear shorts in these temperatures, and Shepherd stopped the study of his fingertips along the curves of Jefi's jaw to pull his wings closer for warmth.

"Look, Shep. Your wings have feathers on them," Jefi said in wonder.

Shepherd smiled and reached out a hand to caress the slope of Jefi's wing. They did have feathers—and musculature and definition. Nothing on their bodies was energy and a wish for a form anymore. Everything about them was muscle, sinew, blood, and bone.

Except their hearts, Shepherd thought with wonder. Whatever was swelling in his chest felt like the swelling chorus of... of... of angels.

For the first time in four millennia, Shepherd understood Jefi's love of music, and he let out a helpless, happy laugh as he buried his face in Jefi's sweaty shoulder. That realization alone was worth the fall.

"Where are we?" Jefi asked, bringing Shepherd to the here and now again.

Shepherd abandoned the idea of warmth and struggled to sit up. "I think we made it to Green's hill," he said with something like hope in his heart.

"You did indeed, my boyos!" There was a man—an elf, in fact, with pointed ears and wide-set, alien features, a pointed chin, and long, long butter-colored hair—sitting on a granite bench with the likeness of Adrian sculpted on the side.

"You're Green," Shepherd said in awe, recognizing him. Green nodded and smiled and offered Shepherd a hand to help him stand up off the grass. Shepherd gratefully took it—and understood it for what it was. He and Jefi had not landed alone. They were not in a terrible, frightening place. They were on Green's hill, Adrian's home. They would be all right.

"I am indeed," Green replied, his voice sounding like Adrian's but different. Different parts of the world had different accents, Shep recalled, even small countries like Great Britain, and Shepherd wondered at the sound of that accent here on a hill a continent away. He forgot that for a moment and bent to help Jefi up. Jefi immediately wrapped his arms around Shepherd's waist and tucked himself under Shep's arm.

"I'm Shepherd, and this is Jefischa." Shep spoke hesitantly, then looked at Jefi to see if this was the right time. Jefi shrugged and nodded, and Shep reached out his hand to Green's cheek. The elf's eyes widened, but he allowed Shep to cup his cheek and then lean in to kiss his temple.

"Adrian says 'Hullo, luv,'" Shepherd said carefully. He was unprepared for Green to close his eyes and trap Shepherd's hand against his cheek with his own trembling hand. Green pulled in a breath that quivered, and let it out slowly.

"Hullo, beloved," he said softly, savoring Shepherd's touch as though it were Adrian's own. "Hullo." Shepherd's palm grew wet with tears, but he didn't move it, not for a long time.


*ADRIAN KNELT on the floor of his room in heaven and pressed his palm against his viewing window as though he really could touch the elf's cheek. "Hullo, luv," he whispered. Through a trick of perspective, for a moment, just a moment, it looked to Saint Peter as though their flesh was really touching. For a moment, Adrian really did hold his beloved's face in the palm of his hand.*

*"Yes," he said out loud to Peter, although Peter noticed he never pulled his attention from the tableau below. "Yes, it was worth all of it, everything, just for this moment." Blood-brine tears dripped onto the*

*back of his hand; he wiped them on his T-shirt and then put his hand back to pretend he truly touched his lover's flesh.*

*Saint Peter watched soundlessly, understanding and accepting at once. Idly he wondered who else needed the prompt to fall, to take a "flesh vacation," as he'd started to think of them, but the question could wait. The fact was, the vampire's ghost didn't really need guarding, and Adrian deserved some time alone.*

*Saint Peter blinked and disappeared, and Adrian continued his vigil at the window to the world of Green's hill.*

Little Goddess: Book One

Working graveyards in a gas station seems a small price for Cory to pay to get her degree and get the hell out of her tiny town. She's terrified of disappearing into the aimless masses of the lost and the young who haunt her neck of the woods. Until the night she actually stops looking at her books and looks up. What awaits her is a world she has only read about—one filled with fantastical creatures that she's sure she could never be.

And then Adrian walks in, bearing a wealth of pain, an agonizing secret, and a hundred and fifty years with a lover he's afraid she won't understand. In one breathless kiss, her entire understanding of her own worth and destiny is turned completely upside down. When her newfound world explodes into violence and Adrian's lover—and prince—walks into the picture, she's forced to explore feelings and abilities she's never dreamed of. The first thing she discovers is that love doesn't fit into nice neat little boxes. The second thing is that risking your life is nothing compared to facing who you really are—and who you'll kill to protect.

Little Goddess: Book Two
Vol. 1

Cory fled the foothills to deal with the pain of losing Adrian, and Green watched her go. Separately, they could easily grieve themselves to death, but when an old enemy of Green's brings them back together, they can no longer hide from their grief—or their love for each other.

But Cory's grieving has cut her off from the emotional stability that's the source of her power, and Green's worry for her has left them both weak. Cory's strength comes from love, and she finds that when she's in the presence of Adrian's best friend, Bracken, she feels stronger still.

But defeating their enemy is by no means a sure thing. As the attacks against Cory and her lovers keep coming, it becomes clear that their love might not be enough if they can't heal each other—and themselves—from the wounds that almost killed them all.

Little Goddess: Book Two
Vol. 2

Green and Bracken's beloved survived their enemy's worst—with unexpected vampiric help.

But survival is a long way from recovery, and even further from safety. Green's people want badly to return to the Sierra Foothills, but they're not going with their tails between their legs. Before they go home, they have to make sure they're free from attack—and that they administer a healthy dose of revenge as well.

As Cory negotiates a fragile peace between her new and unexpected lovers, Green negotiates the unexpected power that comes from being a beloved leader of the paranormal population. Together, they might heal their own wounds and lead their people to an unprecedented place at the top of the supernatural food chain—a place that will allow them to return home a better, stronger whole.

Little Goddess: Book Three
Vol. 1

Humans have the option of separation, divorce, and heartbreak. For Corinne Carol-Anne Kirkpatrick, sorceress and queen of the vampires, the choices are limited to love or death. Now that she is back at Green's Hill and assuming her duties as leader, her life is, at best, complicated. Bracken and Nicky are competing for her affections, Green is away taking care of his people, and a new supernatural enemy is threatening the sanctity of all she has come to love. Throw in a family reunion gone bad, a supernatural psychiatrist, and a killer physics class, and Cory's life isn't just complex, it's psychotic.

Cory needs to get her act and her identity together, and soon, because the enemy she and her lovers are facing is a nightmare that doesn't just kill people, it unmakes them. If she doesn't figure out who she is and what her place is on Green's Hill, it's not just her life on the line. She knows from hard experience that the only thing worse than facing death is facing the death of someone she loves.

Loving people is easy—living with them is what takes the real work, and it's even harder if you're bound.

## Little Goddess: Book Three
## Vol. 2

Cory's newly bound family is starting to find its footing, which is a good thing because danger after danger threatens, and Green can't be there nearly as often as he's needed. As Cory learns to face the challenges of ruling the hill alone, she's also juggling a menage relationship with three lovers—with mixed results.

But with each new challenge, one lesson becomes crystal clear: she can't be queen without each of the men who look to her, and the people she loves aren't safe unless she takes on that queendom with all of the intelligence and courage in her formidable heart.

But sometimes even intelligence, courage, and steadily increasing magic aren't enough to do the job, and suddenly the role of Cory's lovers becomes more crucial than ever. Nobody is strong enough to succeed in every task, and Cory finds that the most painful lesson she and her lovers can learn is not just how to deal with failure. Cory needs to learn that one woman is only so powerful, and she needs to choose wisely who sits outside her circle of family, and who is bound eternally in her heart.

AMY LANE is a mother of two college students, two grade-schoolers, and two small dogs. She is also a compulsive knitter who writes because she can't silence the voices in her head. She adores fur-babies, knitting socks, and hawt menz, and she dislikes moths, cat boxes, and knuckle-headed macspazzmatrons. She is rarely found cooking, cleaning, or doing domestic chores, but she has been known to knit up an emergency hat/blanket/pair of socks for any occasion whatsoever, or sometimes for no reason at all. Her award-winning writing has three flavors: twisty-purple alternative universe, angsty-orange contemporary, and sunshine-yellow happy. By necessity, she has learned to type like the wind. She's been married for twenty-plus years to her beloved Mate and still believes in Twu Wuv, with a capital Twu and a capital Wuv, and she doesn't see any reason at all for that to change.

Website: www.greenshill.com
Blog: www.writerslane.blogspot.com
E-mail: amylane@greenshill.com
Facebook: www.facebook.com/amy.lane.167
Twitter: @amymaclane

By Amy Lane

LITTLE GODDESS
Vulnerable
Wounded, Vol. 1 & Vol. 2
Bound, Vol. 1 & Vol. 2
The Green's Hill Novellas

Published by DSP PUBLICATIONS
www.dsppublications.com

# More from DSP Publications

Blessed Epoch: Book One

For the past few years Yarroway L'Estrella has lived in exile, gathering arcane power.  But that power came at a price, and he carries the scars to prove it. Now he must do his duty: his uncle, the king, needs him to escort Prince Garith to his wedding, a union that will create an alliance between the two strongest countries in the known world. But Yarrow isn't the prince's only guard. A whole company of knights is assigned to the mission, and Yarrow's not sure he trusts their leader.

Knight Duncan Purefroy isn't sure he trusts Yarrow either, but after a bizarre occurrence during their travels, they have no choice but to work together—especially since the incident also reveals a disturbing secret, one that might threaten the entire kingdom.

The precarious alliance is strained further when a third member joins the cause for reasons of his own—reasons that may not be in the best interests of the prince or the kingdom. With enemies at every turn, no one left to trust, and the dark power within Yarrow pulling dangerously away from his control, the fragile bond the three of them have built may be all that stands between them and destruction.

# www.dsppublications.com

# More from DSP Publications

Men of Myth: Book One

Brett Wright and Finn de Morisco come from vastly different worlds. Disowned by his family for being gay, Brett builds both a life on his own terms and walls around his emotions. But nothing can prepare him for the evil that stalks him in the night or from discovering the dark secrets of his heritage.

The youngest of a doting family, Finn lives a sheltered life that allows him to trust easily and makes him quick to jump to the rescue. While using his knowledge of the supernatural world to help Brett uncover the truth of his ancestry, Finn learns nothing in life is as simple and risk-free as he believed.

New knowledge comes with a price—one that may prove too high for them to pay.

www.dsppublications.com